ST. MARTIN'S

MINOTAUR

MYSTERIES

Extraordinary Acclaim for
SCREAM IN SILENCE and Eleanor Taylor Bland

"A fine writer ... A worthy addition to [her] series."
—*Chicago Tribune*

"The twists and mingled plots will keep you entertained to the very last chapter."
—*Rockwell* (TX) *Success*

"Marti MacAlister is a most welcome addition to crime fiction."   —Sara Paretsky

"[Bland is] a fine storyteller."
—*Washington Post Book World*

"Solidly plotted police procedurals with interesting people, packaged in careful, understated prose."
—*Philadelphia Inquirer*

"Her writing is intelligent, sensitive, and sometimes gritty."   —*Quarterly Black Review of Books*

"One of the better new crime writers of this decade."
—*Mystery News*

TURN THE PAGE FOR MORE CRITICAL PRAISE ...

St. Martin's Paperbacks Titles
by Eleanor Taylor Bland

Tell No Tales
See No Evil
Keep Still
Done Wrong
Scream in Silence

SCREAM
IN SILENCE

ELEANOR TAYLOR BLAND

St. Martin's Paperbacks

SCREAM IN SILENCE

Copyright © 2000 by Eleanor Taylor Bland.

ISBN: 0-312-97494-9

Printed in the United States of America

St. Martin's Press hardcover edition / February 2000
St. Martin's Paperbacks edition / February 2001

St. Martin's Paperbacks are published by St. Martin's Press, 175 Fifth Avenue, New York, NY 10010.

10 9 8 7 6 5 4 3 2 1

To Julia, Maude, Lela Jo, Mary Lou, and Sandra,
with love, respect, and tremendous admiration.
You define and transcend the concept of
strong black women.

ACKNOWLEDGMENTS

MANY THANKS—

To my agent, Ted Chichak, with gratitude and appreciation.

To the ladies of Lilac Cottage: Nanatte Borge, JoAn Sabonjian, Lou Smith, and Marge Maxwell.

To my editor, Kelley Ragland, and my publicist, Elizabeth Shipley, for their enthusiasm and expertise.

To Jim Harrington, artist.

To everyone involved with the downtown revitalization of "my town" of Lincoln Prairie–Waukegan, Illinois.

To Torrie Flink and the staff at Lake County Council Against Sexual Assault, who don't let me forget, and especially Jim Zacharius, our angel—rest in peace.

To my family, for always being there for me.

I would also like to thank Rev. Terry McCarthy, Deacon Ron Colaianni, Dr. Robert Kurtz, Dr. Howard Atlas, Mr. Herbert King, Caryn Meyer, Connie Turner, and Chris Johnson for invaluable assistance, concern, and support.

For technical assistance, thanks to Harry Schaefer, Chicago Fire Dept. Ret. and Illinois State Fire Marshall Investigator; Curtis Gentry, ex-Bear; Shelley Reuben; the Red Herrings; Michael Allan Dymmoch, Elroy Reed, Marcella Hardin, Fred Hunter, and Hugh Holton; Louis Berrones, Elliot Dunn, and Michael Waller, attorneys-at-law; Joanne Streeker; and Precious the Pig and Mary.

SCREAM
IN SILENCE

PROLOGUE

He gripped the rough bark and peered around the trunk of the tree. Puffs of smoke hovered like gray clouds in the evening sky. The Warren place was burning. It had been a fine house years ago when the Warrens owned it. Now most of the paint had peeled from the clapboard, and half the shutters were missing. The steps were rotting, and the screen door in the back hung off its hinges. Cardboard and plastic had replaced several windows. He smiled as flames began licking the edges of the roof. People who didn't take care of their homes didn't deserve to have them. Sirens sounded in the distance, nudging him. As he made his way out of the underbrush, dense scrubs scratched at his arms and legs.

He was humming as he jogged along the mile-and-a-half trail, deserted now because it would soon be dark. He ran away from the sound of the sirens, circled around, and then came closer again. Part of the preserve abutted the Warrens' property. He followed the road, which veered toward the burning building, until he was close enough to see the orange-red flames pouring from the roof, the streams of water from the firefighters' hoses ineffective. There was a deep roar, as if the fire was rolling through a tunnel. The smell of wood burning made him tempted to leave the trail and walk through the trees to get a closer look, but he did not. He inhaled deeply and felt a familiar swelling at his groin. The smoke was not close enough to sting his eyes. The heat could not sear his lungs, but the flames—he could see the flames. He leaned against a tree taking in deep gulps of air, savoring the taste of smoke. There was a sudden loud crackling, then a whoosh as a huge plume of smoke rose above the tree-tops. The pleasure these sounds brought made him moan aloud.

When he returned home it was a little after nine. He went into the kitchen and in the light from the refrigerator made two roast beef sandwiches. He topped them with mustard and tomatoes and looked out the window as he ate in the dark. He was always hungry after a fire. He fixed himself a piece of cake, some cookies, and a bowl of ice cream.

He used to come home from a fire, eat, and go to bed—not to sleep, at least not for a while, but to remember. It had been different the last few times and tonight. He felt . . . dissatisfied somehow. He wanted more. This fire had burned longer undetected than any he had set in a long while. It was so powerful—flames leaping above the treetops. He should be happy, but he wasn't. And now that he had eaten, he should be tired, but he wasn't. He felt like running for another two hours. He felt as if he could run all night.

He went to the basement and unlocked the door to his workshop. He had built the heavy table in the center of the room, soundproofed and paneled the walls, and put tile on the floor to make it easier to clean up spills. Locked cabinets were filled with chemicals and supplies. There was a folding cot and sleeping bag for those times when he worked until he was too weary to go upstairs.

His journal was still on the table, open to today's date. He made detailed notes about the fire: which combustible materials he had chosen; how he had sealed the area to restrict the oxygen; the length of time he had stood on the hill and waited before he'd shot the pellets that shattered the windows and caused the backdraft and explosion of fire. That done, he opened the combination lock on an old metal footlocker. He took out a wooden box and sat on the bed with the box on his lap. The box was made of oak, polished to a gleam. He opened it with a small skeleton key that he kept taped to the underside of a lamp on the table. It was filled with newspaper clippings, most of them brief and yellow *with age. There was only one with a picture, the obituary of a police officer who'd died in a house fire. Setting fires could be dangerous. Sometimes the wrong people came around asking questions. He had never allowed anyone to stand in his way.*

He closed the box. There would be another clipping tomorrow. Tonight's fire was so beautiful, it might even make the front page. He felt sad as he returned the box to the footlocker. As wonderful as the fire was, it wasn't the same anymore. It wasn't enough. He unlocked one of the cabinets, removed a shoe box, and put it on the worktable. As he looked at the contents, he felt a surge of excitement. Yes, this was what was missing in his life. Tonight he would find out if that book he'd found in the secondhand store was any good. He would read the directions again, compare them to the checklist he had drawn up based on those instructions. He would make sure he hadn't overlooked or misunderstood anything, then find out for certain if he had succeeded in making his first bomb.

CHAPTER
1

Det. Marti MacAlister parked as close as she could to the area where the bombing had occurred. It was a dark night in an isolated part of town. Dense stands of burr oak and bushes sheltered this part of the road where it ran along the northern perimeter of the Lincoln Prairie Municipal Airport. Branches overhung the street lamps, and few and far between, the houses across the street were further isolated by their distance from the road. Just ahead, red and white lights flashed, blinked, and whirled. No fatalities, the dispatcher had told her, just a mailbox blown all to hell. Just a mailbox—but damned close—not just to some small jets, but also to their fuel source.

Marti rolled down the window as her partner, Matthew "Vik" Jessenovik, approached the car. Vik was four inches taller than her five-ten. He had lost weight during his wife's recent illness, and at 145, was twenty pounds lighter than she was. Almost fifty, he was nine years older than her.

"Vik, what have you got on?" He was wearing a light-weight overcoat over what looked like pajamas.

Wiry salt-and-pepper eyebrows almost met across the bridge of his nose. He had a tendency to lean over and look down at people. Marti called it his vulture look; his craggy face and his beak nose, broken long ago, brought those birds to mind.

"Marti, some idiot set off a bomb thirty feet from the airport. For some reason, that sounded important. What took *you* so long to get here?"

She ignored that. After being a widow for more than four years she had remarried four months ago and Vik was still adjusting. Lately his remarks seemed to imply that she might not be giving the job enough priority. Maybe he was right this time. She and Ben *had* been right in the middle of something.

"What have we got?" she asked.

"There wasn't much damage. I don't know if that's because it was a small bomb or because the mailboxes are out here by the road and away from the houses. I guess we'll find out more about that when the bomb squad and the ATF are through. If they can tell us. The property owner is out of town. Only one neighbor heard anything." He pointed toward the only house with lights on. "There are half a dozen houses along this part of the road, with about a half a mile of undeveloped land behind them. I haven't talked with the people who reported it yet—I was waiting for you—but I woke up everyone else. So far, nobody up late; nobody out late. From the looks of it, they're not your average nosy types. As far as I can tell, everyone has gone back to bed. You'd think they would at least have some outdoor lights on. Maybe they don't want the pilots to mistake the street for a runway. Oh, apparently there is one barking dog—belongs to that house back there." He pointed to the house to the left of the blown-up mailbox.

"Why isn't it barking now?"

"The neighbors wondered about that too, but they were more pleased than concerned. Barking is definitely not encouraged, although I don't know why else anyone would want a dog."

Marti stifled a yawn. She glanced at the clock on the dashboard: 11:57. "What time did the call come in?"

"A little after eleven."

"Maybe we should check on the dog first." She got her flashlight out of the trunk.

They found a small mixed breed under some bushes about fifty feet from the house. The dog was lying in a thicket, like it had been tossed there.

"It looks like its neck was broken," Vik said.

Marti shivered and looked away. People who harmed animals disturbed her.

"Think we should tell them about their dog?" Vik asked. "The place is dark. It looks like they've gone back to sleep. Maybe the people who reported this can tell them in the morning. After all, they're neighbors."

"Whatever. It can wait." She didn't feel much like breaking the news either. Pets were like children to a lot of people.

Yellow tape marked off the area where the explosion had occurred. The mailbox had been attached to a post that was sunk into the ground near a long gravel path leading to the house. All that remained was one jagged shaft of wood pointing upward. There were indentations on the hard-packed dirt where the force of the explosion slammed pieces of metal and wood into the ground, but nearby bushes and trees were undamaged. Marti had worked a car-bombing case when she was on the force in Chicago. She was glad there were no bodies this time. This one hadn't done much more damage than a large firecracker.

"Hell of a place for a bomb," Vik said, gesturing in the direction of the airport. "Too many corporate jets hangared there. Too many politicians flying in and out. It could be some fool playing a joke, or an irate neighbor, or somebody who's ticked off with one of those corporations."

"Or one of those politicians," Marti said. It was warm for the end of April. Spring had come with quiet rain and a slow greening. The mailbox in front of the house next door had petunias planted at its base. A light wind ruffled her hair. She unbuttoned her jacket. Too bad Vik couldn't take his coat off. Pajamas. This had to be his first experience with a detonated bomb; they did respond to calls reporting threats occasionally and she could remember him talking about one that hadn't gone off.

"Just what we need," Vik said. He kicked at the dirt. "Innovation, creativity, stupidity. If this was some damned fool prank . . ."

"And if it wasn't?"

"Come on, MacAlister."

"Nobody's home, Vik. Why do you blow up a mailbox when nobody's home?"

"So they won't get hurt?"

"Then what's the point?"

"How the hell do I know? You think this was political?"

"We'll have a better idea of that when we see the day's flight list."

"Dammit, MacAlister, this is Lincoln Prairie, Illinois, not Belfast or Nairobi. We don't have any terrorists here. No skinheads, no neo-Nazis, no paramilitia."

"No?" she said. "Like hell."

This bomb and a fire earlier this evening, both without injuries or fatalities, along with a drive-by Saturday night with no injuries, made her uneasy. There was such a thing as too much luck. It tended to come in bunches—like trouble.

There was a light on in the den when Vik pulled into the driveway. Mildred was waiting up for him. She must have had a good day. More and more now the days were good. MS wasn't fatal, at least that's what the doctor said. But it leeched away so much of her life. He could remember how she had loved to ice skate, and dance, and take long hikes in the woods. Now she couldn't walk more than ten minutes without her legs becoming weak. And, over time, there would be more changes, more restrictions. Now it was a just a walker, perhaps soon it would only be a cane, but one day it would be a wheelchair.

He let himself into their home and walked toward the light. His den was now their bedroom. As he walked, he heard the thump of Mildred's walker, and before he reached the doorway she was coming into the hall to greet him.

"Matthew!"

In his mind's eye, she was always the girl he'd married. When she smiled, the years fell away and she seemed as young as a bride.

"*Moja serca,*" he said in Polish, going to her. "*Moja serca.*" My heart.

* * *

He listened to the police band on his CB until daybreak. What a stroke of luck, finding that old book in the second-hand store. He had been looking for something to add to his World War I and II collection. All he could see was the spine when he pulled it from the shelf, Bombs Away. He almost put it back when he saw the condition it was in, but the diagrams caught his attention. Step-by-step instructions for making all kinds of bombs. He had to wear latex gloves when he handled it because the cover was so soiled it must have been handled by many people. The pages were dog-eared, and wrinkled and stained where someone had spilled coffee. It wasn't until he called the publisher to order another and was told it was no longer legal to own that he realized how valuable it was. That was two summers ago. Now, after assembling everything he needed, he had built and detonated his first bomb.

TUESDAY, APRIL 27

At eleven o'clock Tuesday morning, Marti and Vik met with Lefty, the sergeant in charge of Lincoln Prairie's bomb squad, and an agent from the ATF (Bureau of Alcohol, Tobacco and Firearms) in Lieutenant Dirkowitz's office. The two of them would have been in court if it wasn't for whoever had blown up the mailbox. The judge agreed that meeting with the ATF took precedence over their testimony in a murder-two case that had been pleaded down to second-degree manslaughter.

The lieutenant's office was at least as big as the one she and Vik shared with two vice cops. Even so, it seemed crowded with three extra chairs. Marti recognized Lefty, though she had never worked with him, and nodded. Lefty was a tall, beefy man with the tip of the index finger on his left hand missing because of some handyman mishap at home. The young man sitting beside him with scraggly, dirty blond hair pulled back in a ponytail and wearing faded jeans had to be the ATF agent.

Dirkowitz was drinking his usual can of diet pop. "Coffee?" he asked. The Pyrex pot and Styrofoam cups were there as a courtesy to the ATF. The lieutenant wasn't big on the amenities.

Marti reached for a cup and wished for sugar as she inhaled the aroma of coffee that was almost as full-bodied as hers. She took a seat and smiled at the ATF agent.

"Dirty Dirk" Dirkowitz ran thick fingers through close-cropped blond hair. He had played football with the Southern Illinois Salukis and still had the build of a linebacker. He made introductions all around. "Sorry to have to bring you out here with something so minor."

"No problem," the agent said. "Especially since it was already detonated. I don't know if I'll come back though, unless you get a live one I can play with."

Marti caught the humor and smiled as Vik scowled. "What have we got?" she asked.

"Nothing sophisticated; just your average homemade toy."

Vik's frown deepened.

"How much did they have to know?" she asked.

"Just the basics." The agent explained the composition of the bomb, how it was assembled, and what detonated it.

The sergeant interrupted occasionally to ask for clarification on a few technical points, but otherwise just listened, nodding his head.

"This sounds sophisticated enough to me," Vik said, when the agent stopped talking.

The agent shrugged. "It doesn't take a degree in chemistry. There are recipe books around, if you know where to look for them. The materials are commonplace, harmless even, until you get the right mix. Nothing was used that we could identify as being imported by paramilitary groups."

"The fuse is what concerns me," the sergeant said.

"Why?" Marti asked.

"He used a chemical fuse," the agent explained. "It has just enough instability to be somewhat unpredictable."

"You mean maybe we'll get lucky and this idiot will blow himself up?" Vik asked.

"Possibly," the agent said. "The fuse does improve those odds. It also improves the odds of doing something the bomber doesn't intend—it goes off too soon. . . . Usually, we can get an ID on the victim, but we find miscellaneous body parts all the time and never know who the bomber was. One time we found two right feet."

"Does this nutcase have enough information to build a bigger bomb?" Vik asked.

"Sure. My guess is this was practice. And I'd guess this guy was a loner rather than part of a group."

"Why?" Vik asked.

"A mailbox?" the agent said. "Groupies own property in isolated areas. They bring their families along and have cookouts and blow up old cars and trees and small buildings."

"You're kidding," Vik said.

"Nope. Wish I was. Then again, this could be some kind of a practical joke."

Lefty distributed some reports and walked the others through them. "If we're lucky, this is an isolated incident, some asshole having fun, and I've told you more about this than you'll ever need to know. The problem is the incident's proximity to the airport and the clientele who have access to it—and not just the politicians. You've got CEOs with companies that manufacture all kinds of things that could piss someone off. You also have corporate types from other countries flying in for tours and meetings. Bottom line—security is going to be damned tight there for a while. If we get real lucky on this one, even if we do have a serious type on our hands, he'll get discouraged and take his action someplace else. On the other hand, if he has a specific target, he might try again."

"Two CEOs flew out of that airport yesterday," Lieutenant Dirkowitz said. "A party of five legislators came in, including a congressman and some executives from a company in the Republic of China. If this isn't an isolated incident, who is he after?"

After Lefty and the ATF agent left, the lieutenant swiveled around in his chair and looked out the window. He had a limited view of Lake Michigan. Today the sunlight made glittering highlights on the blue water. "How long has it been since that kid made that goop stuff and we thought it was nitroglycerin?"

"Last summer, sir," Vik said.

At least a minute passed before the lieutenant spoke again. "I hope it's not a kid," he said. "Let's hope it's not a kid."

"Oh no," Vik said. "It's some prankster or a nutcase."

It presented them with one hell of a choice, Marti thought.

"Damned shame about where it went off," Vik said, as they walked back to their office. "This would have been a lot less complicated, MacAlister, if we didn't have to bring in the ATF."

"Anything that involves the post office involves the Feds."

"Hell, there wasn't even any mail in the box. Besides, our guys can handle it. You heard the ATF agent. This didn't take much expertise. It was just some idiot trying to make a better firecracker."

"You wish. It was a bomb, Vik. A real bomb, not some Silly Putty recipe some kid mixed together."

"I know," he admitted. "Just when you think it's safe to go to sleep at night, we get some damned lunatic on our hands."

"Maybe it's not that bad."

Vik gave her a look that suggested she was the one who had problems with wishful thinking.

Geoffrey Bailey walked up to the gate, unlatched it, and swung it open as if he came here every day, even though he hadn't done more than case the place for a couple of days. This house was ideal, away from the street and almost surrounded by trees. There were places where the sun hardly shone through. The yard was well cared for, and tulips bloomed near the casement. He gave the bell an extra long ring and was rewarded when an elderly woman with a dowager's hump came to the door.

"Good afternoon, Mrs. Jhanke." The name was on the mailbox.

She kept the chain on and looked up at him with watery blue eyes. "My son is not home now," she said. Her voice was loud enough to tell him she was hard of hearing.

"Yes," he said. "I thought you might be alone. I'm with a private security agency, ma'am."

The woman was more interested in looking at him than at the fake ID he flashed. She was probably trying to figure out if he was black. His skin was fair enough to pass, but with his family, there wasn't any point in pretending to be something he wasn't.

"Security?" she asked.

He smiled. His hair, straight and dyed a lighter shade of brown, and his features, inherited from some plantation owner, along with a navy blue business suit, white shirt, and red, white, and blue tie, were usually enough to put them at ease.

"Yes, ma'am. My company wants to help women like yourself, alone much of the time, in neighborhoods that are . . ." He looked about, with an expression intended to convey danger. "Well, you've lived here for a good many years now, haven't you?"

She nodded.

"It's a shame the way things change. Strangers move in, people who don't even speak your language." He had noticed a Hispanic family half a block away. "ElderCare Security wants you to feel safe in your own home, just the way you used to."

"I have no money," she said.

"Why, don't you give that a thought, ma'am." The ones with their own homes always had money. "Our primary concern is your safety, and we are more than willing to make whatever arrangements are convenient for your peace of mind."

"My son handles everything."

"And I'm sure he wants you to be safe at all times, but" —he turned just enough to take a quick look around—"the way this house is secluded from the neighbors, it's great for privacy and peace and quiet but . . ."

"Well, I . . ." Her voice quavered.

She was afraid here. They were all afraid.

"This device is so easy to install that I don't even have to enter your home. All I have to do is unscrew the light fixture and the doorbell." He took two hearing aid batteries and some wire from his pocket. "It is just this simple. You can watch me. Then I'll give you this—" He pulled a beeper from his pocket. "You hear a noise, you push this button, the police are alerted. It's just that simple. Amazing what modern technology can do."

"But I have no money."

"Ma'am, we can work something out."

"No, you don't understand. There is no money. My son has to take care of me. I have nothing in the house. Nothing. He's worried too that someone will rob me."

"And this is such a wonderful device. You would never live in fear again."

"I . . ." She thought for a minute. "Is there any way you

could accept a piece of jewelry, sell it perhaps? It's all I have."

Geoffrey preferred cash, but occasionally he did luck upon a nice antique that he could give to his mother or his aunt. "Only if it's something old that you really don't need anymore. We have to have something to cover the cost of the parts and installation, but we keep the cost to a minimum."

"I'll be right back."

"While you're gone, I'll just install this." He took a screwdriver from his pocket.

She was gone so long he hoped she hadn't had a stroke or a heart attack or something. Her face was flushed when she returned.

"Is this enough?" She held out a ring and he took it, impressed with the weight. The silver was tarnished but there was no mistaking the authenticity of the diamond in the center and the chips that surrounded it.

"Ma'am, this really isn't worth very much . . ." She might part with more.

"It's all I have now. My son put everything else in the vault."

He looked at it for a moment, envisioning it in a different setting but willing to bet his mother would love it just as it was. Mother's Day was still a couple of weeks away, and he already had Mama's present.

"Here's your alarm, ma'am, and remember, just push this button."

"Thank you so much," she said. "Now if anyone tries to get in . . ."

"Just push the button."

He pocketed the ring. Not a bad day's work, even if he didn't have any cash to show for it. He didn't even have to pretend to install anything.

Opal Jhanke stood in the hallway after she closed the front door. Such a nice young man and so helpful. He understood. She *was* afraid when she was alone, even during the day. She looked down at the small black case. Where could she hide it so that Fred wouldn't find it, yet have it close to hand if she needed it? It wasn't that Fred wouldn't want her to have it. If he agreed that she needed it, he would have bought one for her without her even having to ask. But he thought she was safe. He wasn't alone here all day and sometimes most of the night. He could hear every sound and know just what it was. He could see more than shapes when he looked down the hall and into the kitchen.

She felt like a child when the house was dark, not knowing if she was seeing shadows and things moving, or if she just thought she was. Not knowing if a floorboard was creaking or a door opening that she could not hear. She didn't want Fred to know how bad her hearing was, how poor her eyesight had become, or how afraid she was when she was here by herself. Poor Fred, he would worry. And she didn't think he had enough money to do much about it. Just keeping up the house and taking care of her had to be hard on him. He was working two jobs, poor dear. He hadn't even had time for a haircut in close to a month now. His hair had grown long enough to cover his neck and she didn't like the way it fell across his forehead. He looked so disheveled.

She slipped the little black box into her apron pocket. How amazing that something smaller than a pack of cigarettes and lighter than a crab apple could get the police, who were blocks away, if she needed help. Fred would want to know how she had paid for it. Her jewelry, what little she had that Fred didn't know about, was in a false drawer in the small desk in the guest room. She wanted to hide this there, just until she could think of a better place to put it, but she couldn't make it up the stairs again, not today. As she made her way down the hall, past the kitchen to the small porch that Fred had converted into a bedroom, she steadied herself by keeping one hand against the wall. She needed her cane. If she told Fred she had misplaced it, he would find it for her, but she didn't want him to know how forgetful she was.

Opal smiled as she sat in her chair. It was lumpy in all the right places and Bitsy's gray-and-white cat hair had become part of the upholstery. Poor Bitsy, Lord knew what had happened to her, old and arthritic as she was. One minute she was sitting right here on the windowsill warming her old bones in the sun and watching a robin, the next thing she was gone. She must have slipped out when Fred left the door open, though it wasn't like her to go outside. Old, that's what Bitsy had been. Old and confused, just like she was getting to be. And alone, but with this . . . She took the little black box out of her pocket. There had to be someplace she could put this, just for now.

This porch was small, not big like her bedroom upstairs. She couldn't even bring her four-poster down and curl up in the spot where the mattress had sort of caved in from Fred Senior sleeping there all of those years. This chair was the only thing that meant anything to her that Fred Junior could fit in here. She couldn't even read by Grandma's lamp; no room for that either. Course, she didn't read now anyway. The library people had stopped bringing books not long before her last birthday. Eighty must be the cutoff for that, not that she understood why. Her books were upstairs. She had brought one down once, tried to read it, stopped when her eyes began to water. When Fred saw the book, it upset him. He said she was just frustrating herself trying to do things that she couldn't do anymore. She would have asked for new reading glasses, but she didn't think there was enough money. The way Fred dressed these days, in his father's old clothes, she was sure he had lost his job at the office and was doing something menial.

Opal dabbed at her eyes. This wasn't a nursing home. Fred Junior had promised he would never put her in one and he hadn't, but it sure seemed like one sometimes, with everything important upstairs.

It was midafternoon when Marti and Vik arrived at the house that had burned down the night before. Vik referred to it as "the Warren place." Only its chimney was still standing. The acrid odor of smoke and charred wood hovered over everything like a damp cloud. The stench of water-soaked, heat-seared building materials made Marti's stomach churn. Last night this was just another fire, a vacant house that someone had either accidentally or deliberately set afire. But a body had been found beneath the rubble half an hour ago. Now she had to determine if it was a homicide, and if so, if it had occurred either before or after the commission of a felony.

Marti spotted Ben Walker, her husband of four months, standing by the ambulance. She waved. Ben grinned, then pointed to the rear of what was left of the building. Three firemen in full gear were standing there. One gestured toward a bulldozer that had been turned off with its shovel eight feet from the ground. Vik skirted the foundation and avoided the standing water as he walked toward them. Marti held back. She didn't like looking at fire victims.

From where she stood, it looked as if the body had been scooped up with some of the debris, then dumped on the ground. From this distance, it was impossible to tell what had gotten to the victim, fire or smoke. She wanted to keep guessing about that for as long as possible. The coroner's car pulled up behind hers. She waved to Dr. Cyprian and walked over to Ben.

"The fire didn't kill whoever it was," Ben said. He knew how she felt about burn victims. "We found the body in the basement under a lot of debris."

"Male or female?" she asked.

"Female. She was wearing a skirt." Ben was a big man, solid, all muscle. He had a quick smile and an easy laugh, deep and rumbling, and—she had discovered—slow hands.

"What do we know about the fire?"

"We've got two arson investigators working on it. Point of origin was where the house faced the forest preserve. Once it got going, it burned fast. They haven't determined what the accelerant was. There was nothing obvious like a gasoline can. The house was fully involved when we got here last night, and the building was totally consumed. It looks to me like a couple of others we've had recently, but the fire inspectors guess the owner wanted to collect the insurance. That's usually the case with a rapid burn fire in a vacant building." He looked down at her and smiled. "You didn't get much sleep last night. You must be tired."

He stood behind her and kneaded her shoulders and neck until she relaxed and leaned into him.

"Uh-oh," Ben said. "Caught in the act. I think your partner wants you."

Vik was motioning to her to join him. Marti stayed where she was for another half minute, then walked to the rear of the foundation where Vik and Dr. Cyprian were talking.

Dr. Cyprian was their favorite pathologist. He was methodical and thorough and, as his East Indian heritage implied, inscrutable. His suit pants were smudged with soot and soggy at the knees. "A woman," he said. "No burns that I can observe, not that it matters. She was most assuredly dead before the fire started. The body is intact, but there is well-defined decomposition. We will have to clean her up before I can tell you any more than that." Ordinarily, Cyprian never said more than he had to until the autopsy. Lately, however, he had became almost talkative while they were still at the scene.

Marti looked down at the body, which was covered with a soggy layer of soot. She couldn't tell postmortem changes from those caused by heat or falling debris. The victim was wearing a skirt and a jacket, and sensible shoes. Marti wondered if she was middle-aged or young. She wasn't sure why, but that made a difference. More and more often these days, death seemed to come much too soon. Given the circumstances—a vacant house—it was probable that she was part of the transient population. The unhoused, as Vik called them, another phenomenon that was on the increase.

"Make sure the community police units take a look at her when they get her cleaned up," Marti said. "Maybe the shelter workers too."

Marti waited until the technicians photographed and processed the scene; then she shot a role of film too. She watched as Ben eased the body into a bag, zipped it up, and put it on the stretcher. There was a gentleness in the way he handled the woman's body, a respect for the dead, most would say. She knew that it actually was a reverence for life.

By the time Marti and Vik began a canvass of the neighborhood where the fire had occurred, it had been almost eighteen hours since the fire was first reported at 8:20 P.M. the night before. The street where the house was located was beginning an ascent from shabby to yuppie genteel. The Warren property had been vacant without a FOR SALE sign. According to the fire chief, it had been years since the Warrens owned the place. It had changed hands several times, and he had no idea who owned it now.

Vik cupped his hands over his eyes, shielding them from the bright spring sunlight. "So," he said. "What do you think the odds are that anyone saw anything?"

"Maybe we'll get lucky."

The vacant Victorians on either side of the Warren place looked as if they were undergoing rehab, but there weren't any workmen around. The forest preserve stretched for several blocks behind them. Across the street, a small, wood-framed bungalow looked empty. Two larger brick houses were empty, with SOLD stickers on the FOR SALE signs. The nearest house that looked occupied was almost a block away. They headed there.

"Doesn't look like anyone's home," Vik said.

It had been a small house. Two additions had enlarged it.

The garage door was down; the driveway empty. Nobody answered the doorbell.

They walked back to the Warren place. So far they hadn't seen any children or adults, and there hadn't been any traffic.

"We'll have to post uniforms at the entrances of the pre-serve," Marti said. "They close at sundown, so the odds of anyone running or walking through when the fire started are slim, but someone could have been in there. And let's stop by the fire station, talk with the guys who took the call."

Vik raised bushy salt-and-pepper eyebrows, but said nothing. It was the station where Ben was assigned. This was Marti's second marriage, and Johnny, her first husband, Lord rest his soul, had been a cop. She was so used to Vic's spoken and unspoken innuendoes about her marriage that she wasn't even tempted to respond.

Ben was doing something in the ambulance when they got there. Marti went into the kitchen, helped herself to cof-fee, and poured a cup for Vik. When Ben joined them, she fixed another cup with cream and sugar, the way he liked it.

Ben came up behind her and touched her hair. "You've been checking out that fire."

The smoke smell must be in her hair. She didn't have time to have it washed and set and didn't like doing it her-self. Maybe Momma would wash it for her. She sighed and relaxed. Her mother was living with her now.

Ben twirled a curl around his finger then released it and picked up the cup. "I wish there was more left of the place. I think it might have been an interesting fire. Things really got hot at the point of origin."

Marti smiled, remembering a day about four years ago when Ben had taken her on a tour of a burned-out building that had housed a clinic. Although he worked primarily as a paramedic, fire training was also required. It had been quite a while since she had worked an arson case. There were no reports back yet, but the odds were it was either accidental at the hands of some vagrant—perhaps the woman in the base-ment—or deliberate, to get the insurance. There was also the possibility that someone had set the fire to cover up the woman's death, but if that were the case, why hadn't the fire been set when she died?

"It looks like it burned for maybe half an hour before it spread," Ben said. "By then the heat had built up to the point where it damned near exploded. Oxygen must have been introduced. The question is, how did it get that sudden rush of air?"

"What do you mean?"

"I'm not sure." He shook his head. "There's just something about the intensity of the initial burn. Combustion is a chain reaction. The duration of the burn—whether or not the fire goes out on its own—depends on combustible material, an ignition source with sufficient energy to keep it burning, and oxygen."

"Does that mean it's safe to assume arson?" she asked.

"There are no signs of a liquid accelerant. No spill or splash pattern."

"Something spontaneous maybe. An electrical fire."

"Can't say. Maybe when I see the reports." He hesitated, as if he wanted to say something else.

"And?" Marti asked.

"I don't know. I'll have to think about it."

"Today was your day off."

"Right." He grinned. "I'll be home later."

By seven o'clock Marti had found out very little. According to Vik, the Warren family, husband, wife, son, and daughter, had died while trying to beat a train at a crossing. The current owner lived in Florida and had not returned their call. The real estate agent that managed the property knew nothing except that several prospective buyers had looked at it in the past month and yes, it was structurally sound, but in need of many repairs. "If it is arson, Vik, it's not obvious. With a building that old and that isolated, why would anyone bother being clever?"

"Maybe when we find out who the victim is, we'll be able to come up with a better motive," Vik said. "Maybe everything will fall right into place." He snapped a pencil in half.

Marti called the coroner's office again. They had not ID'd the victim.

"Nothing," she told Vik. The odds were slim on finding out anything else today, but she didn't want to leave until she had something. She phoned home. Ben had made it home and was cooking on the grill, and Momma was there. Momma's elderly aunt in Arkansas, whom she'd taken care of for almost five years, had become so incapacitated by a series of strokes that she was now in a nursing home in Little Rock, closer to her daughter. Momma had gotten Aunt Sadie settled in and returned to Illinois to live with them. Marti, who was not big on entertaining, had had an open house so that all of her friends could welcome her.

"Let's call it a night," Vik said. He stretched and yawned.

Marti knew he was trying to get home early enough to spend some time with Mildred. "Sounds good."

He drummed his fingers on his desk for a moment then stood up. "Florida's a good place to be when a rental property you own burns down. So, what have we got? A professional arsonist, an educated firebug, or just an unusual set of circumstances?"

Marti wished they didn't have a victim. Then they wouldn't have to get involved at all.

As Marti turned into the cul-de-sac and looked at their red-brick quad level, she thought of the gingerbread village where she and her two children, Theo and Joanna, had lived before she remarried. They had shared the Tudor with her best friend, Sharon, and Sharon's daughter, Lisa. Now they lived here with Ben and his son, Mike, who was ten, the same age as Theo. It was a big house, mostly brick. Lights were lined up along the driveway and walkway, and motion detector lights came on as she drove toward the garage. They had added a chain-link fence, and Trouble, a large silver German shepherd who patrolled its chain-link perimeters. They had also added an enclosed walkway from the garage to the back door. Inside, an alarm system had been installed. She thought of the "gingerbread village" again, how safe she had felt there until the intruder had gotten in. Now she was watchful.

Momma had her own room in the house, but the apartment over the garage was still empty. Marti was still hoping that Sharon would move up there. She was worried about Sharon. Lisa spent a lot of time here, and she didn't know why. Sharon had never been close to her own mother, and Marti worried that Sharon would become estranged from her daughter as well. Even when they shared the same house there was little time for "woman talk"; now Sharon rarely called, and neither did she. Sharon was in an apartment about fifteen minutes away, and they talked to each other less often than they had when Sharon was in Atlanta attending college.

"That you, Ma?" Theo called as soon as she walked through the kitchen door. "We're downstairs having a picnic!"

Everyone except Lisa was in the den, even Patrick and Peter, the kids next door. Mike had gone from being the class bully a few years ago to a good-natured child, round-faced and chubby. Theo looked just like Johnny, his dad, nut brown with thin angular features.

A red-checkered tablecloth had been spread over a long folding table and covered with food: grilled chicken, brats, corn on the cob, and Joanna's signature touch, vegetable salad and a bowl of fruit.

"And I didn't do a thing," Momma said. Even though Joanna and Lisa helped around the house, Marti was used to seeing her mother busy. It was good to see her sitting in a recliner with her feet up and a tray in her lap.

The four boys were sitting close together at one end of the table and laughing as they popped brats into buns and squeezed on ketchup and mustard. Theo had become a solemn, quiet child when Johnny died. His smile had returned as he and Mike became friends, and then a little of the laughter too. Now, with the addition of these two tow-headed free spirits who lived next door, he was becoming even more outgoing.

Joanna brought down a pitcher of iced tea. "Want some, Ma? Grandma?"

She served Momma first. For a moment their heads were close together and they looked so much alike—same hazel eyes, same long, auburn hair, Momma's twisted at the nape of her neck and Joanna's in one long braid—that Marti almost caught her breath.

The room was crowded, but Marti made her way around the table to where Ben stood with his "Smokin' Fireman" apron on. He put his arms around her and his lips brushed her ear. Ben was a big man, not fat, just solid. He was so easygoing that being married to him after being widowed for more than four years had been an easy adjustment for her and the kids.

"Hungry?" he asked. His voice was low and seductive.

"Ummm."

"For food?"

"Among other things."

"Is that a yes?"

"That's a yes after I eat and spend a little time with the children."

"Sounds good to me." He laughed. "Sounds real good."

Marti looked about the room, feeling relaxed and content until she wondered where Lisa was.

It was almost ten o'clock when Geoffrey swung into the cul-de-sac where Mama lived. Libertyville was just far enough away from Lincoln Prairie—geographically and economically—to give him easy access to his target market and low visibility. It was late for company but Calvin's Benz and Laurence's Beemer were in the driveway. Now what? Last week Calvin had tried to insist that Geoffrey target a date for his college graduation. Big brother even had the nerve to ask what he was going to do with a degree in general studies. As if that was any of his business.

Too bad big brother was here. Geoffrey had spent the weekend in Chicago, then acquired the ring this morning, and now he had to deal with Calvin. At least he'd had a great weekend. He'd told Gayle he was coming to see her, then went to see Kayla instead and said Gayle's name while he and Kayla were making love. Best way to keep a woman in check was to pit one against another. Good thing neither of them knew how much money his family had. They'd be on him like leeches, as well as fighting over him like alley cats.

He parked the six-year-old Toyota he was driving at the curb so he wouldn't have to move it later. As he got out he noticed a few stray grass clippings on the sidewalk. Calvin must have sent someone over to mow the lawn today. Terrific. Worse, Geoffrey was still wearing his jogging clothes. Now he'd have to listen to big brother run off at the mouth about him having plenty of time to go running but never enough time to do anything around here to help out. Then Calvin would start complaining because Geoffrey was still using Calvin's car; wait until he found out it needed new tires. Upkeep goes with borrowing, Calvin would say. The brakes were squeaking too. Maybe bringing up the car wouldn't be such a bad idea. Mama would make sure he wasn't driving around in an unsafe vehicle.

Mama—he fingered the ring in his pocket. He should have gotten a box for it like he'd intended, but that watch switch at the jeweler's was so easy he couldn't pass up the opportunity. No matter, Mama would show the ring to everyone she knew and complain about how much he must have paid for it when he couldn't afford to, which in Mama's mind would translate into how much he loved her. The ring wouldn't really be worth anything until half a dozen church sisters wished it was theirs and Mama's twin, Aunt Precious, got jealous enough to buy one of equal value. Geoffrey did a little dance step as he went up the walk. The front door was ajar. Miles Davis, the little yapper, stood on his hind legs on the other side of the screen and tried to dance and bark at the same time. The mutt with the pedigree as long as his arm didn't like Geoffrey worth a damn.

"Hello, Miles baby," Geoffrey said, as he pushed open the door. "Nice seeing you too." The dog grabbed at his leg with his front paws and dripped a few drops of pee on one of his new running shoes. And folks thought it was easy being the youngest son and still living at home.

Geoffrey heard his name as soon as he stepped into the foyer. But Calvin wasn't calling to him, he was talking about him.

". . . has not done one productive thing in his life. He doesn't have any intention of finishing school."

Not that again. He tiptoed across the marble floor, paused under the chandelier, and listened.

"Mama—" Laurence began.

"This is a sensible plan, Mama," Calvin said. "Are we in agreement?"

What plan?

"Well, I think—" Laurence said.

"Calvin is right, Princess, that boy will never fly from this nest. It's past time he got a little nudge."

Aunt Precious was agreeing with Calvin?

"I suppose you're right, Sister."

Mama too? This was getting out of hand. He rubbed his thumb against the ring in his pocket. Good thing he had some insurance. There was no way Mama could take Calvin's side against him. Damned troublemaker. As if he was so much. Calvin wasn't nothing more than some high-class numbers runner, some flunky stockbroker who'd got lucky with a bull market. Geoffrey checked the time on the Rolex he had snagged and grinned, wondering when the jeweler would notice the fake he had used to make the switch. He had only intended to get the ring appraised. The salesman was so impressed with the perfection of the diamond that he could have walked out with another Rolex, but getting greedy was always a mistake.

Still smiling, Geoffrey walked down the hall. The kitchen was one big room that ran the length of the back of the house. The cooking island and breakfast nook were in the center. Mama spent a lot of time changing and rearranging everything else. Right now there was a family entertainment area to the left with everything Mama could think of to entice Calvin's two kids into coming over. The area to the right was in the experimental stages again. Mama had just had five saucer-shaped lights installed. They hung from the ceiling at different heights above a big round table with a glass top, also new, where everyone was sitting now.

Mama saw him first.

"Hi, baby." She didn't look at him when she spoke.

Geoffrey waved from the center of the room and checked the ovens. He helped himself to greens, dressing, a thick slice of ham, and a wedge of corn bread; brought his plate to the table; then went back for a tall glass of iced tea. Conversation had stopped when he came in, and nobody was talking now.

"Lord, Mama," he said, between mouthfuls of greens, "you outdid yourself. This and a piece of Aunt Precious's Key lime pie . . ." He looked up.

Mama was a tall, slender woman. She had the delicate,

chiseled features and "good" soft brown hair that were throwbacks to their slave-owner ancestors. Daddy had married the prettiest of the Williams twins and Geoffrey looked just like her, right down to her fair, almost white, skin. Aunt Precious, who was seven minutes older than Mama, was large-boned with a round face and full features. She was half a foot shorter than Mama, and had skin the color of pecans, just like Calvin. She looked younger than Mama, but nobody took them for sisters at all, let alone twins.

"So, how are my two favorite girls?"

Mama inspected her nails, lacquered a soft blue with the skyline of Chicago stenciled on in a deeper shade. Aunt Precious seem to be looking just to his left.

Calvin squared his shoulders, gave him a condescending look over wire-rimmed glasses, and cleared his throat, a habit that always annoyed Geoffrey.

Geoffrey managed to bring his fork to his mouth and push the sleeve of his jogging suit back at the same time, flashing the new Rolex.

"Another deal?" Calvin asked.

Geoffrey didn't answer. Mama looked from the Rolex to him, then gave her twin the slightest nod. Equally impressed, Aunt Precious smiled. Geoffrey grinned at Calvin and sucked a bit of food from between his teeth. He was Henderson Bailey's youngest son and more like him than either of his brothers. And Henderson Bailey was the world's greatest hustler, even if he was always legit. Bailey's Real Estate, founded on slum holdings from Chicago to Aurora, had damned near made the old man a millionaire and would have for sure if he hadn't dropped dead of a massive coronary at forty-three. Even so, neither his wife nor his children would ever want for anything, even if it was all held in trusts.

Calvin cleared his throat again. "You know, Geoffrey . . ."

"Have you ever thought of seeing a hypnotist or maybe a psychiatrist for that throat clearing . . . ?" He almost said "shit," but caught himself in time. "Maybe it has something to do with you being the shortest. . . ." He didn't add, and the darkest, like he usually did, because Mama was here, but he could tell by the sour expression on Calvin's face that he had thought of it.

"Geoffrey," Calvin said, "we've been having a family meeting."

"Without the entire family?"

"Something came up and you weren't . . . available."

"Oh? What came up?"

"We thought . . ." Laurence began. Always the sports announcer, he spoke in a deep, resonant voice, not that that ever caused anyone in the family to pay any attention to him. Even when he was sitting, Laurence's height was apparent. He topped seven feet and had played professional basketball. "I think—"

"Aunt Precious has a . . . condition," Calvin cut in.

Geoffrey dropped his fork, jumped up, and rushed over to her. "What's wrong? What is it?" He held her by both shoulders and looked her in the eyes. "Don't try to keep anything from me."

"Geoffrey," Laurence began, "it's just—"

"Cut the act," Calvin said.

"Now, Calvin," Mama said, "you know how close—"

Geoffrey squatted beside his aunt's chair. "Now tell me; what is it?"

"It's just a little heart condition, that's all."

"Your heart!"

"Don't shout, Geoffrey."

"Sorry, Mama, but if anything happened to either of you . . ."

"The doctor says it's nothing to be alarmed about, baby, just something to take care of. You know what a time I have keeping my pressure down."

Geoffrey rocked back on his heels. "You're sure it's not serious? You're telling me the truth?"

Aunt Precious patted his shoulder. "That's my baby. Of course I'm all right."

"The point is, Geoffrey . . ."

"What, Calvin?" The tendons in his feet and ankles were killing him. "Now look," he stood up, "I don't appreciate you having this family conference without me, not when it's about my favorite aunt." His only aunt, and he did love her, no matter what Calvin thought. He had a standing order at the florist's to deliver flowers for her and Mama every other week.

"Oh, Geoffrey," she said, as he gave her a kiss on the cheek. Behind her back, she might be "poor Precious," but her husband had left her plenty. It wasn't close to what Daddy left Mama, of course, but still.

Calvin cleared his throat again. "We've decided that Aunt Precious will move in with Mama."

"Okay. And?" That made sense. They talked on the phone half the day and one of them was always visiting the other, not to mention church, shopping, and vacations.

"And we talked with Sister Shirley Hawkins," Mama said.

"And?" Sister Hawkins was like family.

"She's just a little short of money, Geoffrey, so she's converted her downstairs into two lovely apartments. Separate baths and all."

"And?"

"Calvin rented one of the apartments for you."

"He *what?*" He was careful to keep his voice down, but even he could hear the tremor of anger.

"I've brought some of your things over already," Calvin said. "I couldn't get at the stuff down in the basement; you'll have to move that yourself."

"You *what?*"

"Keep your voice down," Mama said.

"You let him do this?"

"You know, Geoff—" Laurence began.

"Ahem. You're a big boy now, Geoffrey," Calvin said. "Thirty-nine is certainly old enough to leave home."

"Who asked you?" They were not going to put him out of his own home. And certainly not because Aunt Precious was moving in.

"Geoffrey," Mama said, "you know how you get if you're around cats very long."

"Cats?"

"Yes, and birds."

He didn't have allergies to either. That was just his excuse for not having the time to visit Aunt Precious more often.

"Sarah will be coming with me."

"What?" Sarah Vaughan moving in with Miles Davis? That cat and that dog were so spoiled there was no way they could coexist.

"Yes, baby, and Cluck and Hoot."

Good taste and decorum had gone right out the window with cockatoos.

"Ahem. So, you see . . ."

"Calvin . . ."

"I think you two—" Laurence began.

"Now, Geoffrey," Mama said. "Calvin's idea is perfect for everyone. Sister Hawkins has been in that big old house ever since her second husband died. That son of hers moved out a couple of years ago, and he's never there anymore."

Sister Hawkins's son by her first marriage to Reverend Ross. Her son the cop. The tall one who always reeked of Obsession for Men when he ran into him at church. Slim. Now he was supposed to move in with the mother of a cop. Right. Nothing like getting up close and personal with the law, especially in his line of work. Next he would be expected to hold down a regular job.

"You'll be right in the center of town," Mama went on.

Sure, Lincoln Prairie, right in the middle of Scamsville. He should have kept his business ventures in Chicago, but the place was getting too dangerous. Time was a man had to set himself up as a mark before anybody bothered him. Now he just had to be on the wrong corner of the wrong street at the wrong time and he was history. He had been thinking about checking out Milwaukee, but not until next year.

"And you know Deacon Evans."

"Deacon Evans? What about him?"

"He owns the—" Laurence said.

"Ahem. He has that property on Sherman where those black-owned stores are."

"Right." A barbershop, beauty shop, boutique, printer, and a Chinese restaurant. They sure couldn't be talking about a job; no way he'd have anything to do with any of that.

"He needs help," Mama said. "None of us is getting any younger." Her eyes filled as she reached across the table to squeeze her twin's hand. "You're still a young man, Geoffrey. And you've got neither chick nor child. Sister Hawkins will feel so much safer with you and Edna Robinson's boy in the house."

So they had taken care of renting both apartments.

"And Deacon Evans is eighty-five if he's a day. He can't keep up with that property no more. Now that his brother's son passed, he doesn't have anyone."

Not only was he supposed to become some kind of protection or whatever for Sister Hawkins, but he was going to have to be a gofer for Deacon Evans too. Poor man—hah! Old, alone, afraid—just like the woman he had spoken to today. Sister Hawkins and Deacon Evans were just like her. Maybe this wasn't such a bad idea after all. Sister Hawkins wasn't much of a prospect, not with her son the cop around, but Old Man Evans couldn't be too far from passing on. Minimum, he might end up owning some real estate, just like his old man. Geoffrey crumbled the last of his corn bread on the rest of the greens.

"And we can't have you wheezing and sneezing and sniffling because Sarah Vaughan and the birds are here."

If he had known where that lie would lead, he wouldn't have told it. No way he could get away with a miraculous recovery or medical error now. He finished his iced tea. "Lord, that sure was good."

"Would you like some more, baby?"

"Just some tea."

Mama took his plate to the sink and added a slice of

lemon when she refilled his glass. She cut him a wedge of pie too.

"Now, Geoffrey, this is going to turn out to be much better than you think. My big sister just moved in, and the animals will be here sometime tomorrow." Mama gave Aunt Precious a hug. "We've been together since before we were born, and we're going to be together and take care of each other now."

Geoffrey sucked on a toothpick. There was no way he could argue with that.

CHAPTER

7

At 7:00 A.M. Wednesday morning Fred Jhanke arranged Cream of Wheat, a soft-boiled egg, and a cup of tea on his mother's tray. She was sitting by the window, waiting as he entered her room. She smiled as he put down the tray, but there was something in her expression, her eyes. It wasn't pain or fear. She was watchful. Why?

"Morning, Mother," he said. "Your favorite." As he bent over to kiss her cheek, he inhaled, but smelled only camphor, not urine. "You slept well?"

"Of course, dear." There was just the slightest quaver in her voice.

He glanced about but didn't see anything out of place. Turning, he walked from the room. It was cool when he went outside to feed the feral cat that kept the birds away. She had made her home beneath the porch, and he could see her dark bulk and yellow eyes as he squatted to fill her dish. She was heavy with kittens again. Once they were born, he would wait until she left them alone to whisk them away.

At 9:00 A.M. Fred said good-bye to his mother and left the house just as he always did. Before driving to Milwaukee as he had planned, he parked the car half a block away and walked back. He let himself into the house as soundlessly as possible, took off his shoes, and tiptoed to Mother's room.

"Forgot something," he said.

She tried to put something behind her back, but she couldn't move that fast. Fred walked over to her and held out his hand. Without speaking, she gave him what looked like a pager.

"Where did you get this?" He turned it over in his hand. It was too light. "I said, where did you get this?"

". . . I . . ."

He threw it on the floor and it came apart. There was nothing inside. He picked up the pieces and held them out so she could see them. "Mother, where did you get this? Tell me now."

"A . . . a man."

"A man? Someone came to this door and you let him in?"

"No . . . no . . . Fred . . . Of course not. He didn't have to come in to make it work."

"Make it work? Look, Mother, this is just an empty case. There is nothing inside to work."

She blinked rapidly.

"Don't cry, Mother. Don't cry."

"No, dear."

"Now. Tell me about this man."

"He rang the bell. I had the chain on. I didn't let him in. He did something with the doorbell and the light to make it work."

"To make it work? Work doing what?"

"It's an alarm, Fred, that's all. If I were in here alone and someone broke in, I could just push that button and the police would come. I'm alone so—"

"Mother, there is nothing inside. You could have pushed the button until you dropped dead and nobody would come. Do you understand that?"

She nodded.

"Now. How did you pay for this?"

She blinked again.

"How did you pay for it?"

"I . . . I . . . my watch. I gave him my watch. He said—"

"I don't want to hear what he said."

Fred rushed over to her bureau and looked through everything in the top drawer. The watch was gone. At least it wasn't worth much. But this stupid old woman, answering the door to a stranger. He walked toward her.

"Mother, you are an old woman, a very old woman. This man took advantage of you. He sold you nothing, absolutely nothing. He conned you out of your watch. If it wasn't for me, if you were here alone and didn't have anyone to take care of you, you might have had something else to give him, like a blank check or your bankbook." He stopped and looked down at her. He didn't speak until he could tell by the odor that she had lost control of her bladder. Then he said, "Do not open the door to anyone ever again. Do you understand?"

She nodded.

"Good. I'll get you a diaper."

Opal sat at the window and looked out at the pine trees with wide branches that began low to the ground. There were no squirrels this year. There always used to be squirrels scampering about in the yard. What had happened to them? Why had they gone away? And the birds. There used to be such an abundance of sparrows. If they still nested in the fir trees, she couldn't hear them either. Of course with the windows closed . . . but . . . Fred was right. It wasn't safe for her to be alone in the house with any of the windows open. Everything had to be locked, safe, secure. If only this were still the back porch and she could sit out here and feel the breeze against her skin and the sun on her face and listen to the children playing down the street. Did children still live on this block? Had they grown up or moved away? A radio would be nice. But the electric bills would be too high. They couldn't afford it.

Opal sipped tap water from a glass and tried not to wish it was coffee instead. What had gotten into her today? She was feeling old and cranky. If she had known that this was what getting old was like, she would not have wanted to live a long life like her grandparents. Her parents would have lived to be old like she was if it hadn't been for the accident. Now she had lived to be old. Better to have died like her parents, she thought, then said, "Dear God, please forgive me."

She focused on the sunshine, the brightness on the grass, a few places in shadow. Fred Senior should have planted tulips on this side of the house too. She had suggested it but there was something about the pattern of his planting that made him decide not to. Everything had to be done in a neat and orderly fashion to suit Fred Senior. Fred was so much like his father.

A sudden noise startled her. It came again. Just the garbage truck. If it had been closer, if it had been someone trying to break into the house . . . But her alarm was gone. It wasn't fake, like Fred had said. It would have worked. That nice young man would not have just taken her jewelry. Her watch! She had forgotten about that. It had fallen behind the headboard where she couldn't reach it. It must have been a month ago. If Fred found it . . . She trembled. Fred was so angry with her and his anger lasted for such a long time. At least he would be polite about it. Fred got angry just the way his father had.

CHAPTER
8

Damn, Geoffrey thought, as he walked through the apartment. *This sure as hell couldn't be any smaller.* Not that it mattered that the kitchen wasn't any bigger than one of Mama's walk-in closets. He didn't plan to do any cooking. And he didn't need much more than a bed and dresser in the bedroom, although it pissed him off not to have enough room for more of his clothes. But where in the hell was he going to put his stereo equipment? Nice of Calvin to move his clothes and personal stuff here and leave everything important at home. And then there was that little project he was working on in the basement. No way he could move any of that here.

It was worse than a motel. Everything was plain and beige and boring. At least there weren't any frilly curtains or floral wallpaper. And this couch. He sat down. He could feel the spring. He hadn't tried the bed yet. No telling how thin the mattress was. And the furniture. Rejects from a yard sale, all of it. Why had Calvin rented this place furnished? The least Calvin could have done was bring his television over and his stereo equipment. He was going to have to bring Mama here right away. That damned Calvin. How had he managed to talk Mama into going along with this? As soon as she saw these living conditions she would insist that he move back home.

At least there was a telephone. He dialed a number in Chicago, and got an answering machine. Gayle was at work. He left a message. It was always so much fun to see her after spending time with Kayla. She always pretended Kayla didn't exist.

There was a knock on the door.

"Geoffrey." Sister Shirley Hawkins. "I heard you moving in this morning."

She was holding a foil-covered dish. As Mama would say, God bless her heart. "I thought you might not have had time to go grocery shopping, what with getting settled and all." Groceries? They didn't expect him to cook? Sister Hawkins walked right past him and came in without waiting to be invited. Damn, Mama didn't even do that.

He was going to have to get out of here: no space, no privacy, no cleaning woman like he had at home, and from the looks of it, damned little home cooking. He wondered what was on the plate. He couldn't smell anything. He hadn't eaten since he had had breakfast with Mama this morning and it was almost two o'clock.

"Why, thank you, Sister Hawkins." She was a tall, slender woman with dark hair and dark eyes. Strands of gray caught the light, and there were just the beginnings of lines at the corners of her eyes. Her skin was a soft, unblemished amber. She must have been one fine-looking sister when she was young. He would have guessed her age at mid- to late forties if Mama hadn't told him she was sixty-one and had to wait for another year to collect her deceased husband's Social Security.

Geoffrey gave her the wide, dimpled version of his smile. "You're right. I'm starved." There wasn't anything as good as an old church sister's cooking. He took the plate to the table, got a knife and a fork, and sat down. Then he pulled back the foil. What the ... sliced chicken, white meat, no skin, lettuce, tomato, and cucumber, no dressing, and two peach halves. Where in the hell was the food?

"Now if there's anything you need, Geoffrey, just let me know."

"Yes, ma'am."

"I can find my way out. Enjoy your meal."

Meal? What meal? This wasn't even worth calling a snack. He didn't say anything aloud. There was something about Sister Hawkins that didn't invite flattery or cajoling—or complaints. She was more like an army sergeant than a minister's wife. No wonder her son was a cop. This was not going to work at all.

He ate, but only because he was hungry. And he washed the plate before returning it—washing dishes, something Mama never would have allowed. His stomach was grumbling as he went out the front door.

It took Geoffrey a while to locate Deacon Evans. When he did find the old man he was in his backyard planting flowers around the stump of a tree. The rest of the yard was overgrown with weeds.

"Well, now," Evans said. He got up slowly and stood there, holding the small of his back. Geoffrey remembered the deacon as both younger and taller. Evans seemed to have shrunk in his old age. The top of his head just reached Geoffrey's shoulder.

"Well, now," Evans said again. He squinted as he looked up at him, as if he should be wearing glasses. "You're Princess's boy, right?"

"Yes, sir."

"Good. Good. I need some help around here."

"Just what kind of help did you have in mind?" Geoffrey hoped he didn't think he was going to help him with his gardening.

"I've got all this property and just can't keep up with it."

"I don't do maintenance, sir."

"Oh? And just what kind of work do you do?"

"Management, accounting, things like that."

Evans rubbed the gray stubble of beard on his chin. "Well, that's good, since that's basically what I need you for. I was just asking because nobody seemed quite sure of just what kind of work you were in."

"Well, that's it, sir. That's what I do."

"Good, because—" he took in the yard with a sweep of his arm—"this is what I want to do."

Geoffrey thought of the block-long strip of shops the old man owned, with rental apartments right above them.

Maybe he would have his own office. He might even find a place private enough for a workshop. There was no need for him to rush into anything. This looked like one time when everything he wanted would fall right into his hands.

Marti and Vik spent the morning in court. It was early afternoon when they returned to the precinct. They had been in the office for less than half an hour when Janet Petrosky, the coroner, called. "MacAlister? Glad I caught you before you went home."

"Why?" Marti asked.

"I've got news you're going to want."

"Why? What have you got?"

"Virginia McCroft."

"Is that our fire victim?"

"I couldn't believe it, Marti," Janet said. "I just saw her at a city council meeting last week."

"She was on the city council?"

"No, she just went to most of the meetings. And you two need to come over."

There was no need to ask why. The medical examiner had found something suspicious.

"What have we got?" Vik asked when she hung up.

"They ID'd the fire victim. Virginia McCroft."

"Virginia?" Vik said.

"You knew her?"

"She was a couple of years ahead of me in school."

"Oh," Marti said. It was always a kick in the gut, not only when you knew the victim, but when it was one of your peers—when your birth dates weren't too far apart. "Janet wants us to come over. Now."

Vik's hand stopped midway to his coffee cup.

"Son of a gun," Vik said as they hurried over to the County Medical Examiner's Building. "Virginia McCroft."

"How well did you know her?"

"It was impossible not to know her. We went to the only high school in town."

"That doesn't answer my question."

"She was very popular."

She caught him by the arm. "Is that why we're walking so fast? She's now very dead."

He slowed down. "Virginia. Damn. This could be a tough one. My sister-in-law will drive me nuts until we find out what happened. They were classmates."

"What do you know about her?" Marti asked.

"Not much. She never married." Vik shook off her hand on his arm. "Her father was an alderman for years. Died in office. Heart attack." He was walking fast again. "I think that if Virginia wasn't a woman, she would have followed in his footsteps. Not that she couldn't have, but her old man had different ideas about women. Politics was a man's work."

"Like policing?" she said, remembering when he'd said the same thing about their job.

"Something like that," he admitted.

"Vik, there is no need to jog to the morgue. She's not going anywhere."

"She had a letter to the editor in the paper last week. Did that a lot. Something about the leash law this time, I think. The mayor's comment was that she was a public nuisance. I never liked her much, but even a person who inspires that kind of dislike shouldn't be dead."

He all but ran up the steps to the coroner's facility and, once inside, announced that he would not view the body.

"What was it with you and her?" Marti asked.

Vik looked at her. "What do you mean?"

"Come on, Vik. We jogged over here."

"She tried to take me away from Mildred."

"What?"

"That's right." He spoke with pride. "And in those days, Virginia could have had any man she wanted."

"And how old were you when all this happened?"

"We were all in high school. Virginia was two grades

ahead of me. She asked me to take her to the harvest dance. I refused. You wouldn't believe the lies she told trying to get Mildred to break up with me, but Mildred was too smart for that. I gave Mildred a friendship ring the night of the dance. Virginia ended up with that stupid, headline-grabbing varsity quarterback because she couldn't have me."

Marti didn't ask him anything else. The arrogance of the male ego continued to amaze her.

Janet Petrosky met them in the hall. "No purse, but her clothing was still intact. We found one of those check-cashing cards and a cash register receipt in her jacket pocket. Decomposition is pretty well advanced—we are not making any estimates on time of death—so dental records confirmed her identity. And I've got something I want you to look at." She led the way into a room where two X rays hung on a lit viewer. "Look," she said, and pointed. There was a bullet in the rib cage. "The attendants saw the entrance wound when they were cleaning her up."

"Then it is Virginia," Vik said. "And she was shot."

"Yes. We won't know more until the autopsy tomorrow morning."

"You can't say for certain that this killed her?" Vik asked.

"I can't say anything, except that it's there."

"Jeez," Vik said. "She was always so damned . . . right. I can't imagine why anyone would want to see her dead."

As soon as they left the coroner's facility, Marti and Vik drove over to the street where McCroft lived to talk with the neighbors while there was still a little daylight. Virginia Mc-Croft lived on the west side of town in a white-sided colonial with white trim. White shades were aligned at midpoint at all of the front windows, and white sheers or white drapes could be seen below them. The garage door was closed. The street was empty, although some of the other houses had cars in the driveways or the open bays of the garages. Lawns were clipped short and jonquils, tulips, and crocuses were in bloom. There was a notable absence of children and not one driveway with a basketball hoop.

While Vik went around to the back, Marti checked the front door and the garage, both locked. Next she checked the windows, which were too high to reach without a stepladder. None were open; none had pry marks that she could see. An evergreen hedge was planted beneath the front windows as well as those on both sides of the house. The dirt that surrounded them was soft, but Marti didn't see footprints or any indentations that could indicate someone had tried to gain entry. Compared with the neighbors' yards, there was a noticeable absence of flowering bulbs.

"Hey there, miss," a man called. Marti could tell by his voice he was old. "Looking for something?"

She turned. A tall man with longish white hair stood about ten feet away from her. He was leaning on a cane. A sheltie stood beside him, ears pointed, eyes alert.

"Lincoln Prairie Police Department," Marti said. She took out her shield. "Detective MacAlister."

"Don Riley." His hand shook with tremors as he extended it. "Don't tell me someone has gotten around to actually doing Virginia in?" He smiled as he spoke.

"What makes you ask that, Mr. Riley?"

His eyes narrowed. "Are you serious?"

"Yes sir, I am."

"Well." He rubbed his chin. "I've known Virginia all her life, and she does have a knack for speaking her mind, just like her old man. *Has* something happened to her?"

"Do you know of any reason why something might happen to her?"

"There're probably a whole parcel of reasons." He gave a short, dry laugh then cocked his head to one side and looked at her as if he still wasn't sure if she was serious. "I imagine Virginia's managed to be a thorn in the side of more than a few."

"Such as?" Marti asked.

"Well now, let's see. There're those on the county board

who want more land development." He banged his cane on the ground. "Virginia let them have it, all right. Let them know we want a little open space and fresh air. Damned developers just want to make money. Then there were those zoning changes they tried to steamroller through. Condos, I think. Some kind of multiple housing. Like cramming people together is ever a good thing." He paused and looked at the McCroft house, then at Marti. "Really, has something happened to Virginia? Is that why you're here?"

"Mr. Riley, have you noticed anything out of the ordinary lately?"

"Around here?"

"Yes."

"Involving Virginia?"

"Not necessarily."

"No. This is a quiet street, quiet neighborhood. Just about everyone on our block is retired. Biggest thing to happen around here is Sunday visits from the grandkids, and that doesn't happen often enough."

"When's the last time you saw Virginia McCroft?"

He thought for a moment, then said, "Last Friday. She backed that car out of the garage and took off like she was in a hurry. I was out here talking to my nephew about cutting down that tree. It's a Chinese elm, too tall and too brittle. Needs to go." He steadied himself by holding the cane with both hands and rocked back on his heels. "Are you going to tell me why you're asking all of these questions? And why Virginia isn't here to answer them herself?"

There wasn't any reason not to. "Virginia McCroft is dead."

Mr. Riley's hand trembled as he ran his fingers through his hair. He sighed. "I can remember Virginia in pigtails. Heart attack, I suppose, like her father. Weak hearts run in the family. What about her mother?"

"Her mother?" Vik hadn't mentioned her.

"Yes. Someone will have to tell her. I'm afraid I can't suggest who, but there must be someone. Unless there's some kind of legal requirement that it has to be you."

"Where is her mother?" Marti asked.

"Nursing home," Mr. Riley said. "The one on Sunny-brook. My wife and I used to go see her when I could still drive. Virginia was her only child."

"Do you know how old she is?"

"Ninety-two," he said. "Five years older than me."

Too old for a complete stranger to tell her her daughter was dead.

"You never expect to bury your children," Mr. Riley said. "Little Virginia. Cute as a button she was." He sniffed and Marti saw that his eyes had filled. "Guess I'd better go tell the wife." His shoulders were slumped and his pace slow as he walked away.

"Hey, MacAlister," Vik called. She turned to see him stand-ing near the front of the house and walked toward him.

"Get anything out of the old man?" he asked as she neared.

"Not really."

"The kitchen door was unlocked. I called for an evidence tech and a couple of teams to canvass the neighborhood. Let's check the nearest houses while we're waiting."

It was nearing seven o'clock and getting dark when the evidence tech and a team of uniforms arrived. By then Vik had interviewed the people who lived in the two houses across the street while she talked with the neighbors to the right, who remembered seeing McCroft backing out of her garage about a week ago, but couldn't recall seeing her since. The neighbors to the left of McCroft's house were not at home. One lady Vik spoke with remembered seeing Vir-ginia picking jonquils last Thursday or Friday.

"From what I can tell, she was busy," Vik said. "Nobody knew doing what, just zipping in and out all of the time. She took early retirement from her job to take care of her mother, put her in a home when it became too much for her. Accord-ing to the neighbors she didn't have much to do with them beyond hello and a comment about the weather. Too bad. If any of them wanted to know why I was asking questions, they weren't concerned enough about her to ask."

"Mr. Riley seemed a little upset."

"It probably has something to do with his age. There's nobody within whistling distance under sixty-five, but he's the only one who's ninety."

"Eighty-seven," she corrected.

"Ninety," Vik insisted. "Retired minister in the house right across the street said so. They seem to be an interesting bunch for old people, but not a snoop among them. They all seemed to think she had a heart attack like her old man. I didn't contradict anyone, but I did suggest that they keep their doors locked. They looked at me like I was nuts. Of course they keep their doors locked."

"But McCroft's was not."

"Exactly. I'll bet half of them can't remember whether they lock them or not."

"Virginia wasn't that old."

"No," Vik agreed. "She wasn't."

Marti gave up on trying to get home before the kids went to bed and decided to shoot for midnight. "Why don't we go to the nursing home where the mother is while the tech is checking things out here?" she suggested.

When Marti asked to see Mrs. McCroft and explained why, the nurse cautioned that her memory wasn't what it used to be and advised against any mention of Virginia's death until the doctor could be consulted.

"This isn't such a bad place," Vik commented, as they walked down the hall.

"As these places go," Marti conceded. There weren't any odd odors, and she had been able to recognize the meatloaf and mashed potatoes on one of the residents' trays.

Mrs. McCroft was in a well-lit room that she shared with a woman who looked at least one decade younger. The walls were pastel yellow and the curtains cotton with a bright floral print. White and yellow jonquils in a milk glass vase had wilted, while a bouquet of balloons on Mrs. McCroft's nightstand danced in the air currents. There was another balloon tied to the handle of her wheelchair and she was wearing Tweety Bird slippers.

"Well, hello," Mrs. McCroft said, and gave them a bright smile. "It's so nice to have visitors. You're here about Virginia, aren't you?"

Marti hesitated, said nothing.

Mrs. McCroft looked up at Vik. "I remember you from the last time I went to school; now let me see . . ." Her voice was scratchy and high-pitched. "Oh, dear . . . I'm sorry . . . I've gotten so terrible with names." She thought for a minute then said, "What has Virginia been up to now? She is such a good girl, you know. At least when she's at home. High-strung, that's all, and a little impatient at times." She leaned forward and whispered, "She is so much smarter than the other children. That's what it is. Can't you put her in a class with smarter students?"

"Have you seen Virginia today, Mrs. McCroft?" Vik asked.

"Why of course, just this morning before she went to school."

They spoke with the nurse on their way out. She couldn't remember the last time Mrs. McCroft had visited the present, and no, she didn't always know who her daughter was. Mrs. McCroft was frequently unable to recognize Virginia and often mistook her daughter for Lucille, her older sister and Virginia's only aunt, who had died years ago.

CHAPTER
10

Opal wanted to tiptoe to the closet but she couldn't. The house was so quiet that the noise her slippers made scuffing against the linoleum sounded like sandpaper on wood. Whoever was in the house must be able to hear her. She jumped as she opened the door, startled by the rasp of the hinge. He would find her, dear God, he would find her. She pushed at the clothing that brushed against her face, gasping as she walked into the wall. Her heart was beating so fast. She clutched at her chest. It hurt to breathe. The footsteps came closer. The door. She should have closed the door. He would see her feet. He would find her.

He pushed her bedroom door open so hard that the knob banged against the wall. Her knees gave way. She clutched at a coat to keep from falling. He pushed the closet door shut. She felt suddenly safe in the darkness. Then the door opened. She screamed.

"Mother! What are you doing in there? What's wrong?"

Opal almost toppled forward. Instead she hit her shoulder on the door jamb.

"Fred," she said. "Fred, you frightened me so."

"*I* frightened you? How could I frighten you, Mother? I just came home. I do that every day."

His narrow face was stern with displeasure. His blue eyes cold as ice.

"Fred . . . I . . . I . . ." She leaned against the wall. She felt so weak. She had to get to her chair. If she asked him to help her he would put her to bed, and Lord knew when he would let her get up again.

"Mother, you don't look well at all. I think you should lie down."

"No, no. I'm fine, Fred, really. Just fine." She took one step then another. She couldn't lie in that bed again the way she had to last month. There was nothing to look at but the walls and the ceiling, and there wasn't even a picture on the walls.

Her chair. She was almost there. She tried to ignore the pain in her chest and concentrate on putting one foot in front of the other.

"Mother, if this happens again, you're going to have to start getting more rest. Maybe you're spending too much time by that window. You're beginning to imagine things."

Opal said nothing. If she protested, he might even take her chair away. She sat very still and remained very quiet, just the way she would have with Fred Senior. After a few minutes, her son walked away.

Fred went to his room. That stupid old woman. Who had she allowed in the house? Who had she bought that worthless piece of junk from? Who had she given her watch to? That watch wasn't hers to give away. According to his father's will, everything in this house belonged to him. She had no right to give anything away, and whoever came here and took that watch—his watch—had no right to have it. He would find whoever it was. Nobody ever took anything that was his. And nobody ever gave anything of his away.

CHAPTER 11

Geoffrey felt claustrophobic as soon as he sat down in Deacon Evans's office. The room was small and the old wooden desk took up at least a third of the space. There were two wingbacked chairs, one in front of and one behind the desk, both old, like the deacon, the leather cracked with age. Boxes of paper were stacked everywhere. Big, old, thirteen-column black ledgers were piled on the shelves of a bookcase. The ledger he had opened was dated 1987. Only three pages had entries. He reached for one at the bottom of the pile, then changed his mind. From the looks of it, the old man hadn't kept any records in years.

Evans had a bald head. He wore wire-rimmed glasses that he pushed near the tip of his nose so that he could look over the tops when he wasn't reading. Sitting in the chair, he looked small. "Now here," he said. He chose a box and put it on the desk. "This is all of this year's papers."

It was only the end of April. The box, one that a twenty-five-inch television had come in, was filled almost to the top. This was looking just a little bit too much like work. Geoffrey wondered who did Evans's taxes but didn't ask. Did the old man just give whoever it was the whole box?

"Most of this is simple enough," Evans said.

Evans smelled old. Geoffrey couldn't tell what it was, old newspaper, old clothes—he didn't know. But it was a peculiar odor that wasn't masked by aftershave and made him think of death. He tried to aim his nose above the old man's head, while still looking him mostly in the eye. He pushed his chair back a little and just about managed it.

"Now, son, these here are my rent receipts." Evans pulled a shoe box out of a desk drawer and put it on top of the pile of papers. "These folks are all real good about paying on time. I just put 'em right out if they don't. Don't sign no lease or nothing. Handshakes, that's all, gentleman's agreement." He opened another drawer, pulled out another shoe box, and put it beside the one with the rent receipts. "This here is the slips they give you when you go to the bank, and I got all the letters they send in here too."

Bank statements. A good place to start, Geoffrey decided. The old man must have plenty. Did he keep it all in the bank, or did he not trust banks? What were all of these other papers, the ones that weren't sorted? What had he let himself in for? Was it worth it? Did he even know enough to figure out any of this, let alone how to get some of it for himself? He hadn't exactly paid attention when he took that accounting class. He wasn't even sure he had passed. He hadn't even been to school in years now, just let Mama think he was going and pocketed the tuition money Mama gave him.

"Now what we need to do is get this month's rents counted up and make out a deposit slip. I just raised the rents. Do that every year. Nobody is going to think the property is worth something if I don't."

Geoffrey counted the cash, then the old man did as well. Evans put the money into a bank bag. "You just go to drop it off. Bank's the one right up the street."

As Evans leaned back in the old leather chair, Geoffrey realized what a little man he was, short and skinny with an old, dark face, a child's smooth skin, and clear eyes. "Now, son, I know this looks like a lot of work, and maybe it is; but with your schooling and experience and all, it shouldn't be that hard at all. I been talking with Princess about this for a while now. Got to have someone around me I can trust, someone who's already got money and don't need to be trying to steal none of mine. Your mama says you can handle this in your sleep, but I expect it will take you a little time to get it all figured out. Two, three weeks at least."

Geoffrey's head began hurting. He was getting a migraine. No, he didn't get migraines, not really. Maybe he would start now. Who did he know, and how much would he have to pay? No, this was his golden goose. If he let anyone else in on it, he would be worse than a fool. He had never let anybody do anything for him that he wasn't smart enough to do himself. Best way to get cheated. And nobody was going to cheat him out of anything. He'd get a handle on this.

"Now don't you worry yourself none, Deacon Jones. What you need to do, though, is get a computer. Now, for say, two thousand, I can get you something that will work just fine."

"Two thousand? That's all?"

Damn. He'd almost said four.

"I'm talking basic, Deacon."

"Then that will do. I appreciate a man with enough sense to be thrifty."

The old man unlocked the door to another room, closed it behind him, and came out a few minutes later, cash in hand.

"Just in case you need a little extra," he explained, as he counted out twenty-five one-hundred-dollar bills. "With all you know about computers, I wouldn't want you to see something you needed and not be able to get it."

Man's a fool, Geoffrey thought, as he stepped out into the bright early afternoon sun. The wind was blowing cold off the lake. He zipped up his jacket. He would have to drive all the way into the city to hook up with a fence with a hot computer. How in the hell had he ever gotten himself into this? He didn't want to keep old man Evans's books. It would take him six months to straighten out those financial records, if he knew what he was doing. Who knew how long it would take since he didn't. The old fool didn't even balance his checkbook. He had sat right across from Evans, counted up the rents, and palmed two hundred dollars with the old man looking right at him. He didn't like things that weren't a challenge. On the one hand, he made it a point to never take anything from anybody who needed it worse than he did. On the other, he at least wanted to know that he had outsmarted them. Anyone could outsmart Deacon Jones.

As he got into Calvin's old Toyota, he thought about spending the two hundred on a brake job but decided against it. Mama was all set to spring for it. He had just about convinced the mechanic who agreed to work on it to sell him a sporty little Camaro convertible, provided the mechanic could convince Mama that this heap wasn't worth fixing. As guilty as Mama was feeling for having him move out, he didn't think it would be too much of a problem. He stopped at the bank, dropped off the deposit, and tried to decide where to go. He sure didn't want to go to Sister Hawkins's place. Maybe he'd stop by Mama's later tonight and figure out how to stay the night. If he did that often enough, he'd practically be living at home again.

By the time he gave the computer a second thought, he was on Green River Road heading north, the wrong direction if he wanted to shop. For five hundred, he could get just what the old man needed. Then he would have to figure out how to use the damned thing. He didn't feel like driving into the city, even though it was only a little after one and he had plenty of time. The expressway was always clogged with traffic no matter the time of day. Road rage didn't adequately describe how he felt after playing stop-and-go on the Dan Ryan for an hour and covering three miles.

It was too early to go to Mama's. He didn't want her to get the idea that working for Deacon Evans was easy. He thought of the box of papers again. And the shoe boxes. And the computer. He didn't know much more than how to turn one on, and he wasn't sure about that. No matter what Calvin said, there were a lot of things he was good at. This just didn't happen to be one of them.

Geoffrey slowed down. Everything was rural. Small farms. Houses with lots of land between them. He must be near the Wisconsin border. He turned where the road intersected with one going east-west, drove back, picked his mark. It was a small house with a big yard and lots of trees behind it. The nearest neighbor was a farmer with a weather-faded roadside sign advertising pumpkins, squash, gourds, and corn. A field not more than two acres was being readied for planting. Geoffrey checked the mailbox at the side of the road and parked in the driveway behind a 1986 Ford in near mint condition. He was willing to bet it hadn't clocked much more than thirty thousand miles.

An older woman kept the chain on as she opened the door. He guessed her age at about sixty-five. He preferred customers who were a little older.

"Good afternoon, Mrs. Nordstrom. I bet you think I'm selling something."

"And I bet you think I'm going to buy it."

Geoffrey favored her with his best wide-dimpled smile. Within five minutes he was inside. Something crunched under his feet and he glanced down. The carpet was covered with thick, filmy plastic. Before he had had time to look around, a pig came into the room, snorting and grunting, and pushing him until it stood between him and the woman. This was not a small pig, or one of those potbellied Vietnamese pigs. This was a full-sized porker, three hundred pounds if it weighed an ounce.

"This is Babette," Mrs. Nordstrom said. "She isn't very friendly, at least not right away, but as long as you don't try to get too close to me, she won't bite you."

Babette grunted and did what Geoffrey thought must be the equivalent to baring her teeth. He froze and looked around. A Confederate flag hung above the fireplace, with a rack of rifles on either side. What had he gotten himself into, a killer pig and a southern redneck with a Swedish name. Was his slave ancestry apparent?

"You did say I could pay you in kind for this alarm."

"Ma'am?"

Babette butted his leg and he took a step back.

"You said I didn't have to pay cash."

"Oh. Yes, ma'am." He tried to look around to see if she had anything valuable, but Babette was making a chomping kind of noise. He didn't know if that meant she was munching on something or if it meant she was hungry. He didn't want to find out. "Yes, umm, what did you have in mind? I can, umm, just go outside, install this, and be on my way."

"How about these?" the woman said. She walked over to a cabinet and the pig followed. Geoffrey moved and the pig swung its head around. He froze. When the pig turned away again, Geoffrey slid along the plastic without picking up his feet until the front door was right behind him. If the pig charged, he thought he could get the door open and get the hell out before its jaws clamped down on his leg.

"Here we are," Mrs. Nordstrom said. She was holding two candleholders, the kind with a handle. They were gray and made out of what looked to be metal.

What in the hell would he do with something like that? "Why yes, ma'am. This will just take a minute, if I can just go out on the porch . . ."

Without taking his eyes off the pig, he took small steps backward. The pig advanced at the same rate of speed. As he opened the door, it gave a loud snort. His hands shook as he pretended to install the alarm. When he was finished, he grabbed the candleholders the woman held out to him and got the hell out of there.

Marti and Vik returned to the McCroft house when the evidence techs were through with it. As soon as she walked inside, Marti decided that Virginia McCroft was a woman who did not believe in leaving any available space empty. Everything, from kitchen counters to the dining room sideboard and china cabinet and the tables and shelves in the living room, was covered with photos and memorabilia—and vases, large and small, all filled with artificial flowers. Artwork covered the walls. The larger pieces had lights, and Marti guessed that some of it was valuable. Sprays of plastic philodendron had been fastened above the ornate frames and also in corners and above cabinets.

"Jeez," Vik said. "If there are any clues among all this

junk, we'll never find them. She can't have been dead too long. There's not much dust."

Marti wondered how long it took to dust the house. "She must have a cleaning woman," she concluded. That was a place to start.

The four rooms upstairs were as crowded as the three downstairs. The clutter of bric-a-brac repeated itself. Nothing matched and it looked as if furniture from several places had been wedged into each room. Most of the photographs in one bedroom were muted blacks and whites and grays, the women dressed like long ago. Marti thought it must be Virginia McCroft's mother's room, or where she had moved her mother's belongings when she put her in the nursing home. Up here, just as downstairs, there was minimal dust. Only the master bedroom and bath were in disarray.

"Looks like a tornado went through," Vik said.

Marti looked about the room. It didn't look much worse than Joanna's. Virginia McCroft had kicked off her shoes, stepped out of her panty hose, and tossed her blouses toward a chair without bothering to pick them up if they didn't land there. She had also worn contacts, tossed her jewelry in a bowl with an Oriental dragon design, left the tops off of jars and bottles of cosmetics, and used a lot of cotton balls, most of which had missed the wastebasket. For whatever the reason, whoever cleaned the rest of the house wasn't allowed here.

There was a phone in the bedroom, with notes and numbers written haphazardly on a pad and Post-its stuck to the wall. Marti put them into a plastic bag. She went to the room with the desk and love seat where everything was in order. Ledgers and a large checkbook were in one desk drawer, manila file folders with papers sorted into them in another. A manual Remington typewriter was on a stand beside the desk. McCroft's Franklin planner was on the top of the desk, to one side, zippered shut. "That's odd."

"What?" Vik asked.

"She didn't have her planner with her."

"And? Both of us do just fine without one."

"I know, but this thing is supposed to be like an extension of your arm. There is a small notebook that you can use temporarily, but I've never met anyone who did." And this one was closed. Had McCroft intended to take it with her, or hadn't she gotten around to opening it for the day? Marti unzipped the planner and opened it at the plastic marker. Tuesday. Two meetings were penciled in, along with a visit to her mother. Nothing was written in for yesterday. Marti checked the month at a glance. There was nothing there either.

"Which part of the house seems the most like Virginia the way you remember her?"

Vik thought about that then said, "It's kind of funny. Her bedroom is the most obvious answer. She was the center of everything. There were kids all around her, whether she was having lunch in the cafeteria or walking down the halls." He rubbed his chin. "But even though you wouldn't think so to look back at her then, there *is* something about the order in the other rooms—like everything is in its place—that, when I look back, was Virginia too. It wouldn't surprise me if everything that's together had something in common, even though it didn't look that way to us."

When they returned to the precinct, Marti handed Vik the journals, checkbook, and about half of the files. She kept the planner. It was almost nine o'clock. She wanted to see her kids.

"I'm going to go home for a couple of hours," she said.

Vik was already scanning the checkbook, a ledger type with three checks to a page. Without looking up, he said, "Take your time. We're not going to solve this one tonight. Not unless we get real lucky and she wrote the name of the killer on her calendar."

Marti reached for the planner.

"Give that to me, MacAlister. The fire happened last night. We didn't even know she was in there until this afternoon, and we don't know how long she's been dead, but it has been a few days at least. This case was cold when we got it. Go tuck in the kids."

"I'll be back in about an hour," Marti said. It felt strange, leaving the planner and the files on her desk and going home.

CHAPTER
12

Opal clasped her hands in her lap and pressed her lips together. She would not cry. Not now, while Fred was here. He would get upset if he thought she was unhappy. She didn't want him to worry about her any more than he already was. Poor dear. She had given him such a fright today, hiding in the closet. Whatever had made her do that? Just because she thought she heard noises, thought she was alone in the house and someone had come in. Of course it was not the time of day when he would usually be at home, but if she reminded him of that . . . No, she couldn't let on that she even noticed such things. If he thought she suspected he no longer had a job, that would really upset him. Poor Fred. This must be such a difficult time for him, and there wasn't one thing she could say, one thing she could do. If only it hadn't come to this. If only Fred Senior had allowed her to have a job. If only she could have helped to put something aside for this day when they would need money. But then, who would have expected that she would live this long and, thank God, be so healthy.

The door to her room was ajar. Footsteps approached and Fred pushed it open and entered.

"Your favorite," he said, and put the tray with the bowl of mushroom soup on her tray table. The Jell-O was red, as always, and the tea would be tepid and bitter.

Opal smiled but did not speak, just in case he was still upset over the episode with the closet. She didn't want him to dwell on it. If he made too much of it, he might decide that sitting by the window was becoming too much for her and decide that she did need to spend more time in bed.

After he left, she dipped the spoon in the soup and stirred.

Mushroom soup. How she hated it. How she hated Jell-O. Just once she would like to have a hamburger or even a different kind of soup. Vegetable, her favorite. Her own soup, homemade, with beef stock and barley. And sugar in her tea, just a teaspoonful. She sniffed, brushed away a tear. "Old woman," she scolded herself. "Old woman, be grateful. Be grateful. You could be in a nursing home." She picked up the soup spoon. She was hungry. It was such a long time between breakfast and dinner, even if she didn't like what she was served at either meal.

When the tray was gone and the house was quiet, she wondered if Fred was gone. She used to be able to hear the front door close. Now she was never sure. Was she alone? If only she still had that alarm. If only there was some way to make Fred understand that she was frightened sometimes. What if she took sick all of a sudden? She didn't even know if they still had a phone. It had been a long time since she had seen one. Did anyone know she was here? Did they know she was still alive? If only she could find her cane. She could hardly make her way to the bathroom without it. There was certainly no way she could go outside.

It was a little before nine when Marti got home. The house was "coming along," as Momma said. Marti believed in letting a house become itself, gradually gathering what was important. Ordinarily, she would have headed for the family room in the basement first and said hello to Momma, but because the children were still up she went to the middle rooms, as the kids called them, because they were wedged between the ground floor and the bedrooms on the top level.

The adults had settled into the middle room at the front of the house. Ben's desk was centered where the tall, many-planed windows faced the street. Marti's rocking chair and footstool were nearby, along with a card table holding a jigsaw puzzle everyone was putting together. She had put up sheer white café curtains and valances to let in the light, and Momma had hung four large-leaved philodendrons from the ceiling, where they could catch the morning sun. With spring easing in, warmer days and more sunshine to offset the still cold nights, Marti and Ben had taken to bringing their early morning coffee up here.

Joanna's exercise bike was in one corner. Headphones dangled from the handlebars, and Ben had rigged a little shelf so she could read while she pedaled. Goblin, their cat, was napping on one of Theo's sweaters, which she had dragged into the closet. Goblin was cautious where strangers were concerned but affectionate with members of the family. When startled or approached too quickly by someone unfamiliar, she ran away. Tonight she peered out of the closet and stretched, first one hind leg, then the other.

Marti squatted on the braided rug and called to her. "Come on, Goblin, come on." Goblin was either black with white patches or vice versa. "Come on, girl." The cat ran over with a soft meow and rubbed against her when Marti stroked her between her ears.

The boys had taken over the other middle room. Books and toys and games crammed the shelves built into one wall; and the computer was here, as well as a long, narrow table for Theo's experiments, an aquarium with one fat goldfish, and a terrarium with two African fire toads. Theo's model airplane was on one of the shelves. It hadn't been there yesterday. The airplane worried her. Theo and Johnny had been working on it when Johnny was killed. Theo had never finished putting it together. He'd kept it on his bureau after Johnny died. When they came here, he had left it packed in a box. Now it was out again. She didn't know why. Theo was just like his father, uncommunicative, although that had changed just a little since he had known Ben and Mike. The model plane was an uncomfortable reminder for her of the months after Johnny's death when Theo had said nothing at all.

The sound of children whispering distracted her. A friend of Ben's had put in a loft that could only be reached by a ladder. Marti had added a small bookcase, a lamp, and bright, primary colored pillows. Theo and Mike were up there now. She could hear their muffled giggles.

"What's up?" Marti called.

"Ma, wow, you're home early."

Theo and Mike came down the ladder. Both boys hugged her. She kissed their foreheads and rubbed their soft, kinky hair. "Homework done?"

"Hours ago," Theo said.

"Everything okay?"

"Yup," Mike said, grinning.

"How about some cocoa before you go to bed?"

"Yes," Both boys ran down the short flight of stairs ahead of her.

"Grandma made cookies," Theo called.

For the next half hour Marti enjoyed the boys' wide-ranging conversation, saying little herself. The Cubs were going to win the World Series this year. The two of them were going to build bat houses when they went up to their cabin in Wisconsin. One of Jupiter's moons, Io, had active volcanoes; another, Europa, had an ocean beneath its icy surface. Mike had mastered a piece on the piano that Theo was still having trouble with. They had both gotten detention for defending a classmate who was smaller against one who was larger.

Marti refilled their cups and added miniature marshmallows. Theo and Mike had liked each other from the day they'd met. Something about her and Ben being married had solidified that even more. Stability, Ben said. Permanence. She was inclined to agree.

The boys were in bed when Joanna came home. Marti wasn't surprised to see Lisa trailing in behind her. She bit back the impulse to ask if everything was okay.

"How about some cocoa?" she asked instead. "Grandma made some oatmeal date cookies."

Lisa hung her jacket on the back of the chair and stood there, looking everywhere but at Marti.

"So?" Marti said. "You don't like my cocoa?"

Lisa shook her head.

"It can't be the cookies."

She pressed her lips together.

"Sit," Marti said. Now what? The child was obviously uncomfortable. Marti always felt that because they were all women, she should be able to understand Joanna's moods and the nuances of Lisa's behavior. Instead, she was always puzzled. Joanna and Lisa lived in a world that she hadn't even visited at their age. Still teenagers, they already had worries and problems with boys and school and peers that she had never had to deal with. As much as she hated to admit it, she was always in over her head.

"You okay?" she asked. She wished she hadn't because it was a dumb question. She had witnessed enough of both girls' high-low mood swings to know that even though both of them had been laughing when she saw them this morning, that was no reason to assume they didn't have something to cry or feel sad about now.

"I, um . . . I've been here most of the week," Lisa said.

"So I noticed, even though you missed the picnic."

"Don't you want me to go home?"

"This is home, Lisa," Marti said. "This is always home."

Lisa blinked back tears. Marti reached over and squeezed her hand. They were big girls, both of them—Joanna, tall and athletic, Lisa, who seemed short in comparison but was five-seven and solid—capable young women. Why then, did she always think of them as fragile? Because she couldn't protect them. She couldn't shelter them from the pain of a careless remark or a deliberate slight, from the boys who couldn't see enough of them one day and looked right through them the next, or the friend who was unexpectedly sick or ruthlessly shot, and all too suddenly dead. She couldn't shield them from much of anything. And she wanted to. So much of growing up today was different from what she had experienced. They went away too soon. Even though they continued to live at home, they spent so much time away from home, away from shelter, away from love.

Marti smiled at each of them. She got up and gave them a hug, surprised by how fiercely each girl hugged her in return.

Before going back to the precinct, Marti joined her mother in the family room. When Momma came back from Arkansas, she didn't bring much with her, and she didn't want to move into the garage apartment any more than Marti wanted her to. She had gotten used to the upstairs bedroom, and Marti got the feeling that she wanted to be near them more than she wanted to be by herself.

"You're a newlywed," Momma had said a few days after she returned. "And that apartment is just the right size."

"The house is big enough," Marti said. "At least right now. If we start getting in each other's way . . ."

"I'm not in the way, child?" Momma asked.

"We need you," Marti answered. They did. Maybe that

would change with time, but Momma brought something to this house that they all needed.

"Glue," Ben had said.

"Glue?" Marti had asked. "What kind of a word is that?"

"Think about it."

She did. He was right. There was something about Momma being here that made everything come together.

Now Marti leaned back in her recliner, closed her eyes, and listened as a ring announcer introduced the first match on the evening's card. Momma loved wrestling and boxing and one of the cable sports stations broadcast one or the other every night. Some nights Momma watched them in her room; other times she watched them down here. When Marti knew who the fighters were, it was usually because they were reruns. She could remember watching Floyd Patterson on their old black-and-white, and Muhammad Ali when he was still Cassius Clay. Tonight's names didn't sound familiar. One had fought six fights and won them all—four knockouts, two by decision. The other had lost two of his seven fights. That was probably why she had never heard of them.

"Lisa's here," Marti said. "She looked like something was bothering her."

"She's fifteen," Momma said, as if that explained it. It probably did.

"Has she said anything about Sharon?" Marti asked. When she and the kids had shared Sharon's home, Sharon kept her boyfriends, known only as "Mr. Wonderful," away from the house. Now that she and Lisa were living in an apartment, Marti got the impression that she was bringing "Mr. Wonderful" home. Sharon alternated between months of celibacy and brief, ill-fated flings. It was fling time again. Marti assumed that that had a lot to do with why Lisa was here. The cop in her wondered why Lisa didn't want to be around this "Mr. Wonderful." Was it because he was as interested in the daughter as in the mother? Was Sharon allowing him to parent Lisa, tell her what and what not to do? That hadn't been a problem for Marti and Ben, mostly because they were in agreement most of the time, but also, Marti thought, because she wasn't trying to replace Mike's mother, Ben's first wife, and Ben wasn't trying to replace Johnny.

"Do you think everything is okay?" Marti asked.

"With Sharon? Not hardly. But she seems to work her way through it."

"And Lisa?"

"She has a place to come to," Momma said. "Sometimes that's all a child needs, a place where things make sense."

"Maybe I should talk to Sharon," Marti said. They had grown up together, gone through school, marriages, childbirth, divorce, and widowhood together. They were as close as sisters. But lately Sharon had . . . changed.

"The fruit doesn't fall far from the tree," Momma said. "I know a lot of folks seem to grow up and do well in spite of their upbringing, but I'm not convinced. I think maybe some folks are just better at separating the chaff from the wheat and able to glean what they need to survive and even succeed. You and I might see a parent who steals and goes to jail; the child might see someone who is providing for him at all costs and pick up on the root of that as determination, become determined instead of becoming a thief."

"Some children become thieves."

"I know," Momma said. "Sharon becomes more like her mother every day. Maybe Lisa won't do the same thing. I just want to hold onto that child. I tried to hold onto Sharon, but she just wouldn't let me."

Sharon still called her mother Miss Rayveena when she spoke of her. She called Marti's mother Momma. Lisa had started calling Sharon by her first name. Was *she* going to become Ma to Lisa? Marti felt tired as hell as she left to go back to work.

Vik looked up when Marti returned to the office. "Cowboy's been in and made coffee," he said. "He and Slim are off to lie in wait for underaged hookers. What a job."

Marti yawned as she filled her cup, but felt wide awake as

soon as she opened McCroft's planner. Anticipation soon became disappointment. There were few names and addresses and all of those were local. Beside each was a one-word description: neighbor, friend-*M,* or friend-*V.* Neither woman had many friends. Doctors were listed by specialty, as were one electrician, plumber, and handyman. There was no listing for a cleaning woman. When Marti turned to the calendar she saw why.

Each housekeeping chore was assigned an hour and a day. Dusting was penciled in on Tuesday and Thursday mornings from 10:00 A.M. until noon, with a spot check early Saturday morning. Afternoons and evenings were reserved for Mother, typing, and meetings held by various city and county governing bodies—the Forest Preserve Board, the city council—and a dozen organizations, all of which began with "Preservation" or "Restoration" or "Help." There were no names associated with these groups or telephone numbers. The most personal entry was "mammogram."

As she closed the planner, Marti wasn't sure why Virginia McCroft even bothered with it. Everything seemed copied over with rigorous monotony, month after month. And, on paper at least, every human contact Virginia made with any regularity was at a group, not a personal level. Although Marti knew people did kill for causes, none of those listed here seemed that important.

CHAPTER

14

Marti attended the McCroft autopsy alone. Ordinarily she would have thought Vik chose not to attend out of some sense of modesty or decorum, since he had known the victim for so many years and it was a woman. This time she was certain that it was either his own youth or his own immortality that he was avoiding. Vik had known this victim too well.

"No smoke in the lungs," Dr. Cyprian said into the microphone, and later, "The bullet pierced the aorta." The trauma to the body was consistent with falling beams and debris and had occurred after death. Although they would have to wait for lab results to be more specific, Dr. Cyprian did stipulate that death had occurred not more than nine days ago or less than six. The rest of the autopsy was uneventful and Marti reached the precinct in time for roll call.

As soon as roll call was over, Vik sprinted to their office. Marti didn't even try to keep up. By the time she walked in, he was already on the telephone, scribbling notes and interrupting whoever he was talking to with a "Slow down" every few minutes. Their office mates, Slim and Cowboy, both vice cops, were there too. Cowboy was measuring coffee.

"Late night?" Marti asked. Cowboy usually arrived early enough to have the coffee brewing while they were at roll call.

"A wasted night," he corrected. Pale blond hair curled at the nape of his neck. Either he hadn't had time for a haircut or he was letting it grow. Equally unusual, he was wearing aviator-style eyeglasses instead of the contact lenses that intensified the blueness of his eyes. "Word on the street is that we've got some underage hookers working that motel over on Thirty-eighth, but after four nights of damned near all-night watches, I'm beginning to think my informant is wrong."

Marti considered Cowboy and Slim two of the laziest cops she had ever known. There were days when she would have found them insufferable if it weren't for their tenacity when it came to keeping juveniles off the streets.

"You look well rested," Cowboy said.

Slim consulted his calendar. "Her old man's on duty."

Damn. Now they knew Ben's schedule. It was bad enough they had figured out a monthly calendar for her.

Slim was tall and slender with skin the color of caramel. He sauntered over to the coffeepot, poured two cups, and brought one to her. "And I must say that, much to my surprise, married life seems to be agreeing with you. Nothing like a . . . marital relationship." He gave her a full four-dimpled smile and reached out and caught a strand of her hair. "Now that you've kind of got back into the swing of things, so to speak, I'll be right here if you get lonesome."

"Why?" she asked.

He hesitated.

Marti pushed her chair back and stood up. She put her palms flat on the desk and leaned toward him until their noses were almost touching. "Why?" she asked again.

Slim backed away. "Well, I guess I was wrong about one thing, Big Mac. You still can't take a joke."

"Sure I can," she said. "It just has to be funny."

By the time Slim and Cowboy left, Vik had been on the phone for almost an hour. When he finally hung up, he sat back with his hands behind his head and a satisfied expression on his face. "For once my sister-in-law was right," he said. "Nobody liked her."

"Liked who?"

"Virginia McCroft, who else?"

"Why not?" Why was that so important? It couldn't be

because he had turned down her invitation to a high school dance and needed to feel vindicated. Come to think of it, if Virginia was as popular as he said she was, why had she asked *him?*

"Virginia was a snoop, MacAlister, a busybody, and one of those weirdos who pester celebrities."

"Oh?" Marti said. "Which one?" Maybe she should have paid more attention to all of the clutter in the woman's house. She hadn't noticed any movie star memorabilia.

"Virginia pestered politicians."

"Anyone who's been in the national news lately?"

"Local politicians, MacAlister."

"That's great. The lieutenant will love this one. How many of them are possible suspects?"

Vik looked down at a list he had compiled. The expression on his face turned sour.

"Her car might tell us more than any of them," Marti said. "If we could find it." She wished Vik wasn't approaching this from such a personal angle. McCroft's schedule was laid out on her calendar. Ordinarily, Vik would suggest that they use it to backtrack and check out her activities. When Marti suggested that, he frowned and tapped his list with the the eraser end of a pencil. "We've got whoever did it right here. Virginia McCroft had the personality of a lemon, an extremely sour lemon."

Marti tried not to laugh and almost succeeded. "I guess you would know," she said.

After he had looked through the planner, he slammed it shut and gave it a hard push that sent it to the edge of his desk. "She was always organized too. And right. Virginia was always right. Well, the neighbors weren't a damned bit of help. We can start with her friends, both of them."

"I thought she was so popular in school."

He thought about that for a minute. "She was. I don't know. After we graduated, it was almost like she didn't exist anymore." He looked at his notes. "We could start with the board of commissioners, or the members of the city council, or the city treasurer, or the county clerk. They were her primary targets for the past few weeks."

Marti found it hard to believe that McCroft's death was politically motivated, but then again, she didn't know that much about local politics. She voted in almost every election—usually because Theo or Joanna reminded her—and chose people she knew and respected first, then women and other minorities. Those few times when she couldn't make it to the polls, she borrowed one of those "I Voted Today" stickers, put it on her coat, and everyone at home was happy.

"We need to know where the bodies are buried," she said.

"What?"

"If one of our local, friendly politicians did do this, it sure wasn't because of some letter Virginia McCroft wrote or a meeting she attended."

"And?"

"They keep minutes of those meetings, right, Vik?"

"Edited versions, I'm sure."

"Yes, but we would at least have the gist of what was discussed."

"What are you getting at, MacAlister?"

"We need to know what the money issues were, who had something personal vested in the results of a vote, things like that."

"You actually believe that she either knew too much, said too much, or stumbled onto something she shouldn't have?"

"What else is there when you're talking politics?"

"The lieutenant *will* love this," Vik muttered.

Geoffrey took his plate with the two fried eggs over to a chair by the window. This wasn't anything like the breakfast Mama would have fixed for him, but it might hold him up until he went there. He needed some coffee, but he couldn't stand instant and the nearest Starbuck's was a good twenty-minute drive. He *was* getting used to what they served at McDonald's, but even that was two blocks away.

Upstairs, it sounded like Sister Hawkins was moving furniture. Her wake-up calls began with gospel music at six-thirty. If he put two pillows and the blanket over his head, he usually managed to get back to sleep. At seven-thirty she vacuumed, which was when he usually gave in and got up. This morning he had stayed in bed until the vacuuming stopped and she resorted to rearranging the dressers. As always, she dropped something. It sounded like the same thing every time, pots and pans. He turned on the television so she would know he was up. Within two minutes, the noise stopped.

He was sure that he had figured out a way to let Mama know what was going on without sounding like he was complaining, but when he went to the house last night that damned Calvin had been there slapping him on the back and congratulating him on finally becoming his own man—that wiseass, son of a . . . He never got the chance to say anything.

The candleholders he had gotten from the pig lady yesterday were on the coffee table. They looked a little better polished, but he was damned if he knew what to do with them, they were so ugly. Pewter. Who in the hell would want something made of pewter? Neither Mama nor Aunt Precious had anything like it. He couldn't think of one person who did. No way would he just throw them away. There was a fool out there somewhere who would buy them. And if he waited for just the right one, he might make a little extra change.

There was a knock on the door and then, "Geoffrey?" Sister Hawkins. Damn, not again.

"Just a minute." He scooped the last of the egg from the plate, put the dish in the sink, straightened the covers on the bed, put on his bathrobe, and opened the door.

"Good morning, Geoffrey." Sister Hawkins had a smile on her face and a lilt in her voice that she must have been saving until this morning. Her son the cop, tall and unsmiling, stood behind her. Damn. He almost turned to look at the candleholders.

"You know my son, Officer Ross. He works vice with the Lincoln Prairie Police Department."

Geoffrey held out his hand. "Hi, Slim, how you doing?"

Slim nodded. He looked as if this was embarrassing for him too.

"Geoffrey is working for Deacon Evans now."

"You're finally out of school?" Slim said.

"Just about." Geoffrey rattled off the name of the last school he had attended. Would Slim, the cop, check up on him? Oh well, what was one small lie? He could talk his way out of it if he had to. He had outtalked cops before. If only he didn't know this one. And if Slim would just smile. Slim was looking past him and into the apartment. Would he notice the candleholders? Why the hell hadn't he put them in the closet?

"I . . . um . . . just got up."

"Yes, well, just wanted to meet the tenants, make sure everything was okay."

"Oh, yes. Everything is just fine, just fine."

Sister Hawkins just stood there smiling like he had never seen her smile before. Was he supposed to invite them in? It was his apartment. Why should he have to?

"Well, nice seeing you again, Geoffrey. I guess I'll be seeing you around."

Geoffrey nodded. Not if he could help it. He closed the door as soon as Sister Hawkins turned away, grabbed the candleholders, and put them in the farthest corner of the closet.

After talking with the two people Vik had identified as Mc-Croft's friends and several other people they suggested, Marti realized that calling them her friends was, for the most part, stretching it a bit. Virginia McCroft was a person who focused on issues, not people.

"She was the most popular girl in her class," Vik said, as he rang another doorbell. Marti was beginning to think that was how *he chose to remember her,* not how it really had been.

A man opened the door.

"S. J. Rosenblum?" Vik asked.

"Yes. What can I do for you?" Everyone else they had spoken with was a woman. The woman who suggested they speak with Rosenblum did not sound friendly at all.

Rosenblum was a soft-spoken man, sixty perhaps, with graying hair and a receding hairline and pale blue-gray eyes. Suspenders held up brown tweed pants, and the beige sweater he was wearing looked hand-knitted.

"We've come to ask you a few questions about Virginia McCroft."

"Virginia?" His grip on the doorframe tightened. He seemed taken aback. "How did you . . . ? Why are you here?"

"When is the last time you saw her?" Vik asked.

"Why, last Wednesday, of—" He stopped.

Marti thought of the Wednesday afternoon entries on Mc-Croft's calendar. Gardening—every Wednesday from two until four—year-round.

"From two until four," she said.

Rosenblum's mouth dropped open. "That damned planner," he said, and held open the door.

Rosenblum's living room was as sparse as McCroft's was overcrowded, but fussy, with antimacassars on the arms of the wingback chairs, a needlepoint stool, and not one speck of dust on the mahogany tables.

"Please, have a seat." He almost hovered until they sat down, then sat on the edge of a Queen Anne settee upholstered in pale green damask.

"So," Marti said, "you saw Miss McCroft last Wednesday." Rosenblum seemed nervous so she stared at him, waiting.

"Why, yes. Wednesday. Always on Wednesday."

"What about this Wednesday?"

"She—she didn't come." He began rubbing the back of his left hand with the palm of his right hand.

"Was that unusual?"

"Most unusual."

Again she waited.

"I thought perhaps her mother had taken ill. Our mothers are quite advanced in age now. And they don't . . . approve."

"Why not?" Marti asked.

"She's Catholic. I'm Jewish," he said. "My mother doesn't approve. Neither does hers."

Marti found that more than a bit a quaint. "I thought all that changed with ecumenism."

Now Rosenblum was rubbing his hands in earnest. "Nothing is ever that easy."

"How long had you been uh . . . ?"

"Gardening," he said, voice prim. "From two until four."

"Every Wednesday."

"Yes."

"For how many years?"

"Five years, almost six. Before our mothers had to go to Sunnybrook. We met at their gerontologist's office."

Marti wondered where they "gardened" when Rosenblum's mother still lived at home. "But," she said, "this Wednesday she didn't come."

"No."

"Weren't you worried?"

"About Virginia? Of course not. Why should I be?" Marti thought that if he leaned any farther forward he would fall off the couch. "Why are you here . . . asking these questions? What is it? What is this all about?"

"Was Virginia her usual self when you saw her last week?"

He settled back, still rubbing one hand with the other, but calmer, perhaps because of her tone of voice.

"Yes. She was always the same. We didn't—this was our time. Nothing intruded."

"And she didn't seem any different?"

"No. We had a lovely afternoon together, just as we always did."

Marti looked about the room. Everything in its place. Just as everything was surely in its place at McCroft's house, despite the apparent clutter. Two kindred spirits. She wondered if "gardening" included sex, or if their relationship was platonic, but didn't ask.

"Mr. Rosenblum," Vik said, "do you know of any reason why Miss McCroft would go to the old Warren place? It's a big brown house over on Waverly, right behind——"

"The forest preserve. It caught fire yesterday. Virginia and I didn't discuss her political activities. I have no idea why that particular house would be of any importance to her. By the same token, since it does abut a preserve, I don't see any reason why it wouldn't be important to her if there were some plan afoot to destroy or reduce that land." He looked from one of them to the other, then asked, "Something is wrong, isn't it? Can't you tell me what it is?"

"Virginia and I were classmates," Vik said, stretching the truth just a bit. "She . . . um . . . she's dead, Mr. Rosenblum. I'm sorry to have to tell you this, but she's dead."

Rosenblum got so pale Marti thought he was going to faint. Tears began streaming down his face. He sniffed, but did not make any other sound, nor did he wipe the tears away. After a minute or two, he pursed his lips together as if he was holding back a scream. He rubbed the back of his hand with his palm at a furious pace but remained silent.

"Is there someone I can call?" Vik asked.

Rosenblum shook his head. "No," he said in a whisper. "No. There's no one to call."

He showed them to the door without speaking again.

Marti had both of McCroft's file cabinets brought in. She and Vik each took one. Virginia McCroft had dabbled in, made financial contributions to, and written letters about so many issues that Marti didn't know where to begin. She called a friend at the state's attorney's office and asked if there were any hot issues or issues of interest that she should take a look at first. Her friend suggested anything relating to public land—land acquisition, land sales, conservation projects, land trusts—since that was a hot political issue. Marti put everything relating to animals, national politics, and all squabbles over other local political issues aside and focused on land. Within twenty minutes she was amazed by her own ignorance. She didn't even understand the jargon.

"Damn."

"What have you got?" Vik asked.

After she explained, he went through everything.

"There used to be a lot of farmland around here," he said. "Most all of it's been developed now. Here and there there's a farm that's just getting by or going under, and we still have a few family-owned orchards and pumpkin farms, but there's not much more than bones left, compared to what there was." He thought for a few minutes, then said, "It looks like Virginia was identifying whoever owned the property surrounding half a dozen forest preserves. I can't even guess why. The issue swings back and forth. We get a bunch of land-grabbing expansionists in office for a while, and then we vote them out and vote in some folks who want to preserve the prairie or whatever."

"And you?" Marti asked.

He came close to smiling. "Me? I remember Gurnee when it was a rural area with lots of farms, and Washington Street was called Grange Hall Road. And my father, God rest his soul, used to buy eggs at the Moody Chicken Farm in Zion. I'll never see those days again. Now if I want to get a glimpse of what it used to be like around here, I drive up to Wisconsin. Gives you hope, that and driving downstate. There's still land for growing things. There are still a few little patches of God's green earth that don't have concrete and asphalt covering them. Maybe our grandkids and maybe even our great-grandkids will be able to eat real vegetables before they only grow them in some kind of greenhouse, the way they warehouse poultry and animals now."

Was that how Virginia McCroft felt? Marti wondered. Were her inquiries into land ownership some cryptic way of trying to save the land or perhaps expand the preserves? She put everything relating to land to one side. Vik hadn't told her anything that convinced her there was a motive for murder in any of it.

"A pig!" Vik said. "Look at this, MacAlister, a pig!"

Marti took the copy of the *News-Times* that he was holding out. There on the front page was a pig. "Sure, is," she agreed.

It was a large pig, with ears that pointed and droopy eyes. "Looks sleepy," she said. "They must have woken him up to take his picture."

"Her," Vik said. "It's a she. Babette, the pig."

"Is it a pet?"

"Read what it says, MacAlister."

"Well," she said, when she finished, "if it was as smart as the owner says it is, why didn't it figure out that this guy was a con artist?"

"Pewter candleholders," Vik said. "Pre–Civil War. Hard to figure out which of them was the most gullible—him for taking them or her for believing she was getting a real alarm system—assuming that any of this is true. They probably just made it up so that the pig could get her picture in the paper."

Marti flipped through the front section until she found a brief piece on the fire at the Warren place. There was no mention yet of a victim.

Fred watched from the window as the *News-Times* was tossed from the rear window of a green van then went outside and retrieved it. That done, he went down the hall to the porch. Mother was sitting by the window. Old woman, old fool. Worthless. If it wasn't for her he could sell this house and move someplace else, California maybe. He had always wanted to live where there was no snow.

"You look tired," he said.

She jumped. Even though she put her hand to her mouth, he could see that he had frightened her, hear the scream she nipped as soon as she saw it was him.

"I'm worried about you, Mother," he said. "I don't think it's good for you to sit in that chair all day. It can't be good for your back."

Her fingers flexed, just a little, but she sat very still.

"And that sunlight, it can't be helping your eyes much either. Too much of a strain on them, staring out of the window all day." It had been a long time since she'd interrupted him. Now she didn't even speak unless he told her to. Father would have been pleased.

"Mother," he said, "you look tired, very tired. Are you?"

She shook her head.

"Aren't you tired, Mother?"

He took a step closer. She clenched her hands in her lap, but did not flinch or move away from him the way she used to.

"Mother, I think you're lying. I think you're tired."

He took another step. This time she took a deep breath, but she did not move.

"In fact, I think you are so tired that I'm going to have to do something about it. I can't have you sitting here looking out the window all day when you're too tired to be sitting up."

Another step and he was beside the chair. She trembled, just a bit, and there was the quietest moan. Then she sniffled and was still. He stared down at her until the smell of urine told him she had soiled herself again.

"I'll get you another diaper, Mother. And then it will be time for you to go to bed."

He waited. "Well?"

When she nodded, he walked from the room.

Opal slipped into bed and pulled the covers up to her neck. She looked over at the window. Fred had forgotten to close the blinds. If only Fred Senior was here. No, he had sent her to her room too. He had just never made her go to bed. She squeezed her eyes shut and wondered what she would do in the silence. Nothing to read, nothing to listen to, and not much to remember either. She had been in this house for so long, ever since she was twenty-two. It had been an arranged marriage, like her parents' marriage had been, and she hadn't expected more than her mother had expected. She had been, after all, several years past the age when she should have been married. Her life here had been better than her mother's. There was running water and electricity and indoor plumbing and an ice box. If only Fred Senior had been just a little bit younger, not forty-five when he married her and not so set in his ways. It was like marrying her father. And then it had taken her almost four years to conceive. What a disappointment she had been to everyone. Her parents, her husband. Now she was a disappointment to her son as well. All of her life, all she had ever been was a disappointment.

CHAPTER
16

When Marti and Vik went into Lieutenant Dirkowitz's office, Lefty, the sergeant in charge of the bomb squad, and Bartholomew "Tolley" Knauf, the fire chief, were already there.

"When's the last time you two worked an arson case?"

"Involving a homicide?" Vik asked. "There was one a while back. Nothing recent."

"McCroft was already dead when that fire was set," Marti said.

"I know," the lieutenant said, agreeing. "But we're beginning to think we might have an arsonist on our hands connected with this homicide, however indirectly. There is also our mailbox bomber. Even though the bomb looks like a prank, I want Arson, the bomb squad, and Homicide all talking with each other, just in case. The weirdo population seems to be getting younger and increasing." He looked at each of them. "I'd like to keep one step ahead of whatever develops. Since that isn't likely, I don't want to be too far behind."

Marti could think of things she'd rather do, but the lieutenant was right. Tolley might come up with something in the arson investigation that might have bearing on her investigation and vice versa. As for Lefty, maybe they would all get lucky, just one prank, no more bombs, no bodies because of a bomb. They couldn't have a pyromaniac and a mad bomber on the loose at the same time, not in Lincoln Prairie. That thought made goose bumps rise on her arms.

"So," the lieutenant said, "let's begin with the fires."

"It's the MO," Tolley said. "Four vacant houses, four intense, contained burns that just explode when oxygen is introduced."

"So," Vik said, "this guy just wants to torch something and watch it burn. He's not into body counts."

"Apparently not," Tolley agreed. "At least not yet. So far he's picked isolated places: the one by the forest preserve, one condemned building near some farmland that's being redeveloped, another near one of the ravines that had a partial burn intentionally set and hadn't been torn down yet . . ."

"Sounds like he knows the area," Marti said.

Tolley agreed. "We're pretty sure he has to be a local. Maybe someone who moved away and has come back, since this hasn't been going on for too long." He passed out copies of his reports on the fires and explained some of the technical jargon. "What have you got on the body we found?"

Vik seemed reluctant to say anything, so Marti filled him in.

"So," Tolley said, "if it wasn't for this nutcase setting that fire, the body could have stayed there until it rotted without anybody knowing it was there."

Vik winced, but said nothing.

"Lefty?" the lieutenant queried.

"Like the rest of you, I would like to think this is just some kid playing a prank, but the more I look at the reports, the more I think we have someone who knows a little bit about what he's doing. Maybe not a lot because he's using an unstable fuse but enough to put the right chemicals together."

"So?" Tolley said.

"So we wait and see. I'm glad now that it didn't get much attention in the media. Of course that's a mixed blessing. If he *is* a nutcase, he might decide to show us what he can really do. On the other hand, he didn't get that thrill of victory to feed on his first time out. Not that this has to be his first time. I've gone through a lot of reports though, and I can't find anything that tells me this guy did this before, at least not in our area."

"Are we just using 'he' figuratively here?" the lieutenant asked.

"Statistically it's a he," Lefty said.

Tolley agreed. "Not that women don't ever do this, but they tend not to. At the rate the world is changing though, that will change too."

Marti got goose bumps again. She didn't like this kind of crime, one with the potential for so much harm, so many victims at one time. Multiple homicides were still a rarity here. She'd like to help keep it that way, at least on her watch.

"This is a very diversified area," the lieutenant said. "We have a very high volume of noncommercial flight activity at the airport. We have densely populated areas. We have ethnically and economically diverse neighborhoods. We can't have anyone out there playing God and deciding what gets torched or blown up. Vik, I think you and Marti see things from a different perspective than Tolley and Lefty. I didn't include you on this just because we have a homicide victim on our hands. You two are always focused on who did it and why. That's what I expect you to bring to this." He picked up the Vietnam-era hand grenade that he kept on his desk. It was a reminder, not a memento. His brother had died in that war. "Crime is changing and we have to change with it. We can't just cooperate anymore. We have different approaches, different skills, different perspectives, different concerns. We've got to work together." He dropped the hand grenade. The meeting was over.

When Marti returned to her office, Denise Stevens was there. They went back a long way. Denise headed up the Juvenile Probation Department and had been her maid of honor when she married Ben. Denise weighed a few pounds more than Marti and was a few inches shorter. She was "healthy," as Momma would say. Unlike Marti, Denise was uncomfortable with her size. She was an attractive woman with classic features, full lips, and wide, dark, sloe eyes with long, curling lashes and wore hats to draw attention to her face and away from her hips. Today's hat was gold felt with a roller brim.

"How's everything?" Marti asked. It had been a while since she'd seen Denise.

"So-so." Denise helped herself to some coffee.

Marti hesitated before asking about her family, then said, "How's Belle doing?" Belle had sung at her wedding.

"Belle's been here for a few months now. Mama broke her hip in March."

"And Terri?"

"She's in the hospital again."

Terri had been institutionalized following a mental breakdown several years ago. Now she would experience interludes of sanity that lasted several months and then relapse into the mental illness that had been part of her life for years. Denise's mother and her sister, Belle, were raising Terri's daughter, Zaar, who was in kindergarten now and thriving, thanks to their care.

Denise adjusted her hat. Usually she felt comfortable enough to take them off.

"Everything's okay?" Marti asked again.

"Actually, I wanted to talk to you about Sharon's daughter."

"Lisa?" Marti felt the muscles in her stomach tense. Denise wouldn't be here if Lisa hadn't had some contact with the police. "What is it?"

"Keep calm. It's not that bad, but it is bad enough."

Marti took a deep breath. It couldn't be that bad. She had just seen Lisa last night.

"Lisa has been skipping school. Last week the neighbors complained about noise coming from Sharon's apartment. The manager called the police when one of the men got belligerent . . ."

"One of the men?"

"Yes, there were three, none underage, and another girl Lisa goes to school with. Everyone but Lisa was sitting around drinking beer."

"But not Lisa?"

"No. Not yet."

"What did Sharon say?" Why hadn't Sharon told her? Why hadn't Lisa? Did Joanna know?

"I just got the report today. Sharon had to come down and get Lisa released. Juvenile will follow up on it, but it just came to me. It'll be another three or four weeks before they set up an appointment for an interview with a juvenile officer. They'll investigate, make recommendations, the usual."

"Good Lord, Denise. What is happening with Sharon? I've known her almost all my life. I have never known her to be irresponsible, or negligent, where her child is concerned."

Denise looked away for a moment, then looked at her and said, "Sharon has had you to lean on for the past few years, just as you have had her. You still have a support system. Sharon doesn't, with you gone."

"You think this would have happened sooner if I wasn't there?" Or wouldn't have happened at all if she was there.

"You know Sharon's pattern with men, Marti. However, Lisa has been in school every day since this happened."

And at her house every night. And Sharon liked that arrangement.

After Denise left, Marti called one of the deans at the high school, explained that Lisa was staying with her, at least temporarily, and asked that she be called at once if Lisa was absent.

Fred Jhanke read the newspaper article three times. Each time the same sentences jumped out at him. *Mrs. Nordstrom told police that she gave the man the candleholders in exchange for installing an alarm system. Police have determined that there was no alarm system at all.*

This had to be the man who'd stolen his mother's watch, a watch that belonged to him. This woman, this Mrs. Nordstrom, would be able to tell him what the man looked like.

Maybe then he could find out who he was and where he lived.

Fred found the Nordstroms' address in the phone book. When he went there, nobody was home. He decided to wait.

Geoffrey had picked up the computer after he acquired the candleholders. He almost tripped over Deacon Evans as he brought the boxes in.

"Yes sir, I like a man of action," the deacon said. "Say you're going to do it and"—he snapped his fingers—"it's done."

Geoffrey had insisted on having his own space. Not just because Evans's rats' nest of an office was probably a fire hazard, but because he didn't know what the hell he was going to do with this thing and he didn't want Evans to find out how little he knew. His office was a little bigger than a closet, but he had a desk, and Evans had promised him his own telephone line. Now if the old man would just keep out of his way.

"Excuse me, Deacon Evans."

By the time he brought the last box in, Evans had the others opened. "Now just look at this. I must say, you really got a good deal on this. Why, it says 'color monitor' and all. Nothing like having a good businessman around."

Geoffrey had gotten everything for five hundred dollars and pocketed the other fifteen hundred. Easy money. The kind of money he liked. What else did the old man need that he could get for him—cheap?

As Evans hovered over him, Geoffrey unpacked the boxes.

"Well, look a-here, you know just where everything goes. Now me, I haven't even got a clue as to how to turn that thing on. You're just putting everything together like you was some kind of computer technologist or something."

"I've had quite a bit of experience with these, the hardware and the software. Piece of cake, once you get the hang of it." Each of the cords had a little picture at the end and it wasn't hard to figure out where everything went. Turning it on was going to create a problem, but not setting it up.

Geoffrey took a step back, decided he wanted the monitor a little more to the left.

"I guess we need to get one of them computer tables," Evans said.

"Oh no, I like it right here on the desk just fine." He moved it a little more. "I'm going to have to pick up a few small things, a mouse pad, some paper. We'll be ready to go tomorrow."

"Oh," Deacon Evans said, "I won't be here." He sounded disappointed.

"Are you going on that church trip into Chicago to see that play?"

"Yes. I hadn't planned to, but one of the church sisters talked me into it." He giggled.

"Why, Deacon Evans. Still got a little fire burning in the stove, huh?"

The old man smiled and giggled again. "Come to think of it, I've got to give her a call."

Evans was still on the phone when Geoffrey walked past his office as he headed for the door. The old man motioned him in and put his hand over the mouthpiece. "You want to see something funny, take a look at the front page of today's newspaper."

He just wanted to get out of there, but he unfolded the paper—and dropped it. The pig, that damned pig. He retrieved the paper and read the article. Pewter candleholders. The ones that had been on the table in his living room, the ones Sister Hawkins's son the cop must have seen. Damn. Now what?

By the time he reached his car he had decided that the candleholders had been one hell of a mistake. So much for impulse selling. Maybe if he just took them back, but discreetly. Somehow he would have to return them. Maybe then that woman would be happy and shut the hell up. Then again, the way his luck was running, TV cameras would be set up when he got there.

He got the candleholders and drove out there anyway, relieved to see the driveway empty. Maybe they had taken the porker for a ride. It was midafternoon, just as it had been when he'd driven by here yesterday, and again there was little traffic. An older model, dark blue Geo was parked in the dirt road alongside the farmer's field near the shuttered stand where they sold produce in season. But whoever was sitting behind the wheel wouldn't be able to see what he was doing once he pulled into the driveway. He would have to risk it. If he didn't get the candleholders back to her, who knew what the old bag would do next.

He pulled into the driveway and drove until he was alongside the house. There was a porch out back. Maybe he should put them there. No, she might never go out there. He put them between the door and the screen door where she couldn't miss them and backed out of the driveway.

There. She had her damned historic candleholders. Why had she given them to him in the first place if they were so damned important? Maybe now this would just go away. Along with his scam. Damn! His scam, his frigging scam! He'd been working it for months, but now, with everything spelled out in the newspaper, there was no way in hell he could pull it off again. Damn! Now he'd have to come up with something else. Why him? Why in the hell hadn't he just turned around and left when he saw that damned pig?

Fred was whistling as he pulled into the garage. He had kept his distance from the man in the tan Toyota, and lost him when he reached the south side of Lincoln Prairie. But he had his license plate number. There had to be a way to identify him and, if he lived on the South Side, all he had to do was keep an eye out for the car. First, though, he would have to go back and see that woman, make sure that this man was the right one. He hadn't gotten a good look at him either. He needed a better description. Before he got out of the car he reached back and pulled a blanket over the candleholders.

After he lost track of that thieving bastard, he had gone back to get them before the pig family returned home.

Opal tried to control her trembling as she listened to Fred whistling in the kitchen. Whistling just didn't ever bode well. Not when He did it, not when He Senior had. Sometimes, when He Senior whistled, young He was locked in the closet for some minor offense. It didn't take much for young He to rile his father. Sometimes, when He Senior whistled, it was her turn to sit on the floor in the dark and get sick to her stomach smelling cedar and mothballs. Now she listened and trembled and prayed that He Junior wouldn't think of her at all.

Fred couldn't sit still. Out there, somewhere, and not far away, was the man who had stolen his watch from Mother. The people who owned the pig had seen him. They knew what he looked like. He read the skimpy newspaper article again. Nobody cared about the man who lied to the woman and stole her candleholders; all they cared about was the pig.

When he couldn't stand being in the house any longer, he drove back to the house where the pig lived. This time, the woman was at home. She looked at him from the other side of a short, brass chain and would not let him in.

"Could you please just tell me what he looked like?"

The woman shook her head and tried to close the door.

He kept the door wedged open with his foot.

"Now look here, sir. If you don't get off of my property right now, I'm going to call the police."

"No. No. You don't understand. He did the same thing to my mother that he did to you. She's eighty years old. He talked her out of a watch that my father gave her when they were married."

"I'm real sorry about that, but there's nothing I can do to help you. I don't remember what he looked like."

She must have noticed something, the stupid old cow.

"Please, ma'am. The color of his eyes. Anything. If I just had some idea of what he looked like."

"You're sure, about your mother, I mean."

They didn't come much dumber. "Why else would I come here?"

There was a grunting noise. Fred couldn't see the pig, but that had to be what it was.

The woman turned. "Babette? Oh dear, do you have to go?"

She pushed the door again. "If you'll just give me a minute."

"Please. The pig can wait."

"He was colored. He didn't look anything like a Negro. He had hair like us and the nicest hazel eyes, and at the time I didn't think about it. But looking back, I'm sure he was a colored fellow."

The pig grunted again and the woman increased the pressure on his foot.

"He wasn't Hispanic?"

"No. Now please. Babette is about to have an accident in the living room."

Fred pulled his foot away. A Negro. It wasn't much, and it might not be enough, but he did have a better idea of where on the South Side he should look for that car.

Marti was trying to get home more often to have dinner with the family. It seemed simple enough. Stop working, go home, return to the precinct. The problem was what Johnny had called immersion, being inundated with fragments of evidence and information that she could not connect, then getting that one odd connection. Everything not related to the case became a distraction, including home. She called and told Momma she would be late.

"Lord, child, take your time. We're not ready to eat yet anyway."

She could hear the boys in the background. "Is that Peter I hear whistling?" She smiled as she asked. Peter and his older brother, Patrick, lived next door. Peter whistled a lot.

"Marti, they've been busy all afternoon. Patrick and Theo are writing the script. Mike and Peter are making the costumes. They've used up all of the aluminum foil working on swords. I'm not sure what we're going to end up with, but don't worry about missing any of it. They've talked Ben into letting them use the camcorder."

"Sounds like *Star Wars*." All four of the boys loved that.

"That's what I thought, so we're having Martian Meatloaf, Baked Potatoes Uranus, Pluto Spinach, and a Rings of Saturn cake for supper, and none of it's ready yet."

"Momma, you are something else."

"I'm having almost as much fun as they are. Do you think this is the beginning of my second childhood?"

"I wish I were there," Marti said.

"I've been learning how to use this camcorder," Momma said. "Not that that's the same thing . . ."

"It'll be pretty darned close," Marti said. "Bless you."

* * *

There were no leads in the McCroft case. They had not found the weapon, the woman's purse, or her car. All they had right now were dozens of manila files that seemed to contain every aspect of Virginia McCroft's life and her mother's. None of it seemed interesting or important. There was even a file for Bingo, which Mrs. McCroft seemed to have liked fifteen years ago. Losses and wins were recorded, as were the places where she played and miscellaneous costs, such as bingo chips. Vik had such a contented expression on his face that Marti could see he was enjoying every minute of it. The problem was that, so far, there hadn't been anything that either of them could identify as important.

"Who gives a damn about any of this?" Marti said, motioning toward the file cabinets. "This just goes to show you, Vik. There is something to be said for those of us who are not well organized." She put folders *H* through *M* into the drawer. "Ninety-nine percent of what's stored in these folders should have been recycled. And because there is so much useless information, if there is anything important in here, we'll never find it."

"Her budget file is interesting," he said. "Expenses for the house are pretty low. They only owe sixteen thousand on the mortgage, and that's because they refinanced five years ago."

"About the time that her mother went into the nursing home."

"Yes." Vik gave a low whistle. "It's an expensive place, and the cost of keeping her mother there has increased annually."

"What about Medicare?"

"It's a nice place. Medicare doesn't pay for everything. The costs it doesn't cover have gone up every year. Virginia started dipping into their savings to cover the latest increases."

"At the rate those costs are going up, Jessenovik, how long would it have taken before she exhausted her savings?"

Vik scanned the contents of the budget folder. "Four years, five maybe, if she was conservative."

"Would Virginia's Social Security have kicked in by then?"

"No, not for at least another seven or eight years."

"Did she have any other assets?"

"No," Vik said. "Just the equity in the house. I wonder why she retired so early. Then again, if her mother hadn't become senile enough to need a nursing home . . . or if there weren't these annual increases in the cost of her care . . . Without that, Virginia was frugal enough to make ends meet indefinitely."

There were no *N* files, and only Optometrist for *O*. Payroll and pension were next, and soon taxes, which she might pass to Vik.

The payroll records had stopped five years ago when Virginia retired. There were pension records for both women. "That's nice," Marti said. "Five hundred dollars a month."

"For what?"

"Virginia McCroft's pension from Andrew Thornton Inc., Actuary and Accountant."

"Him? Did she work for that dummy?"

"What do you know about him that I don't?"

Vik leaned back and rubbed the stubble of beard that had grown in since this morning. The scratching sound was more familiar than irritating. Neither Johnny nor Ben had fast-growing beards, but she could remember her father doing that.

"There was some problem associated with him. Something to do with taxes. Must have been five or six years ago. I can't remember quite what, but it was in the *News-Times*. I think they dropped the criminal charges, or never had enough to bring any, but he pretty much went out of business after that."

Marti flipped through the file. Copies of the checks were stapled together by year. "He's paying her himself, Jessenovik. It looks like an unusual arrangement to me." She went through the payroll file again. "She worked there for ten years as a clerk. This is about a third of her net pay. She enters it as her pension." Marti checked the prior year's income tax file. "Whatever it is, she is not telling Uncle Sam."

Vik sighed as he closed the file he was going through. "So we talk to Mr. Thornton and find out what was worth five hundred a month."

"If you feel that bad about leaving all of these folders, you can go through the ones I haven't looked at yet and I'll go talk to him."

"No way you're getting out of doing your share, MacAlister."

Before they went over to see Thornton, Vik called someone he knew at the *News-Times* and within half an hour they had faxed copies of the stories that had run in the newspapers about Thornton five to six years ago.

"From the looks of it," Vik said, "Thornton was just plain incompetent. He screwed up a lot of people's taxes." He flipped through a few more copies. "Here it is. Restitution. He had to reimburse the people who'd paid too much."

"Why didn't the IRS give them refunds?"

"Maybe they did. It just says here the reimbursement was equivalent to the amount of taxes overpaid." Vik read through everything again. "His license was suspended. I wonder if that means he got it back?"

Thornton lived in an older home with a closed-in porch that had been converted into an office. A poster board sign in one corner of a large picture window indicated that he was a notary public and an insurance agent. There was no mention of tax preparation or anything related to bookkeeping or accounting. An older model compact, rusting around the edges, was parked in the driveway.

"He's sure not making a fortune at this," Marti said.

"But he was shelling out that five hundred every month."

"And on time."

The man who opened the door was using oxygen.

"Mr. Thornton?" Vik said.

The man nodded and they showed him their shields.

"If I wasn't letting the heat out, I sure as hell wouldn't invite you in." His voice sounded like wind blowing over gravel.

They followed him past the office area, which was cool, and into a small sitting room, which was stifling hot, thanks to a gas heater that burned in a fake fireplace.

Mr. Thornton had long, shaggy gray hair and needed a shave. His face was gaunt, his eyes sunken with dark circles around them. He was wearing a sweater with a million little fuzz balls, and he smelled as if he hadn't bathed in a while. The room they were in was as shabby as he was, with a couple of old, worn chairs and a card table with a deck of cards dealt out in a hand of solitaire. There was an open pack of cigarettes and an ashtray with five snuffed-out butts beside the worn deck of cards. A large, green oxygen tank and a small, portable one were the only other things in the room.

"Emphysema," Thornton said. "Smoke long enough and something will get you." There was defiance in his expression as he looked at them. "So, what do you want now? God knows I've had enough of cops."

"When's the last time you saw Virginia McCroft?" Vik asked.

"Eh?" He sat in a chair and pulled an afghan around his shoulders. "Virginia? Hell, I don't know."

"Guess."

"Probably when she quit." He stared at the doorway to their right as if he was expecting someone to come in. "What's that been, five, six years now."

"I'd think you would know that to the day or at least the month."

He looked at Vik. "Eh? Why's that?"

"Why don't you tell me, Thornton," Vik said.

"Hard worker, Virginia was. And her mother, sick and all." His breathing changed, from shallow breaths to gasps, and he reached for the oxygen mask.

When he took it off a few minutes later, Vik said, "Is that

why you're paying her five hundred dollars a month? It doesn't look to me like you can afford it."

Thornton's face got a little color. "I manage."

"So does Virginia, and quite well. She has a big house, very nice."

Thornton reached for the mask again.

This time, when he took it off, Vik said, "Look, Thornton, why don't you make it easy on yourself and tell me why you were paying Virginia?"

"Hard worker," he gasped. "Good times then; thought I would be rich forever. Promised. Keeping a promise."

"You get it in writing?" Vik asked.

"Didn't have to."

"Then I think you'd better come up with a better reason for doing it."

"Why?"

"Because Virginia's dead, Thornton, and it's not due to natural causes."

Thornton put the mask on again, but he was breathing easier and Marti thought it was just to buy time. When he took it off, he said, "Her father." His breathing was shallow again. "He did me some favors. Early on. Got me started. City business. Promised him. Keep my word."

As they walked to the car, Vik said, "I wanted to leave before he used up that tank of oxygen. What do you think?"

"I don't think he is too incapacitated to have killed Virginia McCroft. She was shot. It doesn't take that much to pull a trigger."

"And he does have transportation."

"Too bad we don't have a weapon," Marti said. Maybe if they dug a little deeper they wouldn't need one. "He would have to have one hell of a good reason to keep paying her; and whatever it is, it didn't go away with whatever happened five or six years ago. He had a reason to pay her last week. And she had a reason to up the ante: her mother's medical expenses."

"Those boxes in McCroft's basement," Vik said. "The attic too."

He didn't sound quite as gleeful when they started going through what was in McCroft's file cabinets.

"I don't think she threw a piece of paper away in her life, Jessenovik. I found a folder marked Fast Food. Guess what was filed there."

"Compulsive," Vik said. "And retentive."

Marti found the extent of Virginia's compulsion for order astonishing. "How in the hell does anyone keep things this tidy?" she wondered aloud. "If this is what people do when they have no kids, no job, and no life, I don't want any part of it."

The boxes were stacked on shelves. They were labeled by year. The ones in the basement were post-1985, and the ones in the attic were pre-1985. They decided to look at the years McCroft had worked for Thornton.

"Another dull but detailed examination of the life of Virginia McCroft," Vik said. "The least she could have done was made up something. She could have pretended to be another Lizzie Borden or something."

"Look at it this way, Jessenovik. Somewhere, in one of those boxes, just waiting for you, is a grocery receipt for every purchase Virginia ever made, along with her grocery list. And, if you're very lucky, they will be sorted by store."

Vik kicked at a box on a shelf near the floor. "Before or after dinner?" he asked.

"After," Marti decided. She wanted to see her kids for a few minutes as much as he wanted to spend a little time with Mildred.

They put a call in for a uniform to pick up the boxes and transport them to the precinct.

Marti called home to let them know she was on her way, and when she got there Joanna and Lisa were setting the table for a late supper. Marti thought about Denise Stevens's visit to her office earlier in the day and wondered about talking with Lisa. She would talk with Ben first. That was one of the things that was different about being married to Ben. He didn't expect her to take care of everything at home. Of course, Johnny had been a narc. He routinely put in longer hours than she did and might spend several days away from home when he was undercover. Still . . . she liked not having to come home and do it all.

Joanna had a basketball game right after dinner. Lisa went with her. Marti thought about Lisa's activities with boys much older than she was and Joanna's relative inexperience. Was she doing the right thing letting Lisa stay here? What else could she do? Protect Joanna? How? From what? What would she learn from Lisa that she didn't already know? Still, Marti suspected that there were areas where Lisa had a lot more experience than her daughter. And, if Lisa made it sound daring and mature . . . No. Marti might as well continue to trust Joanna's judgment, and give her enough limits to make bad judgment difficult.

Aloud she said, "I can't protect her."

"Who?" Ben asked.

"Joanna."

"From what?"

"From anything. I can't protect her anymore. I can try to keep her safe in this house at least. I can enforce a curfew, make a few rules, but I can't really protect her."

"From who, Lisa or herself?"

"Lisa could be light-years ahead of where Joanna is, Ben."

"Yes. I suspect that in a number of ways, she is. But I also suspect that Joanna is light-years ahead of Lisa as well."

"So, what do we do?"

"*You* are doing just fine with Joanna and Theo."

"And you help."

"Good. I want to. But it's not like things weren't going along just fine without me."

"Then things are better now," Marti said. And they were.

She wasn't alone. "What do I do about Lisa? Mind my business? Talk to Sharon? What?"

"I think you should talk to Lisa," Ben said.

"Maybe we both should."

"No, not yet anyway. Lisa seems to be having enough problems with men. I'll just hang around and be the strong, silent type. This is an event, Marti, not a crisis. Lisa's been staying here ever since it happened, which might mean that she knows she's in over her head. And Sharon didn't even mention it when she stopped by, so it seems pretty obvious that she doesn't want to deal with it. You're much better at dealing with the kids than you give yourself credit for." He chuckled and held her against him. "You don't let them know when you push the panic button."

"Which is most of the time."

"I know."

She relaxed against him and wished she didn't have to go back to work.

"Guess what I found today," he said. A low, rumbling chuckle and the way he was stroking her thigh piqued her interest. "More vanilla candles. And . . ."

They kissed.

"And what?"

"I went to Carson's, found this whole display thing with vanilla everything."

"You didn't."

"When you come home tonight, I've got vanilla body wash, vanilla lotion, vanilla splash, vanilla . . ."

Marti kissed him. There was nothing quite like having a man who not only knew how to please a woman but took the time to do it. "Three hours," she promised. "Four max. I'll be home by midnight."

"Don't count," he said. "You'll jinx us."

As soon as Marti stepped off of the elevator and approached her office, she could smell Cowboy's second-watch pot of coffee. The precinct was quiet at night. Vik was there already, with manila folders stacked in neat piles on his desk. Beneath the pleasant mocha aroma, Marti caught an underlying whiff of old paper. She thought of vanilla and wondered how long it would be before she got back home.

Vik was so busy arranging folders in some kind of order that he didn't even look up. By the time she slipped out of her jacket, filled her cup with liquid caffeine, and kicked a box of folders closer to her desk, he was almost smiling.

"You might not have to bother with that tonight," he said. "I think I've just about got it."

"Got what?"

"Give me a couple of minutes."

It was half an hour before he spoke again.

"He divorced the wife," he said. "After thirty-five years of marriage."

"And?"

"Gave her everything in the settlement. Everything, including enough alimony to take care of most of what he'd earned after the divorce. He even gave her the house he's living in now. He also hid some property in blind trusts."

"When was this?"

"About eight years ago. By the time his ineptitude or whatever came to light, he didn't have anything to make restitution with. Virginia made copies of everything, including his income tax returns. He reported a loss for all three years following the divorce. By the time they went looking for assets that could be used to make restitution, there weren't any."

"What about the wife?"

"She went to California. Died there a couple of years ago. According to the copies of the wills, everything passed to the children and grandchildren."

"And Thornton?"

"I have a hunch that they're looking out for him. All we saw was that one room and that beat-up car. And according to this"—he tapped a stack of folders—"he didn't spend that much time here until after the wife died and he got too sick to visit the kids."

"Virginia knew that much?"

"Virginia probably knew what time he went to the bathroom and just didn't write it down."

"How much of this is documented?"

"All of it. I'm not sure how she managed after she quit her job, but she must have had access to everything while she was there."

"How did he get away with it? Couldn't they go after the wife?"

"I don't know. We'll have to have the state's attorney's office take a look at it."

"How long have you been working on this?" Marti asked.

"Over an hour."

"Good job." She needed that shower. She could almost feel the hot water massaging the tiredness from her back, smell the vanilla body wash. "So where are his kids?"

"Thornton's got a daughter in California, a son in Kansas, and another son and daughter in Wisconsin."

"Wisconsin is close enough. Let's find out if their inheritance would be threatened if any of this came out, and let's see what we can find out about Thornton's and his kids' current financial situation. Someone was paying this five hundred dollars. It's not that much when you think about it."

Vik agreed. "Let's take another look at Virginia's finances too. Maybe it wasn't enough."

Marti looked at the boxes on her side of the desk. What else could be in there of importance? There wasn't any good reason to stay here now that Vik had taken care of everything. Ben would be surprised to see her back so soon. Candles would be flickering, oil warming. And Ben . . .

"I wonder if there's anything else? It wouldn't surprise me, Marti, not with all the crap she kept all of these years."

It was hard to imagine why someone would retain and sort and record every aspect of her life like this. Control, Marti decided, or the illusion of control. But why?

Vik yawned and rubbed the back of his neck. "Long day. It's almost eleven. None of this is going away before morning. Let's wait and look at it with fresh eyes after roll call.

Then maybe we can go up to Wisconsin and visit the Thornton kids."

Vanilla, Marti thought, and smiled. She loved the scent of vanilla. When Johnny came back from Vietnam, it had been banished from the house, even when she was cooking. Vanilla plants grew in the Philippines. The smell brought back the nightmares. But, with Ben, vanilla became sensual, erotic. How could the same experience have such a different effect on each of them? Maybe it *was* what Ben had said. *He* had been a medic, not a soldier. He hadn't had to kill anyone. The more she thought about it, the more she realized how much Johnny had paid to fight in the war, and how much he had lost because of it.

CHAPTER
19

He'd done it! He'd built another bomb. He would have to set off two or three more before he understood what the chemicals were doing well enough to begin making changes. This wasn't really his bomb. It was someone else's bomb. It wouldn't be his until he could make up his own set of instructions. The problem was, Lincoln Prairie was too small a town for bombs. A city like Chicago was perfect, but there were too many criminals there. Evanston? Maybe. He wanted to set this one off tonight, and he wanted to be able to read about it tomorrow. Evanston, or someplace on the North Side. They had to believe it was done by someone who lived in Chicago. Nobody would link a car bomb that far from here to the small explosive he had set off in that mailbox.

He exited the Dan Ryan at Diversy and headed east, toward Lake Michigan, then farther north, away from the Loop. He drove until he came to an area not far from the expressway, where there were still a few empty factories that hadn't been turned into condos. There were alleys and abandoned cars here, and the police didn't hassle the homeless as much as they did closer to more highly populated areas. He parked a block away from the car he had targeted for practice, walked back, and tossed the bomb in where a side window used to be. Then he walked back to his car and sat facing his target. He fingered the detonator, not certain that it would work. He hadn't mastered the mechanics of putting one together yet.

He saw something, a shadow, as he set off the detonator. The explosion made his car rock. As a plume of fire, then

black smoke, rose from where the car had been, he waited
for the hardness in his loins, and the release, but it didn't
happen. It hadn't happened with the mailbox either, but that
bomb was smaller than this one.

He slapped his hand against the steering wheel, then
made a fist and hit it once and then again. The bombs were
not going to be enough. They would never be as wonderful
as the fires. He could hear a siren in the distance and started
the car. He saw the house a few blocks away. Brick, abandoned, plywood stripped from the first-floor doors and windows, upper windows broken out. There was too much
oxygen available. It would burn too fast. But he couldn't go
home without . . .

He parked near an alley a safe distance away. His burlap
bag with the gallon can of gasoline was heavy. As he slung it
over his shoulder, his heart began racing. Soon, soon. He
poured the gasoline inside a basement window and became
erect as he waited for the gas to vaporize and spread. Standing away from the window, he lit wooden matches and threw
them inside. The flames flared at once. He backed away
slowly, watching as the flames leaped to the window, seeking
the cold night air that would feed them. He stepped close
enough to feel the heat. The swelling in his groin increased
until he ached. He inhaled deeply, smoke, burning wood,
and heat from the fire. The flames seemed caught in a gust of
wind. The fire reached the ceiling beams and flashed, forcing
him back. It must have hit a gas line. His release was sudden
and unexpected. He stumbled, then lurched away.

As soon as he got back to Lincoln Prairie, he stopped at a
Jewel and picked up some food. He began eating as soon as
he got back in the car. By four in the morning he had gone
through half a gallon of ice cream, an apple pie, and four
cheese and bologna sandwiches. He had never felt so awake
in his life. Everything had changed since the bombs.

When Geoffrey drove past Mama's house and saw Calvin's car parked in the driveway, he went to a coffee shop about a mile and a half away and got half a dozen doughnuts. By the time he came back, Calvin was gone. He rang the bell to let the ladies know someone was entering and let himself in with his key. One good thing about having a cat join the household was that she kept Mama's little yapper in check, and the pest didn't rush over to pee on his jogging shoes.

"Hey, Miles baby."

The little Jack Russell stood there wagging its tail and looking from Geoffrey to the white-and-orange cat, Sarah Vaughan. Sarah didn't have much to do with anybody besides Aunt Precious, a definite plus if they had to have a cat around. Too bad nobody had figured out how to keep the spoiled rotten, overweight fur ball off the furniture.

Mama was redecorating again. From the looks of it, the teeny-bopper idea with every electronic device a teenager could want wasn't attracting Calvin's kids because it had all been moved to an area near the sliding doors and was now crowded out by a conversation pit. Mama and Aunt Precious had their feet up on hassocks. Mama knitted diligently while Aunt Precious did needlepoint. Geoffrey knew that neither woman was doing much more than gossiping, and that this wasn't the best time for a visit.

He kissed them both on the cheek, Mama first, who happened to notice what he was wearing on his feet.

"Good. You're keeping up with your running," she said, as he headed for the kitchen area and food.

"Lordy, lordy, the ladies in my life have outdone themselves today." He helped himself to fried chicken, potato salad, and collard greens. "Blackberry *and* peach cobbler. Now I know you do not expect me to tell you which one tastes the best. Nobody makes cobbler like you two."

Ordinarily they would be waiting on him by now. Whoever they were talking about must be important.

"How you doing, baby?" Mama asked. "Is Sister Hawkins treating you right?"

Just the opening he had been hoping for. "How well do you know her, Mama?"

"Since long before she married Whitman Ross and had that boy of hers."

Damn. That was a long time. He'd have to be careful.

"How long has it been since you've . . . visited?"

"Lord, child," Aunt Precious said, "who has time for that anymore? We're fortunate to see each other at church on Sunday. And with my condition . . ."

Mama reached over and patted Aunt Precious's hand.

Damn. No matter what he said, Aunt Precious and her "condition" would take precedence over everything. And Aunt Precious's damned cat. Why had he told everyone he was allergic to cats? Now he wished he had just gone to see the old bat more often. There was room enough here for all of them, if he couldn't just convince Mama that he needed to come back home.

"Sister Hawkins is on a diet," he said.

"As thin as she is?" Aunt Precious asked.

"Looks like she needs more meat on her old bones, not less," Mama agreed. "How do you know?"

" 'Cause she brings me lettuce and boiled chicken and things like that."

"Good Lord," Mama said.

"Food doesn't come with your accommodations, does it?" Aunt Precious asked.

"No, but . . ."

"Then it is time you found you a good woman," she said. "Or a decent restaurant."

Damn. He'd expect something like that from Calvin but not Aunt Precious.

"You are just spoiled, baby," Mama said. "This move is the best thing that could have happened."

Double damn.

"Deacon Evans says you are doing a wonderful job," Aunt Precious said. "He says he doesn't know what he would do without you."

"He can look after himself just fine."

"Of course he can," Aunt Precious agreed. "But he doesn't have any family left, and he says you're just like a son to him. The Lord is sure going to bless you for this."

It didn't look like the blessing was going to include an invitation to return home. At least not tonight.

"It's about time for the news, Sister," Aunt Precious said and turned on the television.

Aunt Precious was just taking over. Mama never watched the news. Geoffrey wrapped and bagged some food to take with him. Then he fixed a cup of coffee and helped himself to some peach cobbler. Aunt Precious made the blackberry.

"Lord, girl, look at this," Mama said, "a pig. Who in their right mind would live in the same house with a pig?"

A pig? On the news? Geoffrey went over to the television just in time to hear the Confederate from Sweden and his wife discuss the loss of their pre–Civil War candleholders. There was no mention of the candleholders' return.

"Can you believe that," Mama said. "Who would prey on a poor old woman like that? Who would do such a thing?"

"I don't know what this world is coming to," Aunt Precious said, agreeing.

"These folks are our age. And farming people, worked the land. Poor woman just wanted to be safe in her own home and somebody came along and tricked her and stole from her like it wasn't nothing. What kind of person would do that?"

"No home training," Aunt Precious said.

Geoffrey walked back to the table. What would they say

if they knew it was him? What if they knew he was stealing from Deacon Jones? He didn't do it because he had to. There was Dad's trust. He did it because it was . . . fun. He did a lot of things because it was fun and because he could.

" 'A wise son makes his father glad, but a foolish son is a grief to his mother,' " Mama quoted. "I'm glad I won't never have to deal with no foolishness like that."

Geoffrey pushed the peach cobbler to one side. He wasn't hungry anymore.

Opal lay quite still for at least half an hour after the lights went on in the driveway and then went off. That should mean that Fred was gone, but it didn't, not always. He had forgotten to bring her supper. He did that sometimes, and usually it didn't matter much, but tonight she felt hungry. He would get angry if she got out of bed, unless she went into the bathroom, and the bathroom was not that close to the kitchen. If he caught her . . . And what could she eat? Would he notice if it were just bread and jam? Strawberry jam. How many years had it been since she'd had that? There probably wasn't any. But then, maybe there was. She could see it, red with lumps of fruit. Maybe she would just have a spoonful of jam and not touch the bread. No. She needed to think about something else, but the thought of the sweet red preserves would not go away. She waited a little longer and then eased out of bed. She opened the door slowly until it was open just wide enough for her to slip into the hall. She braced herself with one hand against the wall and made her way as quietly as she could to the kitchen.

Without turning on the light, she went to the drawer and got a spoon, then she opened the refrigerator. Strawberry jam. There was some. She opened the jar, put it on the refrigerator shelf, and scooped out a spoonful of jam.

"Mother!"

She screamed. She didn't mean to. She knew he might be there, watching. She clutched the spoon as he came toward her, holding out his hand.

"Could I have this, Fred? Please, could I have this?"

"Sweets aren't good for you, Mother. Don't you remember Father telling us that?"

He blamed her. He would always blame her. But what could she have done? Fred Senior had been bigger than both of them. Fred was still no match for his father in size. How could she have defended him? She couldn't even defend herself.

"Fred, I . . ."

"Give that to me, Mother, and go back to bed. Now!"

Without speaking, Opal obeyed.

There were a lot of police cars in the area when Fred drove over to the South Side. He had to move along as if he knew where he was going, avoid attracting attention, and cover as much of the four-by-eight-block area as he could without the cops getting suspicious. There was little traffic, but more people than there had been during the day. Kids stood in small groups on the corners, all wearing the same color jackets and baseball caps, with the bills at an odd angle. They looked his way and flipped signs with their hands and gave him the finger and laughed. He got so nervous his hands and arms began to itch.

He hadn't noticed until now, but it was getting warmer, even at night. Men and a few women slept in doorways or walked along pulling wire shopping carts, carrying bags. It was quiet, too quiet, but the streets weren't empty at all. There were too many cops. Two on bicycles looked at him as they wheeled by. A few blocks away another pair was on foot. And then there were the cop cars. Too many people; too many cops. He scratched his hands, then his arms. He had to get away from here.

As he turned the corner to head home, a man darted in front of his car. Fred slammed on the brakes. The man grinned at him and tipped his hat, then lurched to the sidewalk with a drunken swagger. Fred's heart was pounding so fast and he was in such a hurry to get away that he drove past the beige Toyota. When he saw the car in his rearview mirror, he almost slammed on the brakes again so he could back up. Instead he forced himself to keep moving. By the time he had gone to the end of the block, his hands were so sweaty he had to wipe them on his pants to grip the steering wheel. He turned and made a wide, three-block circle. This time, when he drove past the car, he checked the license plate. Later this morning, when it was daylight and there were fewer people hanging around outside, he would come back for a better look at the house and to see if he could catch the man.

FRIDAY, APRIL 30

Theo was in the front yard when Marti backed the car out of the garage Friday morning. He was squatting by the flower bed where he had transplanted Johnny's irises. She had brought the rhizomes from their home in Chicago to the house she'd shared with Sharon and then dug them up again and brought them here. A few weeks ago the dirt had finally softened enough and the weather gotten warm enough to put them into the ground.

Marti parked the car in the driveway and walked over to where Theo was inspecting the soil.

"They're not coming up," he said. "You're supposed to plant them in the fall, not the spring."

"I don't think they've been there long enough. It's not time for them to come up yet, is it?"

"No. But they won't."

Theo wasn't usually this pessimistic. He had more than irises on his mind.

"They might stay fallow this year, bloom next spring."

"Maybe." He didn't make any move to get up.

Marti looked down at his dear, bronze face. In profile, he looked so much like Johnny, his face all planes and angles. Dark eyes, pointed chin, high cheekbones, widow's peak. Lord, but he looked just like his daddy. And he was thinking about his daddy again. First the airplane he and Johnny were working on when Johnny died came out of the box and was back on his bureau and now this. She didn't know what any of it meant.

"Are you okay?" Why could she never find the right thing to say to this child?

"Why did Daddy like irises?"

"His grandmother grew them down south. He went there to visit in the summer until he was about your age and she died. After that, he remembered."

"Why do you keep them?"

"Because . . . Your daddy had a lot of memories that made him feel sad, and this memory made him feel happy. I like to remember *him* that way."

"Ben's happy a lot."

"I know."

"He's not much like Daddy."

Where was this going? Did he compare Johnny and Ben just as she did sometimes? And if he did, did he still remember the perfect dad, the dad who helped build model airplanes, just as she remembered the perfect husband for so long? Or was he beginning to remember the long silences, the times Johnny was tired and impatient?

"There are a lot of things about Ben that are different from your daddy but not everything. We are all very important to Ben, just as we were to Daddy. Very important. Ben loves us, just as Daddy loves us from heaven."

"I know." There was something old-beyond-his-years about the way he said it. He was still for a moment, then he stood up. "Grandma said she'd fix pancakes for breakfast. You're going to miss out on them. We'll have to ask her to fix them again when you're home." He gave her a hug and went inside.

All the way to work she wondered what their conversation had really been about.

As soon as Marti walked into the office, Vik said, "Wait 'til you see this." He waved a small diskette.

Poor Vik. The lure of the boxes they had brought in from Virginia McCroft's attic had been too much for him. He had come in before roll call to begin going through them.

"What's on it?"

Vik looked at the diskette, looked at her, and said, "On second thought, maybe I should just tell you about it."

"Give it to me, Vik. Whatever it is, I'm sure I've seen worse."

Their job descriptions hadn't been upgraded to include data entry, so they didn't have a computer. The traffic unit across the hall did. Marti turned it on, booted up the diskette, and watched naked women involved in a range of calisthenics usually reserved for the very supple or the very young. By the time the naked men showed up and began ravaging the suddenly modest nude maidens, she was bored.

One of the traffic cops came in and stood behind her. When he began laughing out loud, she took the diskette out and went back to the office.

"Where did you find this?" she asked. "Stored under *P* for pornography?"

"No," Vik said. "It was filed under *R*."

"For R-rated," she said. "Makes sense. It is that."

"According to Slim and Cowboy, it's pretty mundane stuff. Nothing exotic."

The real question was why Virginia McCroft would have such a diskette. "She didn't have a computer, Vik. At least not at home."

"Now that you mention it, she didn't."

"Oh, and you didn't think of that? What happened? You got caught up in the moment?" She grinned as a flush made its way from his neck to his face.

"I felt like a voyeur, MacAlister. Why would Virginia have such a thing? This Virginia isn't anything like the person I knew when we were in high school. Alive, she seemed so predictable. Dead, she's full of surprises."

"I thought she propositioned you."

"Not exactly. It was just a dance."

"What was she like?" Marti asked. She expected the usual myopic recollections that everyone had when they were too close to the situation to see anything objectively.

After a few minutes, Vik said, "You know what? She wasn't very nice. Popular, but not nice. Mildred didn't have a dozen boys trailing behind her when she went to class, but Virginia did. I think that's what trying to get me to take her to that dance was all about. But why would anyone be that mean to Mildred? I bet Virginia wouldn't have even been there when I went to pick her up if I had said yes."

Occasionally, Vik did surprise her. "Could that be why there seemed to be so few people in her life when she died?"

"Could be," he said. "She sure didn't turn out the way anyone thought she would. She was class vice president, valedictorian, and assistant editor for the yearbook and the school newspaper. She was in the Miss Lincoln Prairie pageant her senior year, first runner-up to the mayor's daughter. I always expected her to marry a lawyer—one who became a judge, or maybe a mayor. I thought she would continue to be . . . important."

"What happened?"

"I don't know." He thought about that while he went through his in basket, then said, "She was supposed to go to college. Northwestern, I think. Nothing ever came of it. It's as if she graduated, then sort of disappeared. I don't know what she did after that. She sure did change."

"Sometimes people become who they are, and we think they've changed."

"Maybe it was all an act?"

"Could have been."

"Then it was a damned good one, Marti." He picked up one of Virginia's folders, read the label, and shook his head. "I talked to my sister-in-law, Essie."

"Find out anything?"

"No. The only time she's seen Virginia since they graduated was at class reunions. According to Essie, Virginia didn't keep in touch with anyone after graduation. Strange."

"Vik, what she was doing with Thornton amounted to blackmail."

He weighed the diskette in his hand. "I know."

"One thing I don't understand is how he paid her," Marti said. "The man gave away most of his assets in the divorce settlement."

"There is property in the land trust," Vik said.

"Property worth keeping to the tune of five hundred a month?"

"Maybe in the long run he was coming out ahead. He owed a number of people money, including the IRS. He gave his wife almost everything. He must have given his kids something too. And they're still alive. We'd better check them out."

"They could have something they want to protect," Marti said. "My other question is, what did she have on him? Five hundred dollars could be a lot or it could be negligible. It's the regularity that gets my attention. It came on time every month."

Marti looked at the file cabinets and the boxes that had been stored in Virginia's attic and basement. They were going to have to go dig through it all again. They had managed to uncover the deal with Thornton and find out about her weekly visits with Rosenblum. Whatever the diskette was all about was most likely in there too.

"How recently was that garbage saved on that diskette?" she asked. "Can anyone tell?"

"Don't know." He made a call then said, "The Web site they downloaded it from has been on-line for about six months."

"Well, that should eliminate the stuff in the boxes. Maybe we don't have too far to look." As she unzipped the Franklin planner, she reminded herself that the Rosenblum assignations had been coded "gardening." As compulsive as Virginia McCroft had been, she had found ways to maintain her privacy.

"Nothing," Marti said after an hour.

"Me neither," Vik agreed.

"There aren't any new receipts or pensions in her account book. Maybe whatever this is about, it just happened."

But nothing different had happened in the weeks before Virginia died. Nor had she gone anyplace or had any appointments where finding something like this diskette seemed likely, still . . . "So," Marti said, "Virginia spent two to three evenings and four mornings a week with her mother and one afternoon a week 'gardening.' She went to the regular monthly meeting of the city council, Park District, Forest Preserve Board, the Downtown Committee, the Water Reclamation Committee . . . what's that?"

"Beats me."

". . . the Historic Society, and half a dozen other civic or government organizations, none of which she belonged to. Somewhere in her travels, she came across this diskette. How? Why? Was she a snoop? Was she looking for something to generate a little additional income? How does one come across this kind of a diskette if one is not ordinarily in the company of those with computers?"

"I've been asking myself a few questions along those lines," Vik said. "Even with what I know about Virginia now that I didn't know before, this one doesn't make much sense."

"Of all of those places, where was she most likely to find this?"

"The city council," Vik said without hesitation. "Or somewhere in city hall."

"That narrows it down," Marti said. "Why?"

"Because they're all politicians. Her father was a politician. That seems to have been her main interest in life, even if it didn't amount to much more than meddling."

"You're a lot of help. Still, I suppose if we knew if and when she had access to a computer . . . ? Whoever downloaded it must have left it lying around; but if they did, how would Virginia know what was on it?" The more Marti thought about it, the more convinced she was that as unlikely as it seemed on the surface, Virginia would have had to have found the diskette at a place she had been to more than once, and she would have to have observed something she wasn't supposed to while she was there. "I think we're just going to have to go to each of these sites and look around."

Vik didn't balk at the idea. He got a call from Wisconsin, and then a fax came in. "Thornton's kids. The daughter's husband owns a dairy farm, and the son owns a real estate franchise."

"Since when?" Marti asked.

"The son has been in real estate for about twelve years, bought the franchise about six years ago when the owner retired. The son-in-law inherited the farm. They faxed a newspaper clipping on local farming that mentions the son, dated . . . yup . . . close to six years ago. He was close to going under until then, along with a few of his neighbors. He's doing fine now."

"Why do I keep hearing the number six?" Marti asked.

"Because Thornton divorced the wife seven years ago and she took the money he gave her and passed it along to the children."

"And we still don't know if their money can be used to satisfy the claims against the father?"

"No, and I suspect that neither Thornton nor his kids pursued that either, or if they did, their lawyer said yes. Otherwise, why would they keep paying Virginia?"

"I don't know, and I don't expect any of his kids to tell us," Marti said. They would have to go to Wisconsin to talk to the two who lived there. She hoped the drive wouldn't take long. "They've talked with their father by now; still we might surprise them if we just show up."

Opal's stomach grumbled as she ate. A custard cup filled with Cream of Wheat wasn't enough to satisfy her hunger. It was the first time she had eaten since yesterday morning and she had stopped being hungry. It would have been better if he had brought nothing at all. Now she was hungry enough to wish for the mushroom soup, as much as she hated it, and to pray to God that Fred Junior remembered to bring it tonight.

The door opened and Fred came in.

"Back to bed, Mother." He picked up the tray. "You look a little rested. Maybe tomorrow, if you sleep well today and tonight, maybe you can get up tomorrow."

Opal nodded. If she smiled or seemed pleased, he would change his mind.

After Fred Junior left, the house was quiet for a long time, but then her hearing wasn't good and the house always seemed quiet, even when Fred was at home. Probably because he spent so much time in Fred Senior's room in the basement. What did he do down there? Why wasn't he working? If he didn't find a job soon, what would happen to them? Maybe that's why he wasn't feeding her. Maybe there wasn't any food. If there wasn't, would he just leave her here to die? What was going to happen to her?

Opal looked toward the window. She pushed the quilt away and sat up with her bare feet on the floor. Did she dare go to the window? If she could just look outside. Even though there was nothing to see, there were people out there somewhere. Could she get help if she needed to? How far could she walk without her cane? Inside, she had the walls to steady her. Out there, she would fall. If only she knew where her cane was. Instead of getting up, she lay down again, listening to a silence that she didn't think would ever be broken and wishing for the sound of someone's voice, anyone's voice, except Fred's.

He read both Chicago newspapers while he was having breakfast. Not that he expected to find anything about the fire or the bombing. The city was too big with too much going on for anyone to take note of something that insignificant. He was surprised to find a mention of the car that he had bombed in the Chicago Sun-Times, *then realized it had to be because someone had been killed in the explosion. That shadow he'd seen just before the car exploded. Whoever it was, was still unidentified. Probably just some street person.*

He clipped the article and put it into the box, separating it from the others and adding it to the yellowed clipping of the cop in the Upper Peninsula who'd died so long ago. The Tribune *had a paragraph on the fire at the Warren place on the page with the obituaries. The body of a woman had been found there. He clipped that too. His best fire ever. One that he had been able to totally control. Soon he would create another fire. He would have to check out the house today and the neighborhood. Then he would have to decide what accelerant would work best.*

Marti and Vik left Lincoln Prairie right after roll call. The drive to Thornton's daughter's farm didn't take long. Although it was northwest of Lincoln Prairie it was located in the southern part of Wisconsin. The weather was still cool but the sun was bright and the grass and trees a brilliant green. Grazing cows paid little attention to them as they drove along the road that led past the barns to the farmhouse.

Marti drove slowly. "How now, brown cow?"

"Jerseys," Vik said.

"Does the kind of cow you have make a difference?"

"Jerseys produce a little less milk than Guernseys, but it's richer, more butterfat."

Marti was impressed. "How do you know so much about cows?"

"We used to have farms in Lake County. We still have a few."

"I didn't think they let them run around anymore. Don't they keep them in stalls with their heads locked in some kind of frame thing?" She had visited a dairy farm once on a field trip with Theo.

"This is called loose housing."

"What does that mean?" Marti asked.

"They get to wander around, go outside."

"I'm counting maybe fifty or sixty cows. That doesn't seem like very many."

"It's about average," Vik said.

"Can he make money at this?"

"Probably not a lot, but from what I can see, that investment six years ago was substantial. These buildings are new, and I'm guessing that what's inside them is too. New equipment to increase production and improve efficiency. In this business you have to maximize everything. Thornton's daughter and son-in-law could be sitting pretty right now."

The farmhouse was a two-story white frame with a screened-in front porch and a brick addition along the west side. The woman who opened the door was so ordinary she would become almost invisible in a crowd. Brown hair, brown eyes, no distinguishing features, average height, average weight. She wore jeans and a long-sleeved T-shirt. She had rolled up the sleeves, and shirt and jeans were dusted with flour.

"Something I can help you with?" she asked, her voice neutral.

"Are you Andrew Thornton's daughter?" Marti asked.

"Poppa!" Her alarm was immediate. "Is Poppa all right?"

"He's fine," Marti said. "We came to talk to you about Virginia McCroft."

"That one," the woman said. She wiped the back of her hand across her forehead. "I suppose you might as well come in. I need to get a batch of bread in the oven."

They walked to the rear of the house through one long family room with a huge fieldstone fireplace. The heads of several deer with modest antlers hung on the wall. It was a lived-in room, with a tall bookcase filled with books near a grouping of comfortable chairs and a sewing machine set up by a window with southern exposure. The television had a thirteen-inch screen and wasn't turned on. Children's coloring books and loose crayons had been tossed in a basket that was on a small wooden table with two chairs. A box overflowed with toys.

They followed Thornton's daughter to the kitchen.

"You've seen Poppa?"

Marti nodded.

"I haven't talked to him today." Six mounds of dough were aligned on a marble cutting board. Thornton's daughter picked one up and began kneading it. Her hands had been shaped by manual labor, thick fingers, large knuckles. They reminded Marti of her grandmother's hands. Grandma had been a laundress most of her life back when there were no washing machines.

"Your name, ma'am?" Vik asked.

"Oona. Oona Amstadt."

"Mrs. Amstadt, we thought that maybe with Miss Mc-Croft asking your father for more money—"

"That witch," Oona said. "Little Miss Efficiency all those years and nothing more than a lying snoop."

"Well, now that she wanted more money . . ." Vik persisted.

"As if there was more to give her. Poppa has never been able to pay her that damned pension, and we had no intention of giving her another nickel, ever."

Marti noted the past tense—*had no intention*—and the *we*.

"Does that mean you were going to stop the pension altogether," Vik asked, "or just not increase it?"

"I told her she would not get another dime out of any of us!" She banged the glob of dough on the marble slab.

"And when did you tell her that, ma'am?"

"Why, just . . ." She stopped.

"It's important that we know when you talked to her," Vik said.

"Oh, and just why is that?"

"Because she's dead, ma'am," Vik said.

"And you think I had something to do with that?"

"Perhaps you could tell me."

"Well, I didn't, but she deserved whatever she got. Holding Poppa to a promise he'd made to her father twenty years ago, and Poppa fool enough to agree. Even the lawyer said it was binding."

"The lawyer?"

"Yes, the one I went to last week."

"And what day would that have been?"

"Tuesday," she said. "Last Tuesday."

"Is that when you saw Virginia McCroft?"

The woman became wary. "I don't have anything else to say to you. If Virginia McCroft got hers, trust me, she had it coming to her."

Back in the car, Vik said, "She's the first person we've talked to who doesn't think McCroft died from a heart attack."

"I was hoping she'd say that Virginia had been shot," Vik said. "A small-caliber gun is something a woman might carry."

"Considering that there won't be anything about Virginia in the news until this afternoon's edition of the *News-Times* comes out, she sure knew a lot, even if she did talk with her father before we got here." Marti thought of Oona's hands, kneading the dough. "If McCroft had been strangled, she would be a prime suspect."

Andrew Thornton Jr. lived about twenty miles from Oona's farm. The real estate franchise he had purchased consisted of three offices, strategically located to draw business from a wide rural area that included a number of small towns. They went to the office in the town where he lived. A secretary who looked like someone's matronly aunt pointed them toward Thornton's office.

Thornton Junior was much more attractive than his sister. There was a boyishness about him that made him seem the younger of the two, although he wasn't. A wide grin was complemented by a cowlick and what Marti's mother referred to as bedroom eyes.

"How can I help you today?" he asked, as he came from behind a semicircular desk polished to a high gleam. "We can meet all of your housing needs, whether you are renting or buying."

He extended his hand. Vik and Marti ignored it.

"Actually," Marti said, "we came to talk to you about Virginia McCroft."

Thornton blinked, then said, "Virginia?"

"Yes, you do know her?"

"Of course. She worked for my father for a number of years."

Marti identified herself and introduced Vik. They showed him their shields.

"Why on earth would you drive all the way here from Lincoln Prairie to talk about Virginia McCroft?"

"How well do you know her?"

"Probably not as well as I know my secretary. She was there when I went to see my father. She typed, filed, whatever."

"How would you describe her relationship with your father?"

He raised his hands, fingers splayed. "I wouldn't. She was the secretary. She was the daughter of a friend of his, if that means anything. Alderman McCroft. He's dead now."

"How well did you know her father?"

"I didn't know the alderman at all. I have a life. My father has a life. Virginia was his secretary. Period. How much does anyone know, or care, about the people in their parents' lives?" He checked his watch. "I've got to show a house in thirty minutes. If there's anything important you need to know, save yourself another drive up here and ask now. I've got to be out of here in six minutes."

He didn't ask about Virginia McCroft and neither Marti nor Vik volunteered the information that she was dead.

"Do you think he was that disinterested?" Marti asked, as they headed back to Lincoln Prairie. "Or had Sis called before we got there?"

"Who knows? He's a salesman. They're all actors." Vik put on his seat belt then said, "You know what I think? There is too much money involved here—with this farm and this real estate business—for it to all have come from Thornton's business dealings. Maybe we should have someone take a look at those files of Virginia's involving land deals. Maybe someone who knows more about it than we do should take a look. There is money in land, and my guess is that Thornton had a lot more cash stashed than the IRS uncovered."

Fred left the house without cleaning the kitchen, determined to confront the man who had stolen his mother's watch—his watch. Anyone who did wrong to a helpless old woman needed to be punished.

It was still cool when he walked outside. He pulled up his jacket collar and rubbed his hands together as he waited for the car to warm up. He didn't know what he was going to say, but he was going to confront the man this morning.

The beige Toyota was parked where it had been the night before. Fred pulled up behind it and waited. By ten-thirty he was hungry. He was in such a hurry to get here. He should have stopped long enough to get a doughnut and a cup of coffee. When a tall, slender, fair-skinned man came out the front door about eleven-fifteen Fred was certain it was the thief because he did look white. He waited until the man went to the driver's side of the Toyota then jumped out of his car and called to him.

The man turned to him with a puzzled expression on his face. "You calling me?"

"Yes." Fred walked up to him. He wasn't as tall as the man, but he was heavier. "You have my mother's watch. I want it back."

"A watch? I don't have anybody's watch."

Fred pulled the pager out of his pocket. "You're the man in the paper, the man who sold an alarm to the woman who owns the pig. You sold my mother an alarm too and gave her this."

"Look, man, I don't have a watch."

"Listen, you lying piece of slime. I know who you are. I

know where you live. And the cops are going to know in about five minutes if you don't give me what's mine."

"Where does your mother live?"

Fred gave him the address.

"Lots of trees around the place?"

"Yes."

"Is she real old, humpbacked?"

"Yes."

The man reached into his pants pocket and pulled out a ring. "I don't know anything about a watch. The woman who lives there gave me this. Here, it's yours. Take it."

Fred did not recognize the ring. His mother didn't own anything like that. "She said she gave you her watch. She doesn't own any rings."

"We are talking about the same house and the same person, aren't we?" The man repeated the address, described the house and his mother.

"But she doesn't . . . "

"Yes, she does. She went inside, got this ring, and gave it to me. She's old. She probably doesn't remember. Maybe she's confused and she thinks she gave me a watch. I'm giving you back what she gave me." He held out the ring.

Fred pushed his hand away. "Give me my mother's watch!"

"I don't have a watch, man! She didn't give me one! Nobody's given me a watch in three or four months now. I'm giving you what she gave me! This!"

Fred looked down at the piece of junk the man was holding out. Chips of fake glass set in fake silver. "This is not my mother's."

"Your mother went upstairs somewhere and got this and gave it to me. It took her so long to get it that I thought she had dropped dead of a heart attack or something. But she did go upstairs and get this, and she did give it to me."

"My mother didn't own anything like this." Mother didn't own anything. All of it was his. "And she couldn't get up the stairs without her cane."

"Look, man, I don't know anything about anything that

you're trying to tell me. All I know is an old woman with a humpback opened the door at the address you gave me, and she went upstairs and got me this ring."

Fred hesitated. She couldn't have made it up the stairs. And if she did, what was up there? His bedroom, some old furniture in his parents' bedroom that he hadn't gotten around to getting rid of. Father might have let her keep a ring. It wasn't worth anything.

"Man, people are looking at us. If I had a watch she didn't give me, I'd let you have it just to get you off my case, but this is it. This is what she gave me."

Fred didn't believe the man. He didn't trust him. "If you're lying to me . . . I'll go to the cops." The man hadn't liked it when he'd said that before. He didn't like it now.

"Look, man, here." The man reached into his pocket and counted out some money. "This is what she gave me, for real. But just for your trouble, I'll throw in a couple hundred, okay? Nothing she had in that house was worth more than that."

Fred took the ring and the money. "I'll ask her if this belongs to her," he said. "If you're lying, I know where you live. You have done something wrong. Be warned: Wrongdoing does not go unpunished."

Fred went back to his car and watched as the man drove away. There didn't seem to be any need to follow him, but he did anyway, continuing past the block-long row of storefronts where the man parked and noting that there was a floor above the stores with apartments. Then he headed home. Home. He didn't want to be here anymore. He wanted to be in California, but he couldn't go yet. Because of Mother. If she weren't here . . . He would go to the bank and go through everything in the safety deposit box. Maybe today, if he had time. He hated this house. Maybe soon he wouldn't have to live here anymore.

Geoffrey could see the man in the dark blue Geo following him. He was sure it was the same car that had been parked over by the farmer's field when he took the candleholders back. Damned if that wasn't nothing but the beginning of bad times. He should have walked away as soon as he saw that pig. The Geo kept going when he parked. He would have waved to him, but the stupid fool definitely didn't strike him as someone with a sense of humor. He thought about driving away and parking someplace else and waiting there to see if the man would come back, park to watch him again; but since the guy already knew where he lived, what was the point? Besides, he'd given him the ring back and some cash. As long as Deacon Evans stayed a fool he could make up the money, but Lord, he'd hated to give up that ring. He had intended to give it to Mama today, instead of waiting for Mother's Day. Nothing was going right where Mama was concerned. She wasn't feeling one bit guilty about sending him to live with Sister Hawkins. In fact, with Aunt Precious there, Mama hardly seemed to notice that he was gone. He slapped the flat of his hand against the steering wheel. Nothing in his life was going right. Not one damned thing.

He needed that ring. Too bad he couldn't have taken the man on, challenged him for ownership of the ring, called his bluff, but the man had said the magic word: cops. Cops. Geoffrey's stomach kicked into gear and began churning so fiercely that he tasted bile. The pig had gotten so much media attention because of the candleholders that if anyone found out he was the mastermind behind the scam, his face would be all over the news too.

What if that joker wasn't satisfied with having the ring back? What if he wanted to get even? No, he was just some religious fanatic. "You have done something wrong. Be warned: Wrongdoing does not go unpunished." Nothing like a little righteous indignation. The fat slob probably thought God would visit him tonight, like the ghosts in *A Christmas Carol*. Weird, both of them, that fool and his mother. He had seen street people who were better dressed. Neither of them had used a comb lately and the smell. The man had definitely needed a bath. Now that he thought of it, he had caught of whiff of something when he was talking to the old woman. Neither of them had used soap or deodorant in a while.

Geoffrey waited a good ten minutes, but the Geo did not come back. He got out of his car and walked back about half a block to see if the man had parked somewhere. When he was satisfied that the Geo wasn't anywhere around, he went inside. His stomach was still upset, and when he thought about having to give up that ring . . . What would he do about Mama? And now he had to deal with Deacon Evans. Listening to that old man run off at the mouth was just what he needed. The place was quiet. Maybe Evans wasn't around.

Geoffrey began by trying to figure out what to do with the spreadsheet program. So far, he had figured out what headers were, and how to change the width of the columns. About all he needed to know now was how to key in the formulas. He was working on that when Deacon Evans came in.

"This is what I like to see," Evans said, rubbing his hands together.

Geoffrey was glad there wasn't enough room for an extra chair. It kept the old man's visits short.

"You're getting more like your daddy every day," Evans said. "Your daddy was a businessman's businessman. Carried all of his business in his head *and* wrote it down on paper. He didn't just do business with anyone either. Couldn't but one man sell him his cars, and one insure his property." Evans chuckled. "What I liked most about him was that he didn't carry himself like no colored man and go around with his hat in his hand. No sir, not your daddy. He wouldn't talk to no one but the president of the bank. He didn't have nothing to say to nobody who wasn't in charge."

So much for what Evans thought he knew about *his* old man. His daddy was a hustler who had dropped dead at forty-three, long before he could teach his sons anything about how he ran his business. Geoffrey remembered a gold tooth flashing and wing-tipped shoes, and he'd always seen his daddy in a suit and tie. Calvin had gotten the fob watch that had hung from Daddy's vest pocket, and Laurence had gotten the diamond stud he wore on his lapel. Geoffrey had his gold signet ring.

"Did right by his family, he did," Evans said. "A good, church-going, family man. And loved his Princess more than he loved life. Lord, but he would be proud to see you now."

They were hustlers, both of them. Was he as good as his old man? Geoffrey thought of the candleholders. At least he had returned them. He flipped through the book that explained the formulas, trying to figure out which ones he should use. If it hadn't been for that pig there was no way those people would have gotten any attention from the news media. That alarm was such a great scam, the best he'd ever thought up. Almost no work, no outlay, just pure salesmanship: him, how fast he could talk, how fast he could think. It was going to take a while to think up something half as good. At least he'd have something to do in the meantime. He picked up the phone and left another message on Gayle's answering machine. Why wasn't she returning his calls?

"Well now, MacAlister," Vik said a few minutes after they got back from Wisconsin, "will you take a look at this. I've got a make on Stanley Rosenblum."

"Rosenblum? What did he do?"

"A widow filed a complaint stating that he'd defrauded her out of some money. He agreed to pay her back and got a three-month suspended sentence."

"Three months," Marti said. "That's odd."

"Not if you've already got one conviction for bilking a widow."

Vik went to the file drawer and selected a manila folder. He put in a call to the nursing home and, after haggling over the privacy act for a few minutes, got an answer.

"The increase in Mrs. McCroft's expenses for the past four years is exactly half of what Virginia has budgeted. What do you want to bet the other half was for Rosenblum's mother?"

After Vik pulled all of the McCroft files relating to land, they drove over to see Rosenblum.

Stanley Rosenblum was not happy to see them. He was wearing what looked to be the same brown tweed pants and beige sweater he had had on the last time they were here. His eyes, a pale blue-gray, were expressionless.

Marti found it odd that he was home during the day. "Do you have a night job?" she asked.

"Not exactly."

"What do you do for a living?"

"I'm a piano tuner."

"Is there a lot of demand for that?" Vik asked.

"There is if you know where to look."

Vik pulled the computer printout on Rosenblum out of his pocket. "Like these two sources maybe." He read off the two widows' names.

Rosenblum's face flushed, but he said nothing.

"How much was Virginia McCroft giving you? Was it only what you needed to cover the increase in your mother's nursing home bill? Or was it more?"

"Look," Rosenblum said, "I do the best I can. My mother has nobody but me. They take decent care of her at Sunnybrook. I couldn't put her in any of those other places. They were too awful. And Virginia, well, she had money, more than she needed. She offered to help me; I didn't ask her to."

"You didn't refuse either," Vik said. "And Virginia didn't have enough money to help you. She was dipping into her savings to make ends meet and would have exhausted that in a couple of years."

Rosenblum looked away. He seemed embarrassed. "I didn't know."

"I wonder who the next sucker will be?" Vik said, as they headed back to the precinct.

"Those gardening sessions of his must be damned good," Marti said.

"Maybe. I don't think he's much of a suspect."

"Remember, Vik, it was a small-caliber weapon, something someone might carry for protection, something they might not think of as lethal. Not everyone who owns a gun wants to kill somebody. It's easy to think of a gun that small as protection."

"I wonder what Mrs. McCroft thought about Virginia and Rosenblum. If she knew. My father always said she was the real politician in the family. Strict Catholics too. All of them. Too bad Mrs. McCroft is so gaga."

"Do you think Mrs. Rosenblum is?"

Vik checked his watch. "Let's eat. Then I suppose we could go and see."

They went to the Barrister. Vik led the way to a corner booth. The lunch crowd had returned to work and business was light. The interior, with dark wood and old pub signs and the dim light from gold-and-brown-toned glass shades hanging from low ceilings, made it seem as if they were entering a cave. The menu had changed under new ownership. Marti ordered shepherd's pie and Vik asked for bangers and mash.

"Trying to find out where that diskette came from is a complete waste of time," Vik complained. His wiry, salt-and-pepper eyebrows almost met in a scowl. "Talk about the proverbial needle in a haystack. Where could Virginia have come across something like that? I checked, and every place she went where there was a computer was business-related. Who looks at porn where they work? And you can't just walk into someone's office and access their computer and watch something like that. That's . . . that's . . . personal stuff. Nobody's business."

Vik's reluctance to name what was on the diskette, to even say "pornography," made her wonder what that said about the owner of the diskette. Many of the flashers, the men who frequented prostitutes, even the men who called and "talked dirty" on the telephone, were getting younger all the time. Some were teenagers.

"This could belong to the son of one of her friends, Vik."

"Virginia didn't have any friends."

"We found a couple. What about your sister-in-law?"

"They haven't had anything to do with each other for years. Virginia got really wrapped up in this political stuff, that and taking care of her mother. Virginia didn't socialize with the neighbors either. We can rule out the politicians she hassled too. Even those who have computers in their offices have secretaries guarding the door." Vik's disappointment was obvious.

"Too bad. She knew so many of them," Marti said. "In Lincoln Prairie that diskette would be enough to keep someone from getting reelected, and she harassed, aggravated, or just annoyed so many of them, even the mayor. And she attended a lot of their meetings. Everything she did involved some political issue or her mother."

"Maybe we can't rule out the politicians."

Marti could see that the possibility pleased him and she wondered why.

"I'm not sure it matters, Vik. What do we do, walk up to everyone with a computer, flash the diskette, and expect the right person to look guilty or blush?"

"Damn," Vik said.

"Do you have any particular reason for disliking politicians?"

"Nah . . . it's them or the sanitation workers. Nobody picks on postal workers anymore."

"Suppose she just had this, Vik, for who knows what reason, but she didn't have any idea of what was on it. She didn't have a computer. Maybe she never looked at it. It was tucked away in a file box filled with junk."

"That still doesn't explain how she got it, MacAlister."

"It could have been accidental. She could have picked it up by mistake. It could have been mixed in with something she bought at a yard sale. I remember buying a bunch of old magazines once because Joanna needed the pictures when she was in kindergarten and there, right in the middle of the stack, were three *Playboys*. Maybe it was something like that."

Their food came and he gave his sausage and mashed potatoes a skeptical push with his fork, then tasted a small slice of sausage. "It's okay, I guess. Good thing they still serve burgers."

"Try this next time," Marti suggested.

The food *was* good and they ate in silence until Vik said, "Suppose Virginia somehow got possession of this diskette, knew what was on it and where it came from, and decided she had another source of income—someone who could somehow be exposed, fired . . ."

"Or seriously embarrassed."

"Which excludes every politician I know. Too bad we

can't walk into the next city council meeting and ask for a show of hands on what they tune into on the Internet."

"What if we're making too much of this, Vik? Because we find it offensive or because it seems so out of character for Virginia to have it unless it was for financial gain. Maybe someone was playing a prank on the local spinster. Any kid with access to a computer probably knows how to pull this stuff up." She thought of Theo and Mike. But they wouldn't . . . She was going to talk with Ben about it tonight.

"I don't think it was kids, MacAlister. There don't seem to be any kids living on her block."

"There's the paperboy, the neighbor's grandchildren."

"Maybe one of the local politicos wanted to get even."

Maybe they were looking at it from the wrong perspective.

It was late afternoon when Marti and Vik visited the Sunnybrook Nursing Home again. They intended to see Mrs. Rosenblum while they were here. Marti shivered as she walked to the front door. She buttoned her jacket and wished she had thought to put on a scarf this morning. The day had begun warm enough, but it had turned cold. Frost was predicted tonight, typical for spring in this part of the Midwest.

Inside, nobody at the nurses' station looked familiar. The three women sitting there were all consulting charts. Since white uniforms and starched hats had been replaced with a variety of smocks, Marti couldn't tell which of the three, if any of them, was a nurse. When she asked for Mrs. McCroft, the woman in the lime green smock said, "Room 219," without looking up.

"How is she today?" Marti asked.

"McCroft? The usual. Out of it. But lucid today. She thinks she's going to Riverside Park with her parents. Humor her."

Mrs. McCroft's balloons were losing helium, and a vase that had been filled with daffodils was empty. The Tweety Bird slippers were nowhere to be seen, and she had on sock-type slippers instead. She was in a wheelchair and leaning so far to one side, Marti was surprised it hadn't tipped over.

"I'm getting a nurse," she told Vik.

"She's fine," the woman in the lavender smock told her. "Someone checks her every half hour."

"Someone needs to see that she doesn't fall out of her wheelchair," Marti said. "And right now."

The woman followed her down the hall and got Mrs. Mc-Croft into a chair, propping her up with some pillows.

"Her daughter did a lot for her that we just don't have time for," the aide said on her way out.

Mrs. McCroft looked at them, then looked toward the door. "I . . . ," she began. Then she looked around, as if she was lost, or confused.

"How are you today?" Marti asked. She wondered if anyone had told her about her daughter, and if she had understood if they did. "Have you seen Virginia today? We're looking for her and we can't seem to find her."

"She's lost," the woman said.

"Are you sure?"

"I sent her to the store this morning to get some bananas, and she hasn't come back yet."

"Can I get a banana for you while you're waiting?"

"Oh, would you? I so love bananas."

Vik volunteered to go to a nearby store.

"Do you have any idea of where we should look for Virginia?" Marti asked.

"She's probably with Essie."

"Do you know where they went?"

"No. They never tell me where they're going. I wish she had gone to the store first." Mrs. McCroft cocked her head to one side as she looked up at her. "They're up in Virginia's room, talking about Jimmy again, and sneaking cigarettes. I know I should go up and do something about it, but I don't know what to do, do you?"

Vik was only gone for a few minutes. When he came back, Mrs. McCroft was surprised by the bananas but delighted to have one.

"Aren't you going to ask me what we talked about?" Marti asked as they waited for the elevator.

"No."

"Just because she's old and senile . . ."

"And in another world."

"No, she's not in another world, Vik. She's right here in this one. She's just not in the here and now. Did you know anyone named Essie when you were in school?"

"That has to be my sister-in-law. What did she say about her?"

"Just that Essie and Virginia were best friends."

"Were? They haven't even talked on the phone in years."

"Mrs. McCroft also mentioned someone named Jimmy."

"Jim was a real common name. There were a lot of them. Maybe they meant Jamesetta. That was this black girl they were friends with."

"What happened to her?"

"Her family was military. They moved away."

"And there's nobody else who stands out."

Vik shook his head. "Virginia was very popular. She went out with a lot of guys. I'll stop by Essie's and see if she can come up with someone in particular."

Mrs. Rosenblum was on the first floor in a corner room larger than Mrs. McCroft's. Peace lilies and rhododendrons were lined up along both windowsills.

"Mrs. Rosenblum?" Marti said.

"Eh?" She was a heavyset woman with a hearing aid in each ear and wire-rimmed bifocals.

A middle-aged black woman was sitting in the corner by the window reading a book. "Can I help you with something? I'm her day nurse."

"We just thought we would stop in and say hello," Marti said, without identifying herself.

"Hi, Mrs. Rosenblum."

"Yes, dear. How are you?" She spoke in a loud tone of voice.

"Speak up if you want her to hear you," the nurse said.

"How are you doing today?" Marti spoke loud enough

for someone two rooms down to hear. "Stanley told us you were here."

"Oh yes, my Stanley. You see what good care he takes of me? And him with a bad heart and all. It makes life a little difficult for him, but he's a good boy, my Stanley."

"We saw Virginia too," Marti said.

"I bet she's a lovely girl, isn't she?"

"That's Virginia," Vik said.

"I do wish they would hurry up and get married."

"You're going to let him marry a Catholic?"

"Why, certainly, if that's what he wants to do. I just wish he'd be quick about it. They've been dating forever and he hasn't even let me meet her yet. If only I were able to get out of here, I'd arrange the entire wedding."

Mrs. Rosenblum's story didn't quite match her son's.

"You should have seen my Selia's wedding. She lives in California now. Four grandchildren. Until Virginia came along, I had given up on Stanley ever marrying. Is she young enough to have children?"

Vik shook his head.

"Oh well, I suppose Stanley is so set in his ways now. I just hope Virginia can adjust to being married to a confirmed bachelor. And with Stanley running his own business out of the house and all. I suppose it's just as well there are no children."

Marti wondered how much "business" could be involved with tuning pianos. A mother's prerogative, exaggerating the importance of her son.

Vik found the pop and candy machines on the way out and made purchases from both. "I can't say I blame Rosenblum for not wanting to marry Virginia," he said, as he handed her a can of Mello Yello. "Who would? Besides, she wouldn't have had time for a husband with all of those knickknacks to dust."

Marti thought of "conjugal visits" penciled in on the Franklin planner and suppressed a giggle. "That probably would have been too much for her," she agreed.

"Mrs. Rosenblum sure has a much better setup than Mrs. McCroft. Why would Virginia help him when she could have done more for her own mother?"

"Love," Marti said. She was certain that Virginia had managed to check out Stanley's mother, especially if Stanley had told her his mother didn't approve of their relationship. She must have figured out that it was Stanley, and not Mrs. Rosenblum, who didn't want a wedding. And Virginia had settled for that; she had settled for what she could get. Marti mulled over that for a minute. It said more about what Virginia thought of herself than it did about what Rosenblum thought of her.

"Love, Vik. She just wanted to be loved." But what made her feel unlovable? "Love," she said again. "Affection, attention, whatever. Once a week, in the afternoon." Some women would kill for that. Unfortunately for Virginia, it had been the other way around. She was the one who was dead. But for love?

CHAPTER
25

"Mother!" Fred shouted as soon as he closed the kitchen door. "Mother!"

There was no answer. He rushed down the hall to her room and caught her getting into bed.

"You were sitting by the window, weren't you?" he shouted. How dare she disobey him. "Weren't you?"

She shook her head. "Th . . . the . . . the window. . . . I just . . ."

"I told you to stay in bed!"

She nodded.

"You admit that you were told to stay in bed and you did not! You disobeyed me!"

She sat on the edge of the bed, not moving.

He walked toward her, hand upraised. "You . . . deliberately . . . disobeyed . . . me."

Instead of hitting her, he grabbed her by her shoulders, lifted her to her feet, and shook her until her head rolled from side to side. He released her and she fell to the floor.

"Look at this, Mother! Look at this!"

He took the ring out of his pocket.

"Yes, I found him. I found the thief who installed your alarm! No one can take what is mine. And look at what he gave me! This!" He held up the ring. "This is what he gave me. This! Not a watch! Where did you get this? How did you get it? Who did it belong to?"

Her whole body was shaking. Good! She was afraid. She should be. She had lied to him.

"Where is your watch?"

"I . . . I . . . I . . ." The smell of urine was strong.

He took her by the shoulder and hauled her up. "Where!"

"Bed."

He pulled her by the arm to her chair. "Sit!"

Then he yanked the blankets from the bed. "Where?"

"Be . . . be . . . behind . . ."

He pulled the headboard from the wall and found it. "You lied! You lied! Where did you get this ring?"

"I . . . I . . . I . . ." She was still shaking.

He leaned down until his mouth was next to her ear. "Where?" he shouted.

She jumped. "My . . . mo . . . my . . . mo . . . mother . . ."

"You're lying!"

"N . . . n . . . n . . . no."

He took a step back. "She couldn't have given this to you. She had nothing. It all belonged to your father."

"Her . . . her . . . her . . . mother . . . the old country . . . her . . . her . . . mo—"

"Shut up!"

He looked at the ring. It was just an old piece of junk. It didn't look like it was worth as much as the Timex. It wasn't worth the time it had taken that man to steal it from him. Junk. That must be why his grandmother had been allowed to keep it.

"You had no right to hide this from Father. You had no right to do that. Do you understand?"

She nodded.

"You lied. You disobeyed. You will have to be punished."

He pulled her to her feet and gave her a push. She fell back across the bed.

"You will be punished for this."

He tossed the ring on the bureau.

"Was this upstairs? Did you go upstairs?"

She nodded.

"Where? Where was it? What else is up there? What else have you hidden from me?"

He went over to her, but he didn't touch her again. Her face was slimy with spittle and tears, and she smelled.

"Lying old woman!" He couldn't think of anything to do to her that wouldn't kill her. Furious, he slammed his fist down on the table, splintering one leg. Upstairs. The man had said she went upstairs. He rushed out of the bedroom and took the stairs two at a time. It couldn't be his room, and his parents' room was empty. The guest room! He had never bothered with anything in there.

He looked from the bed to the dresser to the small writing desk. There weren't that many hiding places. If that man had lied to him, given him this cheap piece of junk jewelry instead of his watch . . . He yanked a drawer out of the dresser. Empty. The other three were too. He turned them upside down and dropped them on the floor when he found nothing taped to the bottom. He looked into the empty spaces where the drawers had been—nothing. The desk was small and so fragile that one leg broke when he picked it up and tried to shake the drawer out. The drawer was stuck. Wood splintered as he forced it out. Two more rings fell to the floor. She did give the man a ring! That lying . . . She'd kept what was his and lied. He picked up the rings. One had four odd-colored blue stones. The other was a band with diamond-shaped red stones. Pretty, maybe, to a woman, but junk or his father would never have allowed her to keep it. He threw the rings on the bureau and went out, slamming the door.

Fred paced from one end of the kitchen to the other. She had to be chastised for this. But how? Her chair. No more sitting by the window. He returned to her room.

"This room smells like an outhouse!"

He picked up the chair. "And you know what?" he shouted. "No diapers! You can stay like that until tomorrow, until next week! You liar! Liar! You kept what was mine!"

He slammed the chair down again and again until it broke. Then he threw it into the hall and kicked it into the kitchen. Troublesome old woman. How many people even knew she was still alive? What would happen if he just walked away from here one day and left her in her room? He could go to California, fill out a change of address for her pension and Social Security, and make sure he paid the property taxes twice a year. Maybe that was what he would do.

* * *

For the second time in her life, Opal wished she were dead. The first time had been two weeks after she was married and she had burned Fred Senior's toast; he'd whipped her with his razor strop for wasting food and locked her in the closet until it was time to cook dinner. Between then and now, she had gotten used to things. She didn't have much to get used to. Being here hadn't ever been much different from living at home with her father. Nothing that mattered had changed, except that she was young then and thought that maybe things could be different. Now that she was old, she knew that they would not.

She couldn't get up, not just because she didn't know what Fred would do to her if she did, but because of her arm and her shoulder. It hurt when she was lying still. When she moved, the pain made her dizzy.

As she had so many times since his death, she wished Fred Senior were still alive. At least she always knew what he would do, and why, and when he was in a bad mood and would be mean for no reason. When he got old and had trouble getting out of his chair, all she had to do was stay out of reach of his cane. Fred Senior was just an ornery old man. He was old when she came here and very old when he died. Toward the end, when she had to do everything for him, he would look at her sometimes in a way that she knew meant that he loved her, appreciated her after all of the years they'd been together. Even though he never said it, she knew that was how he had come to feel about her, even if he did bite her once in a while. Just because he had come to care for her didn't mean he had stopped being ornery. Bedridden, he couldn't be mean to her anymore, no more than she could be mean to him. And in the early days, when he was mean, he wasn't angry; it was just his way. Why couldn't Fred Junior understand that? Why couldn't he be more like his father? Where had he gotten that mean streak?

She tried to move again, and the pain came—so bad she wanted to scream. She couldn't just lie here like this. When Fred came back he would have to let her shower. But how could she? She couldn't even get up from the bed. Dear God, what was she going to do? Somehow she was going to have to do something. If she didn't, Fred Junior was going to kill her.

Marti arrived home just in time to overhear an argument between Joanna and Lisa.

"Get this garbage out of here!" Joanna yelled. Magazines came tumbling down the stairs.

Marti picked one up. It was just one of those teenage magazines. How to apply makeup. How to style your hair. She flipped through it, expecting at least one scantily clad male movie star pinup, but found none.

"If you want to share my room, you're going to have to get your shit together and keep it together!" Joanna shouted.

Momma came out of the kitchen and into the hall. "I figured Joanna would get Lisa straightened out before too long. That child is acting like she's twenty-one."

"What's wrong with the magazines, Momma? It sure can't be that Lisa left them lying around. There's no way she'd find them with Joanna's sweats thrown everywhere."

They both laughed. Marti followed Momma into the kitchen. "Gumbo," she said. There was no mistaking the aroma of crab and shrimp and okra.

"Maybe Lisa shouldn't be here," Marti said. "What do we do if Joanna wants her to leave?"

"Let's see if they can work out whatever this is all about," Momma said. "Maybe they won't sleep in the same room anymore, but I'm quite sure that between us, we can keep Miss Lisa in line."

"Lord, I hope so." Marti was beginning to feel like she was in over her head. She was accustomed to children who at least gave the outward appearance of thinking before they acted. That made it easier somehow. Not that they always made the right decisions because they thought them through first. Sometimes their logic was a long way from what she would have come up with. But at least they weren't impulsive. Sharon was, and Lisa was getting more like her mother every day.

"Miss Lisa could prove to be a handful, Momma."

"I know, child, but where else can she go? We try. Maybe we fail, but we try."

"What about Joanna?" She loved Joanna, and thought she knew her pretty well; but she also knew the odds were almost as good that Lisa would influence Joanna as they were that the reverse would be true.

"I think we can trust Joanna."

"I think so too, Momma, but . . ."

"But you see too much in that job of yours. I'm right here, child. I am right here with these children. You've raised them just fine, just like I raised you. The world is always there. There's not much anyone can do to keep them from it. Better that they learn how to deal with it on their terms and not someone else's."

"I'll talk to Lisa."

"Leave it be for a few days. Someone from the school will call you if Lisa doesn't show up. I'm here when the children are coming and going. I don't go to bed until everyone is accounted for. And Joanna seems to be keeping things between them in check. Be all right, child. Be all right."

Marti rested her head on Momma's shoulder, grateful for a pat on the back and a hug.

"Trash," Joanna muttered, as she walked through the kitchen carrying a stack of magazines that she deposited in the recycle bin in the garage.

"What's wrong with those magazines?" Marti asked. "They are for teenagers, aren't they? There isn't a *Playgirl?*"

"Ma, the cover says *Today's Teen,* but 'Twenty-one Ways to Have Sex Without Having Intercourse'? Come on."

"What? An article like that in a magazine for kids?" She

had picked up the occasional copy herself and brought it home.

"Right."

Momma put the kettle on.

"They tell you what the latest fashions are . . ."

"Ma, where have you been? How about finger orgasms?"

"Girl," Momma said, "I can't believe they would put something like that in a magazine for girls your age."

"Well, believe it," Joanna said. "And I don't need that. I don't need it. This whole dating thing is bad enough."

"Well, let's just sit here and have some tea," Momma said. "There's nothing like a cup of tea to soothe your nerves."

Joanna sat at the table with her chin in her hands. Marti helped Momma get out the mugs and tea bags. "Honey, Joanna?"

"And camomile. My nerves need soothing tonight."

"Now, Joanna," Momma said, when they were all sitting down, "dating is supposed to be fun."

Joanna dunked her tea bag up and down in the hot water so vigorously Marti was sure it would break. "It's fun," she said. "It's lots of fun."

"Tony seems like such a nice young man."

"All young men are nice, Grandma, as long as you keep them in check."

"In check?" Momma asked.

"Grandma, sex is the thing now. Making out. Those who put out, and those who don't. Tony and I have an understanding. I respect him when he behaves like a gentleman. And I have a mother who is a cop and a stepfather who is much bigger than he is."

"That sounds like a reasonable understanding to me," Marti said. How had things changed so much in such a few years? It wasn't that way when she was dating Johnny. Back then, nice girls didn't and those who did didn't bring them home to meet the family. She didn't say this because she knew Joanna would laugh.

"Then there are your girlfriends. The ones who put out, and the ones who don't. Everyone who does thinks you should be like them. Some of those who don't are afraid to admit it."

"It's gotten that bad, huh?" Momma asked.

"I don't know," Joanna said. "Maybe not. I know a lot about sex and contraceptives and all of that, but look at Sharon and look at Ma. Sharon puts out and has all kinds of problems. Ma doesn't and now she and Ben . . . You know, Ma, the whole third level reeks of vanilla."

Momma laughed.

Marti didn't believe what she was hearing. This couldn't be more than the second time she had done something right since Joanna turned thirteen. She had actually done something right. No matter that Joanna had been critical of her decision to have a celibate courtship; now Joanna finally thought it had been the right thing to do. Momma caught her eye and they both grinned.

"What are you so happy about?" Vik asked when she returned to work.

"Joanna thinks I did something right."

"Not bad," Vik said. "I went eight or nine years without either one of mine thinking that. Mildred had it a little easier. I think Christa and Steve felt sorry for her because she was married to me."

"Here." She handed him a foil-covered plate. "Joanna made a carrot cake for dessert."

"With real sugar?"

"I doubt it. She probably substituted a sweetener, but you can't tell."

He peeled back the foil. "The icing looks a little funny."

"That's because it *is* a little funny. She cuts back on the cream cheese and it's fat free, but she makes up for it with the spices. Try it, go ahead."

He took a bite, chewed slowly, said, "Umm," and almost smiled.

"Have you been here long?" Marti asked. "I hope you've

had time to pull together all of those files Virginia has on land trusts and other related topics." She had come to hate Virginia's files and couldn't wait to be rid of them.

"I came up with a couple of lists, but I can't make much sense of them, at least not yet. One's got all of the newspaper articles by date and topic. Another has a list of inquiries she had either made or intended to make about ownership of properties. I don't know if one is relevant to the other, or if Virginia was on a fishing expedition, or just didn't have anything else to occupy her time, or what."

"There has to be something to it. There's too much of it. Then again, where Virginia and her files are concerned, there's too much of everything."

"Well, we're cops, not real estate experts. I made a copy of everything and sent it to the state attorney's office. They've got someone there who will know what she's looking at."

"It'll probably take forever."

"She said she'd do what she could over the weekend. This is a homicide."

The coffeepot was empty. "Where's Cowboy when you need him?" Marti pulled open the drawer with the coffee supplies.

"I would say working, but I'm never sure about those two." Vik tilted his chair back, put his feet on the chair, and reached for the phone. "Are you sure you want to make some? There's always the machine downstairs."

Marti poured an extra measure of coffee into the filter. That done, she went through her notes and the incoming reports on the McCroft case while Vik called around and tried to garner a little gossip on someone who was into pornography. After about an hour and only one cup of coffee, Vik hung up and put his hands behind his head.

"Well, MacAlister, that was a waste. How about you?"

"Nothing on the car. Neither the purse nor the weapon has turned up. They're still sifting through the debris from the fire. Maybe we'll get something. There have been no charges made on her credit cards, no attempts to withdraw money from her bank accounts. We've got the autopsy report, the ballistics on the bullet, and an inquiry from the nursing home as to who will be paying Mrs. McCroft's bills. Does the court appoint someone now? We didn't find a will under *W* or a lawyer under *L* or *A*."

"Wait a minute," Vik said. "There was something." He thought for a minute, then went to the file cabinet. "Here. Elliot Dunn. He's a judge now but he helped her with a problem she had with her mother's Social Security a few years back. I wonder if he still takes his own calls?" He picked up the phone again. "No will there," he said when he hung up. "Dunn hasn't talked with her since they cleared up the mother's problem."

Vik drummed his fingers on his desk.

"Would you please cut that out! Now, method's not an issue. The size of the weapon suggests it was intended for protection. We've got four, possibly five suspects: Thornton, his two kids"—she held up the diskette—"whoever this is, maybe. And, unless McCroft parked her car and left it somewhere, whoever has it."

"Don't write off Rosenblum," Vik said. "They could have had an argument and in a moment of passion . . ."

Marti found it difficult to believe that the man had much passion in him, but he was doing something right. "Why would they be in the cellar of an abandoned house?"

"Leave it to Virginia. She couldn't even die without causing trouble." Vik cracked his knuckles in frustration.

"Stop! You know I can't stand that either." Vik might be getting frustrated, but she was not going to be distracted. "As for motive, our best guess is blackmail, but based on what we know at this point, let's keep an open mind. Which brings us to opportunity. The back door was unlocked. There were no signs of forced entry, which suggests that if the perp came to the house, she either knew or was expecting the killer. As for how or why she was at the Warren place . . ." Marti flipped through the autopsy report. "Lividity indicates that she died at the Warren house and was not moved. She was killed in the basement. She was seen alive last Wednesday, Thursday, and Friday, but nobody recalls anything significant. The fire was set this past Monday. In short, we have quite a bit of information, but we don't know a hell of a lot."

"You've got that right, MacAlister. We are also out of leads, ideas, and suggestions. Let's call it a night and go home."

The house was quiet. Ben and Momma were in the den watching a wrestling match. Marti dozed in the recliner until Ben nudged her. She opened her eyes, feeling wide awake.

"I just missed you at the precinct today," he said as they went upstairs.

"What were you doing there?"

"I had to talk with Arson about that fire at the Warren place."

"What about it? You didn't find a small handgun in the burned-out basement, did you?"

"No. We were just discussing the similarities between that fire and a few others we've had recently and going through everyone's reports and observations. Sort of a task force, but nothing formal yet."

"Vik and I were discussing the possibility of an arsonist with Lefty and Tolley a couple of days ago. Does this mean we definitely have an arsonist on our hands?"

"It looks that way. We'll find out soon enough. You put in a long day. Tired?"

She caught a whiff of vanilla and put her arm about his waist. "I think I was a few minutes ago, but I've got other things on my mind now." There were other fires to be built and put out tonight.

It was just getting dark when Geoffrey exited the Dan Ryan and headed for Gayle's place on East Eighty-third. When he'd called an hour before she had finally answered the phone. Instead of saying anything he decided to surprise her and hung up. He should have planned a big date, dinner at that seafood place, dancing at the Taste, but it had been a long week and he wanted to reserve his energy for what he did best. He liked his women to holler.

He had stayed away from Gayle on purpose. That marriage stuff wasn't what he was about. Nor was he into bringing his women home to meet the family. By now Gayle would be afraid that he had found someone else or that he had gone back to Kayla again. Either way, she wouldn't bother him again for a while about getting engaged or meeting his mother. He had seen Kayla last week. Kayla would always be there, and she never talked about any of that unnecessary shit. Too bad she didn't look as good as Gayle or have a job that paid as much as Gayle's did.

Nightlife on Cottage Grove was fast and loud. Geoffrey cruised along to Eighty-third, more entertained than anxious. Wouldn't nobody mess with him here. Boom boxes and near-naked hookers. Take-out places that sold ribs and catfish and fried chicken, along with collard greens and corn bread and sweet potato pie. Liquor stores three to a block. Currency exchanges waiting to be robbed. Stores with all kinds of cheap goods from clothes to furniture. Squeezed in among all of that, if he looked that close, were a funeral home and a couple of storefront churches. He was smart enough to watch the people, the groups of teenagers, the colors, the gang signs. Years and years ago his daddy had worked these streets, collecting rents, playing numbers, maybe even scoring a little weed. That was small-time compared to the way things were now. Daddy wouldn't have survived on these streets, but he could.

It took him twenty minutes of slow driving and steady looking to catch the flash of the taillights that said someone was vacating a parking space. He drove slow, causing the driver behind him to lean on his horn, and reached the spot just as the other car pulled out. He swung in, made a few adjustments, and turned on the alarm as he got out of the car. He was only three buildings away from Gayle's townhouse. As he got closer, he could see that her bedroom light was on. Perfect timing.

His key didn't fit in the lock. She must have lost her set again and changed it. He rang the bell.

"Something I can do for you, man?"

He was tall, muscular, and not a day over twenty-five. Gayle was standing behind him, making shushing motions with her hands. She was wearing a white negligee that he had bought for her. Geoffrey rocked back on his heels. That son of a bitch. For a moment, a hazy orange filled his line of vision.

"Hey, man, you want something?"

Geoffrey shook his head to clear it. *Your ass,* he thought, *that's what I want.* He unclenched his fist and loosened his tie.

"Kayla don't live here?" he said, just so Gayle would know where he was going.

"There's no Kayla here, man."

"Sorry, I must have the wrong address."

Outside he headed away from his car, taking deep breaths and walking fast. That bastard. That son of a bitch. Gayle was his woman. A cat the size of a small dog darted in front of him. He kicked at it but missed. It turned to hiss at him and he picked up a stone. The cat yowled as the stone hit it in the stomach. He picked up a chunk of asphalt as the cat ran away. Another loud howl told him he had found his mark again. He kept throwing rocks until he couldn't find any more, but either the cat was gone or dead or he had missed. He leaned against a streetlight, panting. "Son of a bitch," he said again. "That dirty son of a bitch." There was a beer bottle in the gutter. He pitched it in the direction the cat had taken, then headed back to his car. To hell with Gayle. Kayla would be damned glad to see him.

When Fred reached the house where the thief lived, his car wasn't there. Maybe it was too early. He would be too conspicuous if he waited. Instead, he drove aimlessly, all the way to the Wisconsin border and back. When he returned, the car still wasn't there. Fred drove around the block a few times without seeing any police cars. When his hands began to hurt, he realized it was from gripping the steering wheel. He wanted to throw something, or break something, or ram the car into the fence that surrounded the house. He wanted to kill that man. If he showed up right now, Fred thought he might choke him to death. But he couldn't do anything. The man wasn't here. He had to do something. He had to.

He put a timing device on the bomb, eased along the driveway, and attached it to the motorcycle. Such an easy target, left outside like this, and in a place secluded enough so that he could work without being seen. He backed away, cut through the yard, and went to a vantage point by a tree about half a block away. Then he waited, hoping that the anticipation would make a difference. It was 10:49 exactly when he heard the blast. There was no fireball, like in the movies, just a loud bang and pieces of the bike flying in all directions. It was noisier than he had expected, but then it was a different kind of bomb from his first one. He felt nothing. Bombs were a big disappointment. He didn't have any more fun tonight than when he blew up the mailbox. Maybe if he tried something bigger. If he had blown up the garage it would at least have burned. Maybe that was it. Maybe a blast from the bomb, and then, right away, a fire. He felt a sudden engorgement in his loins. Yes, that was it. And now that he knew, yes, soon . . . soon. But now he needed some-thing else. The ache would become unbearable if he didn't satisfy it soon. . . .

He found an empty house and realized by its location that it was the perfect place for a fire. There were more people in the immediate vicinity than he would have preferred, but no-body anywhere near the house. Maybe if he went down the alley. Maybe there, he wouldn't be seen.

He turned off his headlights, pulled up to the garage door as if he lived there, and cut the engine. Then he waited and watched. There were no barking dogs, no porch or rear lights on nearby, and the nearest streetlight was halfway down the alley. He took a plastic bag with the quart contain-ers of lighter fluid out of the trunk, put the bag over his shoulder, and headed for the house. Once there, he got in through a basement window with the plywood pulled away. When he turned on his flashlight, several rats about the size of squirrels scurried away. He didn't like rats.

He went to the center of the basement and poured lighter fluid around the thick support beams, giving it time to soak in. Then he saturated a rope and wrapped it around the beams, looping it from one beam to another. He trailed the rope behind him until he reached the window. When he was outside of the house, he lit the rope. Squatting, he watched as the narrow line of fire reached the beams and the beams ignited slowly. He watched until a familiar tension gripped him. Release was swift and sweet. Then he returned to his car. This time he didn't hear the fire engines right away. That was good. The fire had a chance to become strong and fierce and powerful.

By the time he found a place to park and wait, there was a wail in the distance.

It was eleven-thirty when Marti arrived at the site of the bombing. The scene had been photographed, mapped, and graphed. Technicians were standing by ready to bag and label the debris from the motorcycle for reassembly later. Whenever one of the bomb team members or the helmeted firefighters waved his arm, a paramedic or deputy coroner went over to determine if they had found human remains.

There had been a small fire. A motorcycle, burned. The odor of burning wasn't as strong as she expected, but the odor of gasoline was. Lights were set up and there was an odd hush, even though at least thirty people, uniformed and in plain clothes, were milling about, most at the perimeter of the crime scene. Uniformed officers and police barriers kept the curious a block away in all directions. The inability to see much of anything seemed to be keeping the crowd down. Marti didn't hear any crying or see anyone who looked upset or hysterical.

Lefty hurried over. "Well, it's turned lethal," he said. "We've got body parts for the coroner's office to try to re-assemble."

"One victim?" Marti asked.

"Looks that way. My men have talked with the nearest neighbors. They all complained that the bike was noisy. If the driver was the owner, it's a Malcolm Fletcher. He's lived alone since his wife died a few years back, went out every night somewhere between ten and eleven, and wasn't gone long."

Marti made a note of that. Fletcher didn't go far. A nearby convenience store, maybe a bar. "Is this one anything like the mailbox bombing?"

"No. There's a victim." He sounded angry. "If it was the same guy, and he's still out there, no, I don't think so, not unless the mailbox was a practice session for this."

Vik parked and came over while Lefty was talking. He must have been caught in the shower; his hair was still damp. "Same guy?" he asked.

"We don't have much yet," Lefty said. "It'll take a while to figure this one out."

"Any theories?"

"Sure, Jessenovik. Lots of them, but none that's worth a

damn until I get some solid information. And that will take time." He pulled out a pack of cigarettes. "Damn. Need a smoke. Trying to quit," he said, and walked away.

Vik ran his fingers through his hair. For once it lay flat.

"You need to wear it that way more often," Marti said.

"I need to catch this weirdo. What do you think Lefty means by 'time'? Didn't it take about a year to figure out one of those airplane bombings?"

"An airplane is a lot bigger than a motorcycle."

"MacAlister, take another look at this. If a motorcycle didn't have two wheels and less metal than a car, do you think they would have known that's what this was?" Hands on hips, he paced as he surveyed the scene. "This is like something from the ten o'clock news, something that happens in Bosnia or Northern Ireland, not here, not in Lincoln Prairie." He turned away, shaking his head.

Marti didn't know what to say. She had watched her old neighborhood in Chicago evolve from noisy streets where neighbors watched as children played in safety into a place where everyone had learned to stay away from their windows at night and take cover at the first sound of a gunshot, night or day. She was certain that was not what was happening here; but times were changing, and she didn't think this would ever again be the Lincoln Prairie of Vik's childhood.

"Come on," she said, "we've got work to do. We've got to keep this from getting out of hand."

"You don't think it's out of hand yet?"

"No. I think it's still manageable, that we can keep it under control—but we've got to get this guy before he does this again."

Turning to the sidewalks, they began a canvass of the immediate area.

"Damn, MacAlister, here's one for the books. I wonder who lives here."

The house sat back on a double lot and was flanked on one side by a field. Pine trees defined the perimeters of the property, lined up close together on either side of the front gate. The branches swooped low to the ground, and the peaks of the trees were half a dozen feet taller than the two-story bungalow.

Marti could make out a light in a rear window at the side of the house. "It looks like someone is home."

They had to knock for several minutes before they heard a security chain being put on. The door opened less than the width of the chain.

"Sir?" Vik said. "Police." A man was peering out at them. His head was tilted to one side.

"What is it?" His voice was that of an executive, which contradicted what Marti could see of his appearance—shoulder-length shaggy hair and an unkempt beard.

"Could I ask your name, sir?"

"Sure. It's Fred. Fred Jhanke."

"Do you live here alone, sir?"

Jhanke hesitated for a second, then said, "Yes."

"You didn't happen to hear any loud noises tonight?" Vik asked.

The man shook his head. "No sir, the neighborhood has been very quiet. It's always quiet around here." An unwashed odor emanated from his body.

"You're sure about that?"

"The trees," the man said. "They keep out most of the noise."

"You wouldn't have seen anything unusual?"

"No, sir."

Vik took a step back.

"Can I ask what this is about, Officer?"

"Oh, nothing," Vik said. "Just a little explosion by that beige house about half a block from here."

"Mal Fletcher's place?"

"Yes, you know him?"

"We've both lived here a long time. The last time I saw him was at his wife's funeral about a year ago."

"He lives there alone?"

"Yes, sir."

"Did he own a motorcycle?"

"Yes, sir."

"But you haven't seen him in over a year?"

"No, sir. We kind of go our own way. Sorry I can't be of any help. Is Mal okay?"

"Actually he might not be," Vik said. "You might want to check the newspaper just in case."

As they headed down the walk, Marti said, "Looks like this Malcolm Fletcher might be our victim."

"Good thing we've got a name," Vik said. "There sure as hell weren't too many pieces and none of them easily recognizable."

Nobody else knew much of anything either. An older man lived in the house and drove the motorcycle. They had not seen any strangers in the area. They had not seen or heard anything unusual other than the explosion and the sirens that followed.

Vik scratched at his five o'clock shadow. The raspy sound again made Marti think of Ben, who also needed to shave twice a day.

"You know, MacAlister, considering that everyone we talked with was awake when the thing went off, you'd think one of them would have seen or heard something out of the ordinary."

"I think we'll have Lupe come back and talk with that Hispanic family in the morning. They were scared to death of us."

"Let's have her talk to that guy in the creepy place again."

There was no mistaking which house Vik meant. Totally dark, not even a porch light or sensor light, far back from the street, dead center on a double lot, and all but hidden by trees.

They got a call about another fire on the South Side of town, on Eureka Street, before they were finished canvassing for the bomb.

"Probable arson," Marti said. "Vacant house. It's still hot, but unless there were some vagrants inside, we might not have any victims."

"Damn," Vik said. "Not that I wanted to go home or anything. It's only what . . ." He checked his watch. "Twelve-thirty? Is that all? It's been a long night."

"It looks like this bomb went off first," Marti said. "Unless the other fire was smoldering for a while." And what in the hell did that mean? she wondered. She didn't want to think about the implications of both occurring within such a short time.

There was something surreal about driving from one street filled with fire engines and hoses only twelve blocks to another. The fire had not been struck yet. There was a decent-sized crowd. Teenagers hogged the space behind the police barriers. Young children jumped up and down, trying to get a better look at what was going on. Seniors and street people stood in small groups farther away from the action. Marti walked about, trying to catch snatches of conversation. From what she heard, the people in the crowd knew about as much as she did. When she recognized Chief Tolley's hat, she went over to him.

"We've got spotters out there," he said, "looking to see if anyone's getting off on this. Nobody suspicious so far. And we've got a one-block canvass underway."

A quick canvass of the onlookers confirmed the usual: Nobody had seen anything.

"Let's get back to the precinct and get the paperwork done. Maybe then we can call it a night," Vik said. He sounded more dispirited than tired. "Tolley's got everything under control here, and it'll be morning before this cools off enough for anyone to go inside and look for crispy critters."

Marti agreed. As late as it was, it *had* been a long day. She needed a hot shower, a long massage, and the sweet scent of vanilla to get the stench of smoke off of her body and out of her mind.

SATURDAY, MAY I

It was a little before 2:00 A.M. when Marti and Vik reached
Lincoln Prairie General Hospital. They had been called out
while they were still writing up their reports on the bombing. Andrew Thornton Sr. had been brought to the emergency room by a neighbor. They had been stopped en route
for speeding, and the car they were in turned out to be Virginia McCroft's.

"Hell of a night," Vik said. "It's bad when all the crazies
are out and there's not even a full moon."

Marti yawned. "I've given up on getting any sleep."

The waiting room didn't seem that crowded for the beginning of the weekend. Maybe it was the time of year. Winter with its colds and flu had passed, and summer with its
heat-induced short tempers and violence hadn't arrived yet.
An elderly Hispanic couple held hands. He was in a wheelchair and paralyzed on one side. A baby whimpered in its
mother's arms. A teenaged girl pulled a pack of cigarettes
out of her purse and went outside to have a smoke.

Marti was about to speak with the woman standing behind the desk when Vik came out of the emergency room.
"Well, MacAlister, we may or may not get a deathbed con-
fession out of him. Right now he looks comatose. If whatever they're doing doesn't work, they're going to stick a tube
down his throat. Either way, it doesn't look like he'll be doing much talking. At least not for a while."

"Where's the neighbor?"

"Around here somewhere. I've got a uniform keeping
him company. I haven't talked to him yet. Where do you

suppose Thornton was hiding that car? It's not the one we saw parked in his driveway. I didn't notice a garage when we were there, did you?"

Marti had the fleeting impression of a privacy fence on one side of the house and three or four fir trees on the other.

"I bet it's been sitting there all this time, right under our noses, MacAlister. The question is, how did he manage to drive Virginia's car home and get his own car there too? If he drove her car at all. Maybe someone else did."

Marti followed him as he headed for the main lobby, still talking. He sounded wired. They had both had too much coffee and Mello Yello tonight.

"The way our luck has been going on this case, MacAlister, Thornton will be dead and we won't know a damned thing more about the car than we know now. Leave it to Virginia to cause trouble from the grave. Has anyone claimed the body or made funeral arrangements yet? I think she has family up north, Minnesota maybe."

When Marti saw the uniform, a burly young man, she assumed that the gnomelike elderly man sitting on the couch was Thornton's neighbor.

"Sir," Vik said, striding toward him. The man didn't look in their direction.

"Sir," Vik said again, louder.

The man continued to ignore them.

"Hard of hearing and forgot his hearing aid," the uniform told them in a normal tone of voice when they were close enough to hear him. "If you look right at him, enunciate, speak slowly, and talk kind of loud, he'll get most of it."

Vik pulled a chair over and sat in front of the man. "Sir!"

"Eh?"

"What's your name?'

"My name? Ezra, Ezra Downes." The top of his head was bald. A fringe of slate gray hair met his eyebrows and hung to his shoulders. There was a large mole on the side of his nose. "And who are you, young man? Another cop, I suppose."

Vik introduced himself and Marti. "Did you bring Mr.

Thornton to the hospital?" He spoke as the uniform had in-structed.

The old man's head bobbed up and down. "Yes, yes. We were playing cards. Andrew started having trouble breathing and when I opened the windows to clear out the cigarette smoke, that didn't help, so I thought I'd better get him over here."

"Why didn't you call an ambulance?"

"Couldn't remember the number. Know the way to the hospital though. And I still know how to drive. Don't get much of a chance to anymore. My kids took my driver's license and sold my car."

"Where did you find the car you were driving?"

"Find it? It was parked right in the backyard. Been there for a week or so now. Nice car. Engine turned over as soon as I nudged her with a little gas. Rides a lot smoother than that old heap of Andrew's." He rubbed his hands together. "It's been a long time since I drove anything that nice. You don't suppose they'll let me drive it back, do you?"

Vik shook his head.

"A car like that is meant to be driven. Not left to sit and rust."

"Do you know where Mr. Thornton got the car?"

"No. Can't say as I know *why* he got it either. Car he had ain't been backed out of the driveway in two years."

"How did you get the car to the street from the back of the house?" Vik asked.

"Just drove right over the grass and headed for the side-walk. Oh, I kind of nicked one of the trees. I kind of had to squeeze between them. Hope the owner doesn't mind a little scratch."

"Do you know who the car belongs to?"

"No. I asked Andrew that a couple of times. He went to coughing and taking oxygen like he always does when he don't want to say nothing."

Vik asked a few more questions, without eliciting any ad-ditional information, then asked the old man if he wanted to be taken home.

"Home? No. Not 'til I know how Andrew is. He's been running his business out of that house and I been living right next door since our children were kids. No way I'm going to leave him here alone."

"Did you call Wisconsin, talk with his daughter or his son?"

"Oona said they was coming. I'll wait right here 'til they do."

Vik told the uniform he could leave.

"What? You ain't going to arrest me or nothing? I was going a little fast."

The uniform stopped near the exit. "You were doing seventy, sir," he said, without turning around.

The old man rubbed his hands together again. "Great little car," he said. "Built for speed."

As they headed back to the emergency room, Vik said, "We finally get lucky and it's the Mario Andretti of the prune juice and oatmeal generation."

"Virginia did drive an Escort, Vik? I did read that right? We're not talking about a Porsche or a Jaguar?"

"MacAlister, the last time that man drove a car it was probably an Edsel. At his age a ten-speed bicycle must seem fast."

The news wasn't good when they spoke with the nurse. Thornton had been intubated and was sedated. Perhaps they could see him tomorrow; then again, maybe not. The car had been impounded. An evidence tech would give it a thorough going over first thing in the morning. And there were always the neighbors. Perhaps one of them had seen something. Meanwhile, there was nothing to do but wait until Thornton's son and daughter arrived from Wisconsin. Not that Marti expected either of them to admit to knowing anything about Virginia McCroft's car or how it came to be parked behind their father's house.

When Oona and her brother Andrew arrived at three in the morning, Oona glanced in Marti and Vik's direction but didn't nod or speak. "I'll check on Poppa, Andy," she said. "Maybe you should keep an eye on the vultures."

Andy came over to where they sat. "Any particular reason why you two are here?" he asked, without any pretense at being friendly.

"Several," Vik said.

When he didn't elaborate, Andy said, "Mind telling me what they are?"

"Yes," Vik said.

"You don't actually expect us to allow you to speak to our father tonight?"

"No," Vik said. "I don't think he'll be talking to anyone for a while."

"Then why are you here?"

"It's as good a place as any."

"I think I have a right to know why you are hounding my father when he's at death's door."

"Could be," Vik said.

Andy Thornton looked from Vik to Marti and back at Vik. "Cops." He said it like some people say 'shit.' Oona called to him and he turned on his heel and walked away.

"They're taking him to Intensive Care," Oona said. "Maybe he'll get a little privacy. We'll have to talk with a lawyer in the morning and see if they have any right to do this." There was an edge to her voice. She sat in a chair on the other side of the room, with her face in profile, arms folded. Every few minutes her shoulders shifted as if she was about to turn and look at them, but she did not. Andy did favor them with an occasional angry look. Vik stared him down.

Another half hour passed before Ezra Downes shuffled in. His movements were slow and deliberate; his shoulders were stooped and his eyes rheumy. If his pants and jacket were any indication, he had shrunk over the years. Nevertheless, Marti smiled as she thought of a young Ezra flooring the accelerator on a Model-T.

"Ezra," Oona said, "what on earth are you doing here?"

"Me? I drove Andrew to the hospital. We had a police escort and all."

"You drove? In what?"

Andy said, "Does Poppa's car even start?"

"Andy, shut up. Ezra, how did you get him here?"

"In that car that was parked back behind the house. Great little car. I hope the owner doesn't mind that I got a speeding ticket and . . ."

"A ticket? For speeding? Ezra, you . . . you old fool. Do you know—"

"Oona!" Andy grabbed her by the arm.

"You stupid old fool," Oona said. "Poppa just feels sorry for you. He isn't really your friend. Nobody is your friend. None of us can stand you. Get out of here, now!"

"Oona! Shut up!"

Andy pulled her away. As brother and sister walked down to the elevator, Vik said, "Well, they found out why we're here."

"Officers," Ezra called, "are you leaving now? Could you give me a ride home?" There were tears in the old man's eyes.

Ezra didn't remember anything useful on the way. In fact, they had trouble getting him to say anything at all. Marti thought she heard a few sniffles from the backseat, but she didn't call attention to it by offering him tissues. When they got to Thornton's place, Marti got the flashlights out and they took a look at where the car had been parked. The tree branches were so low they had to duck beneath them.

"I bet Virginia's car has a few scratches on the roof too," Vik said.

They stopped when they reached the corner of the house and could see into the yard. The grass was sparse and still brown in places. They didn't see anything lying on the ground.

"We'll have to send a tech out here too," Vik said. "Just in case."

That done, they headed to the precinct to pick up their cars and go home. If they moved fast they could skip roll call and get three, maybe four hours' sleep. Their reports could wait.

He waited in a doorway not far from the station parking lot until the two cops who had been asking questions at the fire got out of one car together and headed for separate cars. It was real easy identifying them, a black woman and a white man. He wrote down the make and license plate numbers as each car drove past the place where he stood. Then, using his binoculars, he did the same with the car they had been in together. They were the same two cops who had been knocking on doors after the bomb went off. They were asking too many questions, just like the cop in the Upper Peninsula had. They would have to be stopped. He was certain that nobody had seen him, certain that they would never find out who he was. But why take chances? This was going to be so easy. He would go home and make the bomb, hook it up to the car, and everything would be okay by tomorrow.

It wasn't long past daybreak when Marti met Vik at Thornton's house. The state's attorney had called at six-thirty to let them know the judge had approved a search warrant. A fine mist had greeted her when she backed out of the driveway, but the weather had settled into drab and overcast now.

"We'd damned well better find something," she said, as they followed two uniforms inside. "Judge Kelford has a long memory."

They walked into the room where the card table was set up. One hand of poker was neatly folded. The other was scattered on the floor.

"Miss Oona will not like this little visit," Marti said.

"I just hope she didn't get here first."

Marti didn't think Oona was the brightest person she had ever met, but Marti didn't want to underestimate her either. "Her father is still in critical condition. With luck, she's too worried about him."

There were three rooms in addition to the one they had seen the last time they were here. The den had a thirty-five-inch television and a reclining couch where Thornton could watch in comfort with a couple of friends. The bedroom was as comfortable, and the kitchen had been remodeled recently.

"I had a hunch that front room was for show," Vik said. "There's nothing poor or bankrupt about anyone in this family."

There was also a storage area the size of a walk-in closet, stacked with half a dozen boxes filled with manila folders and loose papers, and a four-drawer file cabinet.

"If we don't find anything incriminating," Vik said, "we'll have to leave all of this here."

For the first time since Marti could remember, Vik didn't seem to relish the idea of going through someone's records and files. A couple more finds like this, or another case with similar demands, and he might be cured of his love of paper and paperwork.

The uniforms were efficient and didn't make too much of a mess. Within half an hour they found Virginia's wallet in the oven of an unused stove on the back porch. But they didn't come up with a gun.

"No purse. No gun," Marti said. "But at least Judge Kelford won't be ticked off." They had a case coming before him in two weeks and neither of them wanted to give him any unpleasant memories this close to that trial.

Virginia's driver's license, two credit cards, a debit card, four check-cashing cards, and $17.43 were in her wallet.

"This tells us a hell of a lot," Vik said, complaining. "I wonder where her purse is."

He instructed the uniforms to look again. Marti took two rooms and he took the other two and they tried to find some odd place where the purse might have been stashed.

"Nothing," Marti said.

Vik agreed. "Except for more damned papers. What was wrong with these two, couldn't either of them throw anything away?" The expression on his face suggested that he had just tasted something sour.

Marti didn't try to spoil his mood by saying something positive. She found herself wishing that Oona had come while they were here. She would have liked to have seen her reaction.

Back at the precinct, Vik sat and stared at the diskette while they waited for Thornton's files to arrive.

"This is a dead end, MacAlister. This is just a dead end. We're never going to be able to connect this to anyone. Why would Virginia even have this?"

Marti wished he had never found it. It was worse than the proverbial needle in the haystack. The way Vik kept coming back to it—he wouldn't call it intuition, or even a hunch, but it made her wish they could connect it to something too. She glanced at the clock, disappointed because it was still so early in the day. Ben was coming over at noon to take her to lunch—if she could take time out to eat.

The lieutenant called an 8:00 A.M. meeting with Marti, Vik, Tolley, and Lefty to discuss last night's bombing and fire. Firemen were still going through what was left of the building. So far they had not found any bodies.

"If these aren't isolated incidents, Vik . . ."

"Then we've got at least one psychopath out there, possibly two."

She caught the touch of sadness in his voice. "Hey, this happens everywhere. No place is immune anymore."

Vik's scowl deepened. He didn't answer.

Lefty, the head of the bomb squad, and Tolley, the fire chief, were already there when Marti and Vik arrived at the lieutenant's office. Lieutenant Dirkowitz had not only coffee this morning but doughnuts as well. Marti took this as a signal that this could be a long meeting. She nodded to Lefty and Tolley and reached for a Styrofoam cup. "Dirty Dirk" Dirkowitz had an expression on his face that matched his nickname. Mad as hell. His muscles bulged beneath his shirt, and he kept clenching and unclenching his fist. He had earned his nickname as a football player. If Marti had seen him coming at her during a game looking the way he looked today, she would have run in the opposite direction.

She poured a cup of coffee for Vik. He had had about as much sleep as she had and looked the worse for it, with dark pouches under his eyes. Vik frowned because there was no sugar, but didn't refuse the caffeine fix.

The lieutenant popped open a can of diet soda. "So, what have we got here?" he asked. "An increase in gang activity? Unrelated incidents? A pyromaniac? What?"

Everyone was in agreement that this was not gang-related activity. Local gang members tended to limit their warfare to fights and an occasional drive-by. Shooting, not arson, was their overwhelming method of choice for maiming, killing, and getting even. There wasn't anything in the recent past that connected gangs with bombs.

Dirty Dirk massaged the sides of his neck. His eyes were bloodshot, as if he hadn't had much sleep. Marti didn't want to think about how her eyes must look.

"Let's start with last night's bomb," Dirkowitz said. "Lefty, do you think this could be the work of the same perp who set off the mailbox bomb?"

Lefty was tall with a lot of bulk. He shifted his weight in the chair and tested the temperature of the coffee. "It was small," he said.

"What does that mean?"

"There were enough explosives to take out the bike but not enough to damage anything else. That's the only similarity that I can see right now. We're working on it."

"Work faster," Vik said. "We've got to nail this guy."

"Look, Jessenovik, we've got a motorcycle that's in a hundred different pieces and a corpse that's almost as bad. We're working as fast as we can."

"Can you give us anything else?" Dirkowitz asked. "Any reasonable assumptions that we won't hold you to later but might get us moving?"

"My guess is that it blew when the guy turned on the ignition."

"So," Vik said, "assuming that this guy isn't a hit man for the Mafia or some other type of professional assassin, what are we talking about in terms of a bomb?"

Lefty gave them a few possibilities.

"Was it something I could put together in my basement?" Vik asked.

Lefty nodded. "There are books out there—"

"Don't remind me," Vik interrupted.

Dirkowitz turned to Tolley. "And the fire?"

Tolley ran his fingers through his bristling, buzz-cut black hair. "Different MO."

"How different?"

"The fire at the Warren place and the fires that preceded it smoldered until they built up enough heat and combustible gasses to flash over as soon as air was introduced. This fire didn't. No similarities."

"How important is that?" Vik asked.

"I don't know. The other thing is that the other fires were set in abandoned buildings in isolated areas. This one was set in a heavily populated area."

"Which bothers me," the lieutenant said. "How consistent is an arsonist?"

"A pyromaniac gets off setting fires, sir. They like rituals. Repetition. Predictability. There was a ritual in the way the Warren fire was set and also in the way the previous fires were set. And all of them were in less populated areas. This fire was set in a hurry."

"But it was also in an abandoned building," Vik said.

"True. And it's just cooling down. We haven't fully inspected the interior yet."

"He was more likely to be seen this time," Marti said.

"Which is exactly what he doesn't want," Tolley said. "This guy is a control freak. The odds that he would put himself in a situation he couldn't control are slim to none."

"But *could* this be the same perp?" the lieutenant said.

"Could be," Tolley conceded. "But right now the only compelling reason I have for thinking so is that it's probably the first time we've ever had two fires within five days that were deliberately set in unoccupied buildings. We're thinking insurance fraud on this one. That's the most likely possibility."

"Yes," Marti said, "I like that. It beats the hell out of the alternatives."

"How would Homicide proceed with this one?" Dirkowitz asked.

"Another canvass," Marti and Vik said, almost in unison.

"And talk with the beat cops," Marti added.

"Good. Better yet, since that's a community-action area,

we'll let those uniforms handle it. Marti, you and Vik follow up on it." The lieutenant reached for his defused hand grenade. "And you, Tolley?"

"Right now, our focus is on the scene itself; what it can tell us. And how fast we can get the owner for having it set to collect the insurance."

Dirkowitz weighed the apple-shaped grenade. "Okay, pending further information, I'm willing to concede that this fire is unrelated to the others. But can we get a more detailed profile on the arsonist?"

"Beyond being a loner? I'll get someone working on it."

"So we're back to the bombs," Dirkowitz said. "Bombs. Incredible, isn't it? What in the hell is going on out there?" He toyed with the pin on the grenade. "Shouldn't we be able to apply the same logic to a bombing that we do to a fire?"

Lefty leaned back and stared into his cup for a moment. "In this case, I think the targets are important."

"The guy who blew up the mailbox has it in for the government?" Vik asked.

"Not necessarily, Jessenovik. Everyone has to start somewhere. The two bombings could be unrelated or related. The mailbox could have been practice. The motorcycle was a targeted act. The focus of my investigation will be there. The victim's death was directly related to the timing of the detonation."

"Because you think it went off when he started the motorcycle?" Vik asked.

"I think that's a given," Lefty agreed. "And if we can figure out why, we might even be able to determine where our bomber will strike next."

"He," the lieutenant said. "In both instances?"

"Fits the profile," Lefty said.

Tolley agreed that in both instances they were talking about male perps.

"And you think he'll do it again?"

"Hell," Tolley said, "the arsonist and the bomber will if we don't stop them."

Lefty and Tolley distributed reports on everything they knew to date. There wasn't sufficient information on the bombings to see a pattern. The two most recent fires seemed unrelated, but the investigation on last night's fire had just begun.

"What was the extent of the damage this time?" Marti asked. "How soon was it called in?"

"It burned for a while. The way it was set, it went unobserved until it had had time to generate a lot of heat."

"Doesn't that make it similar to the other fires?"

"In intensity, yes. In MO, no."

Ben had been at both fires. The Warren fire had been on the perimeter of his district; last night's was in the center. If he couldn't make it for lunch . . . she was looking forward to a little time alone with him away from home, even if it was just the Barrister.

"We need to nail whoever set this one," she said. "If it had spread . . ."

"If it's the same perp . . . ?" Vik said.

The lieutenant dropped the grenade on his desk. "We're not going to stay lucky much longer," he said. "We're going to have a significant body count if we don't catch them."

Geoffrey was late getting to work. He caught himself thinking that, late for work. Damn. What was happening to his life? Nothing he had planned, that was for sure. Meeting up with that pig was the worst thing that had ever happened to him and nothing good had happened since. He was beginning to think someone had worked root on him or invoked some kind of hex. Gayle was a thing of the past. There was no way he would take her back after last night, and he hadn't been able to find Kayla. And now, double damn, Deacon Evans was waiting for him.

"Geoffrey, you're running late today. Must have got something going last night with your young lady."

"Something like that." It had been about ten when he'd gotten back from Chicago, an early night, especially for a Friday.

"How bad was the fire on your street? It wasn't even a block from Sister Hawkins's place. Good Lord, you even smell like smoke."

Did he? He thought he'd taken care of that when he showered. The fire was great, the only good thing to come out of the entire evening, but he didn't say so. The whole street had come alive. Fire engines and hoses. People standing around in nightclothes, street clothes, and a couple of hookers who might as well have had on no clothes. All that was left of the house was charred wood, two toilets, and a bathtub. He thought about calling Mama to let her know what had happened but figured the shock effect would be greater if she heard it from somebody else and then realized how close he might have come to being dead. Just living in a neighborhood where a fire could happen so easily, and had the potential to spread fast, would be enough to have Mama begging him to come home where it was safe.

"I was expecting to see you at nine o'clock sharp, with this being your first time collecting rents and all."

"Sorry about that. I know I said I'd be here, but with all the excitement . . . they've still got a fire truck there."

He was exhausted by the time he got to bed. He had counted on Sister Hawkins to wake him up this morning, and for whatever reason, she hadn't. Good thing the old man didn't take it upon himself to collect his rents. He had rigged the formulas in the spreadsheet to deduct five hundred dollars from the total of the rents due. If the old man collected the rents himself, and counted it . . .

"No matter, Geoffrey. You can just go on and take care of it now. A few of the tenants might not be around to pay you, and they have until the fifth day of the month, but I'm always there on the first. Most of them just hand it over. Be more cash than checks, but it's okay to take checks from them, just get it all to the bank real fast." He picked up Geoffrey's first spreadsheet. "I see that computer is paying for itself already. You won't even have to count it." He shook his head from side to side. "Amazing what the world is coming to. Before we know it, folks won't have to be thinking about nothing at all. They'll have a computer they can take wherever they go to think for them."

"Seems likely," Geoffrey said.

"Your mother is so proud of you," Deacon Evans said.

Not that again.

"Laurence has been something of a disappointment. Calvin, too."

"Calvin?"

"Well, you know how it is when all the church sisters get together and go to bragging about their children and grands. Princess never has had much to say, unless she's talking about you."

"Really?" That was a surprise. If it was true. "But Laurence is on cable network news every night. And Calvin, he's rich."

"I know, but Laurence is also . . ." He twisted his hand in the gesture for a homosexual. "And Calvin, well, his wife is from Finland. Why, when my nephew was in the navy, I heard him tell that coloreds wasn't even allowed to get off the ship when they pulled in there."

"That had to be a long time ago. And this is the first I've heard of it. Your nephew could be exaggerating."

"Exaggerating or not, there're enough of us who have heard him say it. Poor Precious, got a son a rich man, richer than her husband, and ain't got no bragging rights at all. When folks get to talking, it's your name Princess and Precious say most often. And all those gifts you give her . . . She shows them to everyone."

And he'd had to give back the ring. A perfect diamond, the jeweler had said. Damn.

After the meeting with the lieutenant, Marti made a quick sweep of the neighborhood surrounding the site of the bombing, while Vik and Lupe Torres did another canvass. The Mini-mart/gas station where Malcolm Fletcher bought his nightly newspaper and a pack of cigarettes was three blocks from where he lived. The owner looked like he was from the Middle East. He was a local, had owned the place for eleven years, and knew exactly who she was talking about. He called the night manager, who confirmed that Fletcher hadn't shown up the night before.

"Most unusual," the owner said. "Most unusual indeed. He always comes here, always comes. He has been coming here for years. Very polite. Quiet, not much to say, but always 'please' and 'thank you.' "

She met Vik at their unmarked car. "Where's Lupe?"

"She had to get back to her beat."

"Did she get anything out of the Hispanic couple?"

Vik rubbed at a stubble of beard. "Just that the motorcycle was noisy, and the man went out the same time every night. Nobody around here saw anything, or if they did, they're not telling."

"Did you find out where he kept the bike?"

"In the driveway unless the weather was bad."

"So it wouldn't have been too difficult for our mad bomber to access."

"Don't say that, MacAlister." Vik's voice was sharp. There was a twist to his mouth that she didn't see very often. He didn't like being reminded that Lincoln Prairie was no longer the same town he grew up in.

* * *

Marti had a message from Ben when she got back to the precinct. He would be there at twelve-thirty. It was twelve-fifteen now. She called to check on Thornton, who was still in Intensive Care and on life support, then went through the evidence tech's reports on Virginia McCroft's car.

"No purse, no gun," she told Vik. "But he picked up lots of trace fibers and a variety of soil samples when he vacuumed." She tried to call him and left instructions when he wasn't there. "His lab partner says he's at the McCroft place collecting samples to run against what he found in the car. I told them to have him go over to Thornton's place too."

The door opened and she looked toward it, expecting to see Ben, but it was just Slim and Cowboy.

"Oh," she said, disappointed. "It's you."

Slim sauntered over. "Glad to see me, huh?" He took a step back. "Say, what is this, a new suit?" He gave a low whistle. "Those slacks are fitting good. Old man's been after you to lose a little weight, huh? Or is it just from getting a lot of exercise?"

Without looking at him, Marti said, "Actually, it's none of your business."

Then she turned and looked past Slim. Ben was standing in the doorway. A slight narrowing of his eyes and the tilt of his chin told her he had heard what had just been said.

Cowboy winked at her, cocked his hat back on his head, and grinned.

"Looks like we got company, partner."

Slim turned. "The little man. My pleasure. Quite a woman, isn't she?"

Ben came into the room and sat down at Slim's desk.

"Hey, man," Slim said. "Sorry. My space."

Ben pushed the chair back and put his feet up on the desk.

"Say, Ben," Slim said.

"Yes, Officer Ross?"

"Wrong desk. Your wife's desk is over there." He pointed.

"My wife? You mean Detective MacAlister?"

If it wasn't for his eyes, Marti wouldn't have known he was

angry. She knew that Ben knew he didn't need to protect or de-fend her. She also understood that there was something totally different going on between the two men, that Slim had gone where a man did not go with another man's wife and Ben had to reestablish the boundaries. Vik got her attention and winked.

"Yes," Slim said. "Detective MacAlister. She sits over there."

"She. My wife, Detective MacAlister."

"Yes, yes."

"And you sit over here."

"Right."

"Oh, I see. My wife sits there. You sit here. I've got that right?"

"Yes, you've got it right." Slim spoke with exaggerated patience.

"You're sure about that?" Ben asked. "You're sure about who sits where?"

"Look, man . . ."

"Just answer the question, Officer. You are *sure* about who sits where?"

"Okay," Slim said. "Okay, man, okay."

"No, it's not okay. But now that I know that you know where everyone's place is, I guess I can let you have yours."

Ben took his time getting his feet off the desk and getting up. As he walked past Slim, he brought his hand down on his shoulder. "Nice meeting you, Detective Ross."

Slim didn't answer.

Vik gave Ben a thumbs-up.

"Are you okay with that?" Ben asked as they walked to the elevator. He smelled of smoke.

"This time," she said.

"I know you're used to male cops behaving that way and you can handle it, but this wasn't about that."

"I know. It's one of those male-bonding things, right?" she joked.

Ben put his arm around her. "That's close enough, Officer Mac."

* * *

They walked the block and a half to the Barrister. Gray clouds were still gathered overhead. They seemed more sad than threatening. Marti didn't think it would rain. This part of town was all brick and mortar—the precinct, the county jail, city hall, the county building, the coroner's facility. Most Saturdays there were few pedestrians. Today they were alone. She had been hoping that the sky would clear, but yesterday's sunshine and relative warmth had gone the way of fool's gold. It was overcast and chilly and just dismal enough to seem more like late fall than the first day of May. The city had put waist-high planters made of pebble-incrusted concrete along the sidewalk, but with the temperature still descending to frost levels at night, the annuals hadn't been planted yet. Marti linked her arm in Ben's and they talked about going north to open up the cabin in a couple of weeks.

Saturday business was less than brisk when they reached the Barrister. Marti recognized a judge, a couple of lawyers, and a bail bondsman. The Saturday morning court session, which was primarily for setting bail, with occasional interruptions for marriage ceremonies, must be over. Ben led the way to a dimly lit booth away from the others. Crocuses bloomed in a small bowl on the table and a fire crackled briskly in the fireplace. Marti suggested the shepherd's pie. Ben ordered bangers and mash.

After the waitress poured coffee, Ben said, "The real reason I wanted to have lunch with you was to talk about Momma Mac."

"My Lord, the thrill is gone," Marti said with a deep sigh. "Not even six months and the honeymoon is over. We're talking about the other woman in your life already."

Ben grinned. "Next Sunday is Mother's Day and the men's choir is having something special for the church mothers after services. Momma Mac will be included."

"Oh, Ben, Momma will love that. How come I'm just hearing about it now?"

"I can't say anything in front of her."

"We are alone every so often."

Ben chuckled. "I've been distracted." He leaned toward her and whispered, "By the sweet scent of vanilla and a very sexy lady."

Marti laughed. "I'll make sure nothing keeps me from services next Sunday, not even the scent of vanilla."

"Nothing will keep you away," Ben said. "Promise?"

She promised. "Nothing."

"Not even a dead body that's still warm?"

"No."

"Even if they find it in the county building?"

"Nothing."

"Even if it's a state attorney?"

"No way."

"A circuit court judge?"

"Nope."

"Deal!"

He frowned when the sausages and mashed potatoes came.

"Vik tried that and didn't like it. Maybe you should have ordered the shepherd's pie."

Ben jabbed at the potatoes with his fork, then sliced off a hunk of sausage and popped it into his mouth. "Umm, spicy. Beef. How's Vik's wife?"

"Mildred is doing much better. Her MS is stable again."

"Good. Vik's okay. Too bad the same can't be said of Officer Ross."

"I've traded insults with experts."

"I know." Ben looked at her without smiling, then reached out and touched her cheek.

She grabbed his hand and held it.

They talked about the fires and bombings over coffee.

"The lieutenant called a meeting on it this morning. Tolley said the MO on the fire over by Eureka was different from the fire at the Warren place. He's not sure if it's the same person."

"Let's hope it's not."

"Why?" She didn't know a lot about arsonists.

"It could mean he's losing control."

She watched the flames flickering in the fireplace. There was a sizzling sound and the fire flared up as one log broke apart and another burned brighter.

"What's your gut feeling about this, Ben? Do you think the same person set all of the fires, or did someone set this one on Eureka for the insurance?"

"I think it's the same guy."

"Why?" Nobody else did.

"The point of origin," Ben said without hesitation. "I've seen all of them. The heat is so intense once he strikes that match . . ."

"And you think he set this one too?"

"This one bothers me."

"Why?"

"It's a digression from the pattern. I think his target changed or his motivation. I think this might have been personal somehow. The arsonist gets so much satisfaction—not just from the fire, but the whole process of setting the fire, watching it grow, the excitement of firefighters on the scene—that he always gets that rush, so what he does becomes predictable, what he knows will work."

"And if last night's fire was set by the same guy?"

"Then he's stepped out of that pattern. Something else is going on—anger, revenge, hatred, fear, whatever. He's doing something he has to do, the same as he has to breathe, but he's not doing it in the way that will give him maximum satisfaction. He's bound to get frustrated, fast. Then, too, there's the other possibility . . ."

"That he's out of control." She didn't want to think about the implications. But she had no choice. They would have to increase the patrols in the area where this latest fire was set, whether anyone agreed with her about the arsonist or not. That neighborhood was too densely populated to take the risk. But would increased patrols do any good if he was, in fact, out of control?

"What do you know about mad bombers?"

Ben laughed. "That's an interesting way to change the subject. Nothing like being married to a cop. I know a little about bombers, not much. I suppose they are a lot like arsonists except for a preference for the big bang theory of mass destruction. You've got that motorcycle fatality now too, haven't you? Are you getting anywhere with it yet? It takes a while to get everything reassembled and sorted out."

"Unofficially, we agree on the probability that the same person blew up the motorcycle and the mailbox."

"I guess now that you've got a victim, it's a lot less likely that we've got a junior mad scientist giving us a crash course in chemistry one-oh-one."

"Anything is possible," Marti said. She yawned, then spooned extra sugar in her coffee.

"Four hours' sleep isn't enough," Ben said. "Or was it three?"

"Something like that."

"Are you anywhere near solving anything?"

"Probably not," she admitted.

Ben motioned to the waiter for more coffee. He looked tired too.

"What are you doing today?" she asked.

"I'm off until Monday."

The waitress came over with a full carafe. Marti pointed to her cup. She felt as if she was somewhere between exhausted and comatose, and it was going to be a long day. "Have you got anything planned?"

"Theo and I are going to finish that model airplane he's been working on forever."

"You're kidding."

"No."

"Did he ask you to help or did you volunteer?"

"He asked. Mike is going to make one too, and then we're going to try them out when we go up to Wisconsin to open up the cabin."

Marti tried to correlate this with her conversation with Theo yesterday and could not.

"Why are you shaking your head?"

She told him about yesterday and gave him the history of the airplane.

"I think I'll leave that alone," Ben said. "Just go with the flow, finish the airplane, and fly it. It sounds like it might be something good. It might mean that he likes me."

"You already know that."

Ben covered her hand with his. "Yes, I know that," he said. "But even though everything seems to be going well, I don't think this is that easy for any of them. I think that they want us to be a family, thank God, but they have memories, the same as we do, and regrets. Theo and Joanna have to miss Johnny, just as Mike has to miss Carol."

Marti felt too tired to deal with any of that today. It was enough that the model plane would finally be completed. And then what? There was no point in thinking about that. Enjoy the moment. "I think this thing with the airplane is good," she said. "I have no idea what it means, but something tells me it's okay."

Slim and Cowboy were gone when she got back to the precinct. Vik had manila folders lined up on all four desks.

"I think I might be onto something," he said. "The trouble is, I'm confused."

Marti left him to whatever he was trying to organize and went through her in basket looking for reports on the Mc-Croft case and the motorcycle bombing.

"Nothing," she said. She'd been saying that a lot the past few days.

"I wish nothing really was nothing," Vik said. "Instead of nothing useful, or nothing we can figure out, or nothing that makes any sense."

He rearranged the folders, moving them from one desk to another for over an hour before he sat down and began massaging his neck. "There are papers in his folders and papers and clippings in her folders that seem to be about the same thing. The trouble is, I can't find anything that explains what Virginia's folder with a newspaper clipping so brittle the paper is ready to crumble has to do with Thornton's folder that has a survey plate of the same place."

"We're back to this land business."

"Yes. If there is any land business. If it does make any sense. If, if, if."

"Well, if there is, it looks like you've got it all organized. How do we find out whether we've got the whole puzzle here and it doesn't mean anything, or if we've still got a few pieces missing that could mean something?"

"You're asking me, MacAlister? Well, guess what: I don't know. Virginia's dead. We need a motive. This is as close as we've come to having one. And if there is a reason buried in here somewhere, then God help us because I just don't know."

Vik was still puzzling over it when they got a call that Oona Amstadt wanted to see them. She was pacing in the interview room when they went downstairs. Her face was drawn, and she looked at least five years older than she had when Marti had seen her at the farm. She wondered if the child's toys she'd seen there were for Oona's child, or grandchild, but didn't ask. The room was so small that pacing consisted of three steps from the door to the table, a right turn, and three more steps to the wall.

"You," Oona said, as they walked in. "I wanted to see your boss and make a formal complaint, but the lieutenant isn't available. I'm going to call the mayor's office to complain about his not being available first thing Monday morning. If I still lived here, I'd know who to call now."

Arms folded, Marti leaned against the table. Vik straddled a chair.

"How dare you search my father's house? I don't know who you think you are but—"

"We're peace officers, ma'am," Vik interrupted.

"We serve and protect," Marti added.

"Don't you get sarcastic with me."

"We had a search warrant," Vik said.

"My father is in the hospital."

"And you're here?" Marti said.

Oona took a step toward her. Marti eased away from the table. Oona backed away.

"Why don't you have a seat?" Marti suggested. The woman was making her twitchy.

Oona sat. "Why don't you leave my family, my father, alone?"

"Things don't seem to be working out that way," Vik said.

"Why? Because of that selfish, greedy woman's car?"

"That's a place to start," Vik said.

"Maybe she drove the car there herself. Nobody saw how it got there."

Marti thought that was an interesting observation. She looked at Vik. He rubbed his thumb against his index finger. He had picked up on it too.

"You can't think my father did this. Does he look like someone who could drive a car? What do you think he did with his oxygen tank, tied it to the roof maybe?"

She looked from Marti to Vik.

"Since you think you're such smart sonsabitches, you figure out how her car got there. A car and a wallet and you think you know it all. Well, know this. That's my father's house, and he's too sick to tell you anything. And guess what? My brother and I don't know."

With that, she left.

"For someone who doesn't know anything," Marti said, "she knows quite a lot."

Vik agreed. "She even knows things we haven't told anyone." Nobody else knew about the wallet.

"She didn't mention the purse though. Or the gun. I wonder how much she knows about them?"

Calvin and Laurence were there when Geoffrey arrived at Mama's. It was only the first of May and a lousy day for cooking out, but from the sounds coming from the backyard, they were grilling on the patio. If he just had that ring. This would be the perfect time to give it to Mama. He'd be moving back in tonight if he still had that ring. That damned pig.

The yapper Miles Davis didn't greet him when he let himself in. Sarah Vaughan sat haughty and indifferent by the staircase. He flipped the cat the finger, headed toward the sound of voices, then stopped. The last time Calvin had been here, he had accidentally overheard everyone talking about him. This time he decided to eavesdrop. He made his way to the back of the house and paused near the curtains drawn at one of the windows where he couldn't be seen. Calvin was talking, of course. Little big man—the oldest, the shortest, the darkest, and the one with the biggest mouth.

". . . don't think it's a good idea for you to go over there tomorrow, Mama."

Go where? To see his place? Damn. That was just what he wanted; and soon, while the air still smelled of burned wood and the gutters were filled with sooty water.

"He's not—" Laurence began.

"We have known Shirley Hawkins for a long time, Princess," Aunt Precious said. "Long enough to trust her to look after Geoffrey."

Look after him? Nobody looked after him, certainly not Shirley Hawkins.

"If you go over there now and every little thing isn't perfect, you'll start worrying yourself about his comfort. A man needs to worry about his own comfort."

"And—" Laurence said.

Calvin cleared his throat. "A man isn't a man until he can take care of himself."

So, this wasn't Mama's idea. Calvin and Aunt Precious were running the show.

"I know I've done too much for Geoffrey," Mama said, "but he was just a baby when your daddy passed. I know he needs to be out on his own."

"We—" Laurence said.

"We all had a daddy long enough to know how to grow up and become men," Calvin said.

Like either of them would know. Even when Daddy was here, by the time he was born, the man was on the road traveling most of the time, keeping up with his real estate investments.

"Now, Princess," Aunt Precious said, "I couldn't love him more if he was my own, but you do want a few more grandchildren, don't you? Maybe even a grandson who looks like his grandmother? Geoffrey is the spitting image of you."

That wasn't fair. Just because Calvin's wife was from Finland and Mama couldn't brag about their kids like she wanted to, that didn't mean he was responsible for perpetuating the family name. They had to be out of their minds.

"Once Geoffrey doesn't have his mama babying him, Princess, he is going to find himself a wife."

Aunt Precious. He couldn't believe it. Why was she here? Uncle Frank had been dead for at least fifteen years. Now all of a sudden she has to live here instead of him. Why? She put him out, that's what she did, and now she was encouraging Mama to keep him out.

"Be honest, Mama," Calvin said. "Do you feel bad because Geoffrey's not here? Do you miss him? Or are you just feeling guilty for making him stand on his own two feet?"

Geoffrey waited. Everyone was quiet until Mama said, "I am so blessed to have you here with me, Precious. It's just like when we were growing up. With Geoffrey here, I was alone."

Well, damn them all, Geoffrey decided. He slipped down to the basement, and using the keys he'd kept, unlocked the door to his office and worked on his latest project for a couple of hours. Then, briefcase in hand, and still wearing his running shoes, he left as quietly as he had come. Damn them all.

CHAPTER
32

When Vik began kicking Thornton's file cabinet, Marti decided it was time they took a break. Vik had worked through lunch. She should have brought him an order of bangers and mash. She ordered pizza instead.

"I feel inundated with paper," she said. "Let's forget about it for a few minutes. Focus on something else."

"What we really need are a few witnesses," Vik said. "I can't remember a case like this where everything happened in such isolated areas that nobody saw anything. We can't even get a witness at McCroft's or Thornton's place, where there are neighbors."

"I think we have to go back," Marti said. "Maybe we didn't ask the right questions. Maybe we weren't there at the right time of day."

"Maybe we wait for the pizza and I eat something first."

Vik's growing dislike for the paper in this case had not yet overcome his curiosity or his compulsiveness to read everything. The question was, were Thornton and Virginia just compulsive collectors of worthless information?

"The one thing McCroft's and Thornton's files have in common, Vik, is land. Even though we can't figure out any correlations. And that's also what the state attorney suggested we focus on."

"Look, MacAlister, neither of those two were involved in any land deals. From the looks of the mega mall and strip malls and new housing developments, there aren't many more deals to be made around here. My guess is they were both angry because so much has changed. Virginia spent a lot of time writing letters and going to meetings where land acquisition and the use of land was decided. She was real big on conservation. Both of Thornton's kids are doing something that involves land. Maybe they got that from him. Maybe we're just looking at this the wrong way. Maybe they just care about what's happening to the land. I don't think land had anything to do with why Virginia was killed."

"Or anything to do with why Thornton would want to see her dead?"

"If Thornton killed her, he had a much more practical reason than that. Like not forking over five hundred dollars a month."

Marti found her copy of the correlations Vik had identified between land mentioned in Thornton's files and land mentioned in Virginia's. Vik was probably right, but even so, it was the one thing they knew of, other than Virginia's pension, that McCroft and Thornton had in common. And right now, the Thorntons were their only logical suspects.

When Marti parked in front of the McCroft house, Virginia's neighbor Don Riley was leaning on his cane and watching as a younger man turned the soil in a flower bed. A woman who was Riley's height stood next to him. She had a blue rinse in her gray hair. They both wore corduroy slacks and turtlenecks and heavy cable-knit sweaters. It was late afternoon. The morning's overcast sky had shifted to gray clouds with patches of murky blue. Marti buttoned her London Fog and tied the belt.

"Officer MacAlister." Riley held out his hand. "This is my wife, Mary Margaret."

Mrs. Riley wore glasses with thick lenses in frames studded with rhinestones and shaped like cat's eyes.

"That's my nephew, Bobbie."

"Ma'am," Bobbie said, his back to them. He kept working the dirt with a spade.

The sheltie was half in and half out of a doghouse not far from the front porch. He looked up at the sound of Mr. Riley's voice, then tucked his head between his paws.

"I haven't read anything else about Virginia in the papers," Riley said. "I guess that means you still don't know who did it."

"Not yet," Marti said.

"I suppose you're wondering if I remember anything," He ran his hand through longish white hair. "Trouble is, there's nothing to remember."

"We didn't see much of Virginia anymore," Mrs. Riley said. She had a strong, resonant voice that dispelled any impression of fragility. "Before her mother went into the nursing home, she'd bring cookies over when she baked and sometimes even a casserole. She'd see if we needed anything when she went to the store, things like that. But once Libby went into the nursing home, we hardly ever saw Virginia anymore."

"Always going someplace, Virginia was," Mr. Riley said.

"And you last saw her a week ago Friday."

"Right, I was trying to decide whether or not to cut down that tree over there."

"Not last Friday." His nephew Bobbie straightened up and twisted around to look at them. "That was Thursday."

"Friday," the old man disagreed.

Marti reminded herself that this was the man who either couldn't remember or lied about his age. She took a closer look at Bobbie. She guessed his age to be a few years either side of fifty.

"What makes you think it was Thursday?" she asked.

"I know it was Thursday. I came over to take a look at the tree to see if me and a couple of friends could take it down. On Friday we all took off from work early and went up to the cabin to get in a little fishing. Remember, Uncle Don? I stopped by Saturday evening with some trout."

The old man rubbed his chin.

"Bobbie did bring us some fresh fish last Saturday, Don," Mary Margaret said. "I deep-fried it for supper."

"Then I guess that's right," the old man said.

Marti asked a few more questions, hoping the younger

man might remember something else, but she didn't find out anything further.

"Well, that's more than I got," Vik said, when they got back in the car. "Virginia was seen at the nursing home on Thursday too. So, she could have been killed Thursday night, instead of Friday. Not that one day makes any difference with what we've got now. Let's take a look at what we know about everyone's whereabouts on Thursday. With what, four known possible suspects, that shouldn't take long."

Reports from Lefty, the bomb squad captain, and Tolley, the fire chief, had been delivered when they got back to their office. Marti scanned hers, then gave Tolley's a closer look, reading it twice.

"Hey, Vik, if you look at the next to the last page of Tolley's report, where he lists everything unusual that was observed by people accessing the forest preserve at the entrance nearest the Warren place . . ."

"What about it . . . oh, black vehicle, older model . . ." He scanned the report again. "No mention of it anywhere in the interview notes. I'll give Tolley a call."

When he hung up, he said, "It should have been deleted from the report. The witness, a Mr. Becker, reported seeing the vehicle the week before the fire."

Marti fingered the pages for a few minutes, then said, "Virginia McCroft drove a car that fits that description and she died a week before . . ."

"I know, I know."

Becker's address and telephone number were listed at the end of the report. Marti picked up the phone. Mr. Becker was just leaving for O'Hare Airport.

"Black car?" he asked. "They said it wasn't important. Wrong day."

"What day was that?" Marti asked.

"What day did I tell them?"

"You weren't specific."

"No? Perhaps when I get back . . ."

"Can you remember the day?"

"No."

"It could be important. This is a homicide investigation."

"I don't know. I flew in from Japan on Monday . . . Wait a minute." He called, "Hey, Liz," then said, "We had dinner with the Penobscots on Wednesday and went to the theater Tuesday, right?"

Marti couldn't hear the answer.

"What about Thursday?"

She waited.

"It had to be Thursday," Becker said.

"You're sure?"

"Positive."

"What time?"

"Before dark."

"How long . . ."

"I have no idea. After five, before seven."

"Did you see anyone in the car?"

"I've got a plane to catch."

"Did you?" Marti persisted.

"No. Nobody but the driver." Muffled sounds indicated that he was speaking to someone else with his hand over the mouthpiece.

"Can you describe the driver?"

"A man."

A man. Great. If he was correct, there went her Oona Amstadt theory. "Can you remember anything about him?"

"No, nothing. He was leaving. I saw the back of his head. Look, I have to go. If you have any other questions I'll be back next Wednesday." With that, Mr. Becker hung up.

"See, it's just a coincidence, MacAlister. The driver wasn't even a woman. What would Virginia have been doing there anyway?"

"Why was she found dead in an abandoned building not more than a block away?"

Vik snapped a pencil in half, then he picked up Tolley's reports. "I'll take the top half of this list. You take the rest."

One other person recalled seeing the car. He was certain it was a Ford Escort. He'd seen two women sitting in the front seat, but couldn't remember what either of them looked like. "Older," he said. "They weren't dressed for running, and they were arguing. That's what made me notice them in the first place."

Vik broke another pencil. "Typical answers. No two people ever see the same thing. Even if it was two women, it still doesn't make sense. Suppose it was Virginia and Oona. Suppose Oona did kill Virginia. What did she do then? Drive to the Warren place and dispose of the body?"

Marti thought of Oona's hands as she kneaded the dough. "She's strong enough and the Warren place is isolated enough, even during the day."

"We don't have enough to bring her in."

Marti was forced to agree. "I don't think we want to alert her to the possibility that we might want to either." There was something about Oona that bothered her. Was it something she'd said? Or was it just her personality? Or was it intuition? "Maybe when we get the evidence tech's report on Thornton's place there will be some matches to what we found in the car. Then we can talk to her."

Vik leaned back and clasped his hands on the top of his head. "Too bad we don't have a reason to check her house. The likelihood of fingerprints is slim. Does that report say they found any traces of flour?"

"Don't get sarcastic, Vik." She couldn't remember the last time they had had a case where so much had to have happened and so few saw anything at all.

"Land," she said.

"The forest preserve?"

"It covers a lot of land."

"I am not going through those files again, MacAlister."

"But, Vik, there are so many pieces of paper."

"Then maybe the state attorney I sent copies to will come up with something."

Marti wondered how long his stubbornness would last, if

the thrill of the paper chase had been eradicated or just temporarily suppressed.

Vik picked up his copy of the list of those who had been interviewed by Tolley's and Lefty's teams. "I guess we have no choice but to talk with these people again." He didn't sound eager to do that either. "Another waste of time. Maybe instead of having one person who saw a man and another who saw two women, we'll get an ID on two dwarfs and a giant."

Marti gulped down another cup of coffee and grabbed a candy bar. Vik was in a great mood to go out and meet John Q. Public. It looked like she was going to have to do all of the talking.

The sky was overcast when Marti and Vik approached the large, brick Tudor on Elderberry Street. A fine mist was falling when they got out of the car, and Marti put on her rain scarf. They had called everyone on Tolley's and Lefty's lists and narrowed it down to those who were at the forest preserve on the Thursday before the fire at the Warren place and those who were there the evening of the fire. They had spoken with all but four people without results.

Sharon Zamberlan was a middle-aged woman with braces. She was reed thin, without any sign of a middle-aged bulge. She had a jogging suit over one arm and a glass of tomato juice in her hand. Running shoes had been discarded near the door. Marti was always a little put off by people who were into healthy lifestyles. She wasn't sure if it was her inability to stay away from fast food or living with her own health food nut, Joanna. She wondered if the tomato juice was laced with vodka, knew that wasn't nice, and didn't care.

Zamberlan admitted them to the foyer after they showed their ID. A dog barked from somewhere inside the house and a fat marmalade cat that must have weighed at least thirty pounds was sprawled on its side on an Oriental throw rug. Smart cat, no healthy diet for it.

"I don't mind taking the time to answer your questions, Officers, but I'm afraid I don't think I can help you. I run for an hour every morning and every evening. I'm training for a marathon. I'm afraid I don't pay much attention to whoever else is there."

"Do you always go to the same forest preserve?" Marti asked.

The woman nodded.

"Do you drive there?" She lived at least nine or ten miles away.

"Yes, of course."

"Do you always park in the same place?"

"What on earth are you getting at?"

"And other cars are in the parking lot."

"Of course."

"But nobody takes your spot?"

"Occasionally, but not often."

"So you've seen the same cars there. If, for example, a red Geo was parked two spots down from where you parked every Tuesday and Thursday and it wasn't there one night, you would notice."

Sharon Zamberlan raised the glass of tomato juice in a small salute. "I see." She thought for a minute, then described all of the cars she could recall that were usually parked there when she was there and on which days. Among those she remembered were a black Ford Escort that she had never seen before as well as a dark green sport utility vehicle that wasn't familiar. She did not remember seeing anyone in either.

As they walked back to their car, Vik said, "Whoopee! This was a great idea, MacAlister."

Harry Tompkins lived in an apartment house on the southwest side of town. He was not as friendly as Sharon Zamberlan. He did not invite them into his apartment and stood with them in the hallway instead. Mr. Tompkins remembered a dark-colored car leaving as he was arriving but had no idea who was driving it. He was certain that only one person was in the car. Tompkins also recalled seeing a green sport utility vehicle parked and unoccupied. He noticed it because it had Wisconsin license plates.

"Wisconsin plates do not a Thornton suspect make," Vik said, as they returned to their car.

Marti didn't answer. The eleven regulars they'd spoken with were solitary runners who didn't socialize with anyone and paid little attention to their surroundings. She doubted that they would have paid any attention to the cars in the lot if they'd walked there instead of driving. The fact that two of them had seen something out of the ordinary was enough to convince her that Virginia had parked there. Marti felt just the slightest spike of adrenaline. They were beginning to get somewhere.

The last two people on Tolley's list had seen nothing unusual. Vik gave her a "What did I tell you?" look, but said nothing. Marti glanced at the dashboard clock. She had missed dinner. Worse, she didn't even want to go home. Not now. Her tiredness had been replaced by an adrenaline flow that would compel her to keep moving until she had more answers.

"So, Vik, we find out if one of the Thorntons owns a green sport utility vehicle. We see if there are any fiber matches between Thornton's house and what was found in McCroft's car—and let's talk with Ezra Downes again, see if we can pin him down on exactly when Virginia's car showed up in Thornton's backyard. He was a little vague about that. When we finish with that, I bet we'll be ready to have another talk with Oona and Andrew."

Vik's wiry eyebrows almost met in a scowl. "We need a motive," he reminded her. "That and a weapon would be nice. Not to mention McCroft's purse. Discontinuing that five hundred dollars a month isn't reason enough, not based on what they have going for them, and we haven't been able to uncover any pressing financial need. Even if Virginia was leaning on them for more money so she could keep subsidizing Rosenblum, I can't see any of them killing her because of it."

"People do get greedy, Vik."

"True, but I don't see Oona or Andrew Junior doing anything stupid. It would be smarter to pay her than to jeopardize what they have."

"Oona's impulsive," Marti said. "And I've got a hunch Andrew's been relying on charm for a long time now."

Nobody was at home when they stopped to talk with Ezra

Downes again. The rain had stopped but the air was damp. Marti wasn't ready to return to the precinct. Vik was still scowling, and she didn't feel like being cooped up with a grouchy partner.

"We really should stop by last night's . . ."

"Good idea," Vik said.

". . . fire scene before it gets dark."

Maybe he wasn't ready to be cooped up with her either.

There was a lot going on at Eureka Street. It was one of the main north-south streets in an aging part of town that wasn't showing any signs of being revitalized. The corner grocery stores had been converted into rental units with painted-over plywood where plateglass windows had been. Most of the single-family homes on untidy plots of land had been compartmentalized into efficiency apartments. Those still occupied by their owners were recognizable by swept sidewalks and well-kept yards, newer siding, paint that wasn't peeling, windows neat with blinds and curtains, and for those with porches a variety of chairs.

Despite the unfriendliness of the weather—more like April than early May—people were outside. Perhaps it was the lack of a biting winter wind and ice-glazed snow or maybe it was the promise of the warmth and sunshine that would soon come. Children rode bicycles and Rollerblades or tried to dig holes where frequent footsteps had eroded the grass and beaten the dirt into compacted trails. Teenagers performed their perpetual pantomimes of constant motion as they stood on front stoops and near doorways. Marti marveled at their inability to be still. Hands waving, mouths moving, legs jiggling, a sudden outburst of dance steps. She wondered if their movements stopped even in their sleep. She drove slowly. The constant motion of the street reminded her of growing up on a similar street in Chicago.

As she turned the corner, wide rivers of dirty water ran alongside the curb and led her to the burned-out house. Little more than the outer walls and the chimney remained. After eighteen hours, give or take, the place no longer held any interest for the locals. A red station wagon with the Fire Department emblem was parked out front. Marti pulled up behind it.

"It looks like the arson investigators are still here," she said, as she turned off the ignition. "Maybe they found something."

"Let's hope it isn't a body," Vik said. "Not that anyone could cause as much trouble as Virginia has, dead or alive."

A fireman in full gear walked to the front of the building while they were standing there. He reeked of smoke. Marti wanted to take a few steps back but did not.

"Find anything?" she asked.

"No crispy critter this time."

"Thank God!" It was bad enough they had an arsonist on their hands. They didn't need another victim.

The fireman confirmed what Tolley had already told them. The point of origin was a foundation beam at the center of the cellar. The fire had burned intensely when set, then spread vertically and horizontally until the structure was consumed.

"Was there a sudden influx of oxygen?" Marti asked.

"You mean like at the Warren place?" The fireman shook his head. "No, it had to be the saturation level of the fuel."

"We've got a smart arsonist," Vik said.

"It looks that way."

"Smart like at the Warren place?"

"No. This one was definitely set for profit."

Two teams of uniforms who worked the area as part of the neighborhood policing program joined them, and they began canvassing in a three-block radius. The sounds of the street seemed subdued when Marti compared them to her neighborhood years ago. The kids' conversations were quieter and seemed more conspiratorial. There were fewer adults, and those who were out walked as if they had someplace to get to in a hurry. Parents weren't seen or heard at all. When she was a child, their parents called to them in code—their first name if it was routine—their first and middle names if they were in a little trouble—all three names if they were in serious trouble. Anything more than their first names meant come here now and move fast, and they did.

When asked, most of the kids skating and biking up and down the street and along the sidewalk said they had come out during the night to watch the fire. None of them admitted to being outside before it started. There were a few scattered teenagers, some wearing gang colors, who said they had spent the evening indoors. Legitimate business and industry had left the immediate area long ago, with the exception of one beauty/barber shop, a liquor store, and one small, corner grocery store with the windows boarded up and the boards covered with wire grating. If it wasn't for the kids coming out with candy, Marti would have thought the store was vacant. Neither she nor Vik found one person who had seen anything until they stopped a tired-looking, brown-skinned woman, who was pushing a baby carriage with a sleeping infant at one end and a sticky-fingered toddler at the other.

"No, I ain't seen nothing you'd be interested in," the woman said. "Not unless one more drug dealer makes a difference." When pressed, she described an older model dark blue car that had been "spending too much time in the neighborhood not to belong to nobody who lives here." Marti made a note of that and when they met with the beat cops, she asked about it. Three of the uniforms had made note of the car. One had run a make on it. "Belongs to a Frederick J. Jhanke Senior," he said and gave them an address.

"That's the guy who lives in the creepy house," Vik said.

"And not only does he live near where a motorcycle was bombed, but it looks like he also drives around near houses that are burned down."

"Jhanke." She didn't feel prickly or twitchy yet, but her antenna was definitely going up.

Even in broad daylight Jhanke's house seemed creepy. Tall yews, with a grayish cast to their wet, green branches, stood sentry on three sides of the fenced-in property and had been planted in a row not more than fifteen feet from the front of the house. There was a stillness about the place that made it seem desolate. No chirping birds; no scampering squirrels. Nothing, just the weighted-down silence of the encroaching trees. They were parted by a narrow, concrete path that led to the front door.

Vik scuffed the bottom of his shoe on the doormat. "Gum," he said. "Must have picked it up on Eureka. When we were kids we would have called a place like this a haunted house and driven whoever lived here crazy sneaking up to peek in the windows."

Marti rang the bell, then knocked, while Vik went to the detached garage.

"No car here," he said when he came back.

"And nobody answering the door."

"Is it locked?" Vik asked.

"Of course. Let's go around back."

There was a considerable amount of property. The owner, or some previous owner, liked a lot of personal space and privacy. Crab apple trees and burr oaks were planted in an orderly stand that blocked the rear of the house from the neighbors behind it. A chair that looked as if someone had taken an ax to it had been tossed on the grass. It seemed odd amid the order of grass cut low and tulips blooming in precise rows of twelve with a measured space between and beside each row.

Nobody answered the back door. Marti looked through the window. The kitchen seemed in perfect order except for the garbage overflowing the wastebasket in the corner and the stack of dishes in the sink. Marti knocked, waited, knocked again.

"Nobody home," she said. If someone was at home and just not answering, there was nothing she could do about that, at least not yet. They had no reason to request a search warrant or enter the premises without one. Even so, their previous visit had been to make inquires about the motorcycle bombing, and now they were here because of the owner's possible proximity to a fire caused by arson. Coincidence? Marti stopped halfway down the walk to turn and look at the house again.

Foreboding, she thought, *a foreboding place.* A cold wind gusted and caught at her jacket. She pulled it closed and shivered.

When Opal heard someone knocking on the front door, she remained very still. The least movement of her arm made her shoulder hurt so bad when she tried to get up to use the bathroom, she had fainted. When He let whoever it was in, did she dare try to let them know she was in here? The knocking stopped before she could decide, but she didn't hear any voices. Was He at home? She hadn't seen him since He'd hurt her.

The knocking began again. Closer this time. The back door. This time she did try to call to them, but her call for help was just a raspy whisper. How could she let them know she was in here? Opal turned her head from side to side, looking for something she could reach. There wasn't anything but the tray on the table that He had brought her, yesterday or perhaps the day before. The empty bowl was arranged the way He liked it, with the used tableware beside it and on the soiled but folded napkin. There was a little tea in the cup. If only she could reach it. She tried not to think about how thirsty she was. Help. She had to get help.

The knocking seemed louder. She couldn't just reach for the tray and knock it over. She would pass out from the pain. Instead she tried to scoot nearer. When it hurt too much, she waited. They knocked again. She tried to cry out again. Not loud enough. Every time she moved, her shoulder hurt. Slowly. She had to move slowly. When she was close enough to reach out her hand and tip over the tray, she realized that the knocking had stopped. She waited, listened, nothing. They were gone. Gone. Dear God, whoever it was, was gone. She tried not to cry, but tears slipped down her face and became itchy as they reached her neck. They were gone. He was gone. She was alone. She was going to die.

There was a police car driving slowly along the street as Fred reached the corner where he turned to go home. The car came to a stop at his house, paused, then drove on. Instead of turning the corner, he drove straight ahead. Cops. Why? Did they know Mother was inside? Why would they come here? How would they know? The bank. Maybe that was it. That was only the second time since Father died twenty years ago that he had gone to the vault. He had to show ID and sign both of those cards. Maybe they had to notify the police. If they did, then this must just be routine. But he didn't want anyone to know about Mother. If they started asking questions . . . He circled the block a few times, then decided to park his car a safe distance away, someplace where it wouldn't be noticed. There was a large grocery store eight blocks away. He left the car there and walked home.

It was getting late and dark outside when Marti and Vik returned to Ezra Downes's house. Not only were most of the lights on, music was blasting as well. When the old man opened the door, he said loudly, "Why, Officer MacAlister and Officer Jessenovik. How nice to see both of you again." The music stopped as soon as the first "officer" left his mouth.

"Mind if we come in?" Marti asked, in a voice as loud as his. She wanted to see who had turned off the noise.

"Well, um . . ." the old man hedged. His movements were slow as he tugged at the belt of a black bathrobe made of a satiny fabric. Marti could almost hear Vik saying that it was as shiny as his bald head. "I'm sort of . . . entertaining."

"Oh, sorry we interrupted." Now she really was curious. Who could someone this old be entertaining?

"Mr. Downes . . ."

"You don't have to yell. I got a new battery in my hearing aid and it's working just fine."

A light went off in a room down the hallway. "Ezra?" a woman called. "Ezra?" She stepped into the hall and took a few steps toward them. In the bright light, Marti could see that the woman was very blonde, thanks to her hairdresser, wore her hair in a style reminiscent of the Andrews Sisters, was heavy on the eye shadow and lipstick, and had to be at least sixty years old. She was wearing a long, black negligee. It wasn't see-through, but Vik looked away.

Ezra didn't say a word. The woman stepped back into the room. When she emerged again, she was wearing a comfortable, fuzzy pink bathrobe. Ezra turned and looked at her, then held the door open so they could come in.

The lighting in the living room was dim. A bottle of wine and two half-filled glasses were on the coffee table, along with what was left of some Chinese take-out. Ezra waved them to the chairs and sat on the couch beside the blonde. She was taller than he was, and he seemed like a wizened boy beside her. The hand he placed on her thigh was knotted with thick veins.

"How's Mr. Thornton doing?" Marti asked. "Have you seen him today?"

"Not good," Ezra said. "Not good at all. I told him them cigarettes would kill him. Cut back on them myself years ago."

"His children are still here." Marti caught just a glimpse of an expression on Ezra's face when she said that. It came and went too quickly for her to interpret, but it reminded her of Oona's disrespect last night.

"Oona seems very . . . protective," she said.

The woman snickered.

Marti thought back to her previous conversation with Ezra. He had been a tiny bit forthcoming. No, he had told her exactly what he wanted to, no more, no less. If she could approach him the right way this time, he might do the same thing again.

"I know how the car left the yard and how it got there, but what I need to know, Ezra, is when?"

"Thursday," the woman said, surprising her. "A week ago Thursday, before it got dark."

Ezra did not interrupt or seem annoyed by the woman's response. Maybe he did want them to know something, but wouldn't tell them himself because of his friendship with Thornton.

"I don't think Mr. Thornton's going to make it," Marti said. "They can't get him off of the respirator and breathing on his own."

"I know," Ezra said. "He got sick like this before, but he don't look good this time. He don't look good at all." He sounded more pragmatic than sad, the way people some-times did once they began experiencing the loss of family

and friends. "Poor old Andy, just couldn't leave them cigarettes alone. We are friends. Good friends. Have been for
years." He was remembering what Oona had said at the hospital.

"I know, Ezra. I could see that. Anyone could. We had to
search his house."

"It was because of the car, wasn't it?"

"The owner of the car is dead," Marti said.

Ezra stroked his chin. "I figured it must be something, the
way Oona came tearing into the yard and hid it like that."

Marti was careful not to react when he said Oona's name.
Instead she nodded her head. "Yes, we know. She was seen
driving the car."

"Funny kid, Oona," Ezra said. "Always getting the other
kids to do things they didn't have no business doing. Used to
play with my kids up in the tree house and had them doing
all kinds of things I didn't know nothing about. Good thing
there wasn't none of that marijuana floating loose back then.
Bad enough there was cigarettes and booze. All of them got
drunk and sick one day messing around with my wife's
cooking brandy."

"Tree house?" Marti asked. Was the old man telling her
something or just making conversation?

"Yeah, I built one for my kids out back. That was their secret place. They went up there even when they was
teenagers. My oldest daughter got herself pregnant up there.
Course we got her married right away, but it would have
been nice if she had gone to secretarial school like she'd
planned to."

He tugged at the robe where it was separating at his
knees. His legs were bare and spindly. Marti refused to think
about what she might see if the robe came open.

"I climbed up there a few years back," he said, "to see if
the wood was rotten. It was still as sound as when I built it.
Their old footlocker was still up there, still full of whatever
they hid up there. I left it there without looking at what was
inside though. Knowing Oona, figured there was likely to be
something in there I was best off not knowing about."

"Can we see the tree house?" Marti asked.

"Sure can. Climb right up there, both of you, if you want." The look Ezra gave Vik suggested that he didn't think Vik could make it.

Vik got their high-beamed flashlights out of the trunk.

"I can't believe this," he said, as they headed for the backyard. "Entertaining a floozy at his age."

Marti tried not to laugh.

"It's not funny, MacAlister. First speeding and now this. The man needs to be in a nursing home with someone to keep an eye on him."

"You're absolutely right, Vik. Ezra might die a happy man if they don't lock him up somewhere." She hoped she and Ben were just like Ezra and the blonde forty years from now. She wondered if Joanna would still approve. "What's a 'floozy'?" she asked.

Vik didn't answer.

The tree house was wedged between two tree trunks that grew in a vee. Boards had been nailed into one of the trunks as footholds. The tree house was longer than it was wide with a sloping roof, and protected by overhanging branches that extended high into the sky. Vik went up first.

"Ezra was quite a carpenter," he said, as Marti followed him inside. There was enough room to stand up. The door had a lock and there were glass windows that could open. As far as she could tell, it was watertight and there were no signs of squirrels moving in. Except for the footlocker, an oblong metal box, dented and scratched, that looked like army issue, the tree house was empty.

Vik tugged on the padlock, then got out a penknife and unscrewed the hinges.

"Well, take a look at this," he said. He held up a black leather purse. "I wonder who this could belong to?"

Marti didn't have to wonder why Ezra wanted them to find it.

It was after nine o'clock when they returned to the precinct. They drove past the Jhanke house on their way, but it was dark. The garage door was open, the garage empty. Marti had the dispatcher contact a patrol unit and request additional surveillance.

As soon as she reached the precinct, Marti called in a technician to go over Virginia's purse. There were no additional reports from the technician who'd collected the evidence from the McCroft car. Vik called him. "We've got some fiber matches from the Thornton place," Vik said.

"Let's see what we get from the purse, then I think we might be ready to talk with Oona. Let's hope she's still at the hospital. That would be a lot simpler than trying to bring her here from Wisconsin."

Opal thought she heard music. It was a strange sound, like a voice above the wind. She tried to sit up and see where the sound was coming from, but she wasn't sure where her legs were or her arms. Where was she? Where was He? Was He the one who was singing? No, it wasn't He. As she listened, the voice began to sound like her mother's. Mother only sang when Father was away. She would wait until he had been gone for a while, then she would sit Opal on her lap and brush her hair and sing the sweetest songs. *Angel music,* Opal thought. *Mother had the voice of an angel.* And now she was an angel, with God. Mother was singing to her now, just as she had years ago. Calling to her, singing to her. Mother. Mother. Here I come.

When he drove past the house where he had set the fire the
night before, cops seemed to be everywhere. He hated it
here. He wished he never had to come back to this neighborhood again, but there was another house that had to burn.
What should have happened before had not. The pounding
in his head was easing up, but the headache wouldn't go
away until he had taken care of what had to be done. For
now he would have to go home. No. He didn't want to go
there. He didn't want to go there ever again. He stopped at a
gas station, filled the tank, and bought half a dozen doughnuts. A familiar restlessness took hold of him. He got the
empty gasoline container out of the trunk and filled it. Then
he headed north, toward Wisconsin.

When he pulled into the driveway where the pig people
lived, the house was dark and quiet. Their car was parked
alongside it. It was so quiet here, so still. No houses nearby,
no people, just peace and quiet away from everyone. Why
should they have this when all he had to go home to was . . .
it wasn't fair. Nothing in life was fair. They'd crowded his
best fire out of the news with their story about their stolen
candleholders and their stupid pig. If it wasn't for them he
would have made headlines. These people who already had
more than enough were still taking what was his.

He opened the trunk and took out the rest of the lighter
fluid, then closed the trunk quietly. When he walked to the
back of the house, he was alert for the sound or movement of
a dog. Then he thought, But they don't have one: they've got
a pig. He poured the lighter fluid along the foundation at the
rear of the house and used a rolled-up newspaper as a torch.
Once the fire was going, he got back into his car, backed

down the driveway, and circled around the wide, furrowed fields of a farm until he reached a point where he could see the back of the house and watch the flames spread.

Marti was waiting for Vik to get back with some Mello Yello and hoping they would hurry up and hear from the technicians when Tolley burst into the office. "We've got another one," he said.

"A fire?"

"Yes. I just got a call from Pleasantdale Meadows."

That was a small town near the Wisconsin border.

"What's that got to do with us, Tolley?"

"It was the people who owned the pig."

Now she had lost him. "What pig?"

"The pig that made the news because someone conned the owners out of their candleholders."

Two things occurred to her. She didn't know Tolley very well, and she was close to exhaustion. What was the man talking about? "A pig? Candleholders?"

"Yes."

She was missing something. "And their house caught fire."

"No. The fire was set—deliberately."

"What has that got to do with us?"

Tolley sat in the chair between her desk and Vik's and ran his fingers through his close-cropped, bristling black hair. "I don't know."

"Then what . . ."

"Everyone got out okay, even the pig. In fact, the pig woke everyone up and that's how they escaped. The department up there put in a call to us because the woman was hysterical. She kept insisting that someone was out to get them. Everyone assumed she meant the con artist, but she said no, that he was just a thief; he wasn't crazy. She said it had to be this weird guy from Lincoln Prairie who set the fire, said he came to their house and pleaded with her to tell him who had taken the candleholders. He told her that whoever it was had conned his mother out of a watch. She said the man was all wild-eyed, and he looked like a bum. And he drove a small, older model, dark blue car, with rust."

"Frederick Jhanke Junior," Marti said, just as Vik came through the door with four cans of pop.

"What about him?" Vik asked.

This was one coincidence too many. "I think we'd better have a talk with him."

It only took the state's attorney an hour to get a search warrant. The Jhanke house was so dark and so isolated that Marti felt apprehensive as they pulled into the driveway. She radioed the others. Extreme caution. Six units went in, guns drawn, with two back-up units outside. Vik and Marti waited in their unmarked car. They were too tired to back anyone up, and Vik had agreed that once this operation was completed and secured, they were both going home to bed.

Marti could hear a siren in the distance when the uniform came out of the house and walked to the car.

"We found an old lady inside. A real old lady. She's in bad shape, but she's still alive."

Vik rubbed his eyes. "An old lady? Then who in the hell is Frederick Jhanke?"

"We'll get that sorted out, sir. Right now, an ambulance is coming."

The house seemed creepy from the outside with the lights out. Inside, with the lights turned on, everything from the overstuffed furniture in the living room to the mahogany sideboard and china cabinet in the dining room reminded Marti of an old movie. There were even two lamps with metal bases and fringed shades. Marti followed the paramedics, both of whom she knew. They worked with Ben.

The woman was very old. She was lying on a bed in the back room. Her mouth was partially open, but her eyes were closed. Marti wasn't sure if she was breathing. She was so thin, so frail, that they should be able to see her chest move if she was. The room smelled of urine and something else harder to define. Sweat. Scared sweat or maybe sick sweat. She wasn't sure.

"Is she all right, Allan?" she asked.

"Can't tell yet." he said. He began taking her pulse. "Thready," he said. "Let's start an IV."

The woman was wearing a nightgown. Her wispy gray hair was dirty and either sweaty or oily from not being washed. She smelled as if she hadn't bathed in a while, and her skin was dry and flaking.

"This will feel a little cold, ma'am," Allan said, as he began attaching the EKG leads.

The woman moaned when Allan tried to move her.

"Does this hurt, ma'am?" he asked.

She moaned again.

"Something's wrong here. Tell me when it hurts. Does this hurt?" He began with her right hand, repeating the question as he progressed to her wrist, then flexed her right arm at the elbow. She didn't moan again until he touched her left arm. "It's her left arm or shoulder," he said. "Something might be broken."

The elderly had brittle bones. She could have broken a rib during a spasm of coughing.

Allan had a hard time finding a vein. "Dehydrated," he said. He numbed the back of her hand before starting the line.

Marti would have felt better if Ben were here, but Allan was doing a good job. She would have to remember to tell Ben that. He was Allan's supervisor and had helped train him.

While Allan worked on the old woman, Marti took a quick look around. This was a closed-in porch, small. Just a table and a dresser besides the twin bed. Dirty dishes on a tray. The tableware held her attention. The knife and fork were on a used napkin that had been smoothed out and neatly folded. Along with the spoon, everything was aligned on either side of a custard cup.

She took another look around. A quilt was folded at the foot of the bed. A pair of sensible shoes and a pair of slippers were neatly aligned by the wall. A brush, comb, lotion, powder, toothbrush, toothpaste were arranged on the small, three-drawer dresser. They were in alphabetical order—by accident or design? Her skin prickled.

Vik came to the door. "Her name is Opal Jhanke. She lives here with her son, Fred Jhanke Junior. Her husband is deceased. Is she going to be okay?"

"We're stabilizing her now," Allan said.

Marti asked for some gauze pads and moistened them at the kitchen sink. She returned to the backroom and washed Mrs. Jhanke's face. Then she found a Chap Stick in her purse and applied it to the old woman's lips.

Allan looked up and smiled at Marti. "From the looks of it she's been here unattended for a while. I'll swab out her mouth as soon as I get this IV going. She's gone a long time without anything to drink."

Opal wished for the energy to open her eyes or say thank you. The warm water felt so good on her face. It had been so long since she had had a bath or a shower. And her lips, they had been so dry. Now if she could just have some water. She tried to speak but could not. He had finally come home and called an ambulance. He hadn't left her here to die. He'd seen that she had hurt herself and gotten help. He was a good boy. She had always known that. He hadn't meant to set the fire that destroyed their cabin in Wisconsin. He had just been playing with matches. All children did. They almost hadn't made it out, but there he was, waiting for them in the yard when they did. He had run to the neighbors to get help. She understood that. She understood that children did leave their skates on the basement steps when He Senior tripped on them and broke his leg. She knew that children were mean to each other and made up stories. She knew they were lying when they blamed Fred Junior if their kitten or puppy or rabbit ran away.

He had been a difficult child to love sometimes, but he was a good boy. He was quiet and much too serious, and she could hardly ever make him laugh or smile. He'd refused to be cuddled or comforted or held. He wouldn't sit on her lap or let her sing to him. He wouldn't even take her breast when he was a baby. But he was her child, a good boy, and she loved him. And now she knew beyond any doubt that he really did love her too.

He went to the same doorway where he had stood the night before and pulled out his binoculars. Their car was not parked in the same place. He scanned the lot for fifteen minutes without being about to determine which car was theirs. He would have to get closer. He might have to walk through the parking lot a few times to find it. He waited, watching to see what foot traffic was like, surprised when nobody went into or out of the station. The county jail was three blocks away. He decided they must take prisoners there when they were arrested, and for a moment he felt safe. Then an officer in a uniform came outside. He would have to be very careful. Two sides of the parking lot were close to the street; one side was right next to the police station. He chose the side that was abutted by some municipal buildings.

A car pulled into the parking lot, and the cops who had come to his house got out. He stepped back into the doorway, out of sight, as they went inside. His heart began beating so fast that he had to breathe fast. The car he was looking for was parked in the second row from the municipal buildings, three cars from a side street. His feet felt like lead as he lifted one, then the other, then carefully crossed the street. His head throbbed as he got under the car. By the time he'd decided on the left rear wheel and attached the bomb, he was drenched in sweat. He stopped, listened for anything that might mean someone was nearby, and when everything stayed quiet came out from under the car and walked quickly to the sidewalk. He wanted to run as fast as he could, but he did not. When he was two blocks away, he looked at his watch. Ten minutes—it had only taken him ten minutes to attach the bomb. Whistling, he went into an all-night burger joint and ordered a cup of coffee, three fish sandwiches, and two orders of fries. He had gotten lucky once tonight. If he got lucky twice, the car and the cops would be history by this time tomorrow.

*   *   *

The house was dark and everyone was in bed when Marti got home. She and Vik had both agreed that it was time to pack it in. They had left Tolley and his men and a couple of uniforms tossing the Jhanke place. Once again she thought of Pandora's box. Time enough to find out what was inside tomorrow. She felt so tired she didn't think she could function with a couple hours of sleep. And, conversely, with the adrenaline still pumping, she wondered how she would get to sleep at all. She turned the house alarm off as soon as she went inside then reset it. As she went upstairs, she thought about taking a shower. Her shoulders ached, her legs ached—later. She was too tired. She thought about the model airplane project and went to the boys' room. Adrenaline combined with apprehension as she opened the door. Why had Theo asked Ben to help him? Two airplanes were on the bureau. She went over to Theo's bed. He stirred when she sat beside him, then opened his eyes, said, "Hi," and closed them again.

"You finished your airplane," she said.

He nodded. "Ben helped. Mike made one too."

She wanted to ask him what that meant, but she didn't think he would be able to tell her. Instead, she sat beside him and began stroking his short, kinky hair.

"Your daddy loves you," she said. "He loves you so much, and he is so very proud of you." She didn't use the past tense, because she didn't believe the dead were that far away. They were just in a spiritual dimension.

Theo's shoulders began to shake and she saw that he was crying.

"Come here, sweetheart," she said. And he came into her arms and sobbed. *Such a hard thing for a little child,* she thought, *losing a parent. Such a hard thing to get used to.*

When she got into bed, she snuggled against Ben. He turned without seeming to waken, and she curled her body against his. She thought of their children safe in their beds, of the airplanes on the bureau waiting for flight. Of Johnny, the husband who was no longer beside her and never would be again. Of Carol, Ben's first wife, who would never be here again either. Then she thought of Ezra Downes and his floozy and hoped that at their age she and Ben would feel that romantic about each other. Then she thought of Opal Jhanke. She felt the warmth from Ben's body and the weight of his arm around her and was grateful. "Thank you, God," she said aloud.

"Amen," Ben said, and held her closer.

SUNDAY, MAY 2

Marti's beeper went off at quarter to six Sunday morning. As she reached for it, Ben stirred beside her. She caught a whiff of vanilla as his arm went around her. She resisted the impulse to ignore the call and checked the number. It was Vik, of course. Who else? "Now what?" she demanded when he answered her call.

"Two things. The first one will keep. Thornton died. I sent someone over to pick up Oona and bring her in for questioning before she has a chance to go back to Wisconsin."

Marti lay back against the pillow. It was a struggle to keep her eyes open. "I understand the logic, but I think it's a bit premature."

"We've got enough to hold her on suspicion." His voice sounded hoarse, but she guessed it was fatigue, not a cold.

"I don't want to talk to Oona, Vik. Not until I see what they come up with on the purse. We still don't have the weapon. We don't know how strong the fiber evidence is yet." Maybe bringing her in wasn't such a bad idea. Oona tended to get emotional. She also had a tendency to keep talking when she should keep her mouth shut. A few hours in a confined space could increase those possibilities to their advantage.

"Second, it looks like Jhanke is our bomber. Tolley called, wants us to meet him there."

"Where are you?" she asked.

"Still at home."

"Do we have a warrant out for Jhanke?"

"Yes."

"Good. That means we're looking for him and there's not a lot we can do until we find him. I need a couple more hours of shut-eye. So do you. Let's plan to meet Tolley at the Jhanke place at ten."

"Sounds good," Vik agreed.

Ben reached out and took the receiver. Eyes closed, he replaced it. "I barely remember you coming in. What time was it?"

"Close to three."

"Three hours' sleep and you're not ready to get up?"

"I don't even want to open my eyes yet." The days were gone when she could function at full capacity after going three or four days without getting enough sleep. These days she worried that she would overlook something because she was too tired to notice. "Are you going to church?"

"Yes, but you were right about getting more sleep. I'll reset the clock for nine-thirty."

"I'll miss roll call."

"They won't fire you." Ben reached up and changed the alarm.

She wanted to tell him about Allan. Later. She needed more sleep.

Momma. She would have to make it to church today. Three o'clock.

Vik's car was parked in the driveway when she reached the Jhanke house. The rain had stopped and the skies were a pale blue. In a few hours they might even have a little sunshine.

Tolley met her at the door. "Wait until you see this, MacAlister. Your partner's still in shock."

"Don't tell me we've got another Gacy?" she asked. Her stomach lurched.

"Nah, this isn't Chicago."

"Not yet," Vik said.

She followed him and Vik through a kitchen that was in

perfect order except for the dishes in the sink and a waste-basket filled to capacity. A door opened onto a flight of stairs that led to the basement.

"In here," Tolley said.

They entered a room in the middle of the basement with a large, homemade worktable in the center and a cot with a pillow and folded blanket off to one side.

"Take a look." Tolley opened a cabinet.

There were bottles of what looked like chemicals and all kinds of electrical things inside. Marti checked the labels. Again, everything was in alpha order. "And?"

"Aren't you the one who thought Jhanke might be our mad bomber? This is a bomb factory, MacAlister."

"You're kidding."

"What?" Tolley said. "Don't tell me a big-city cop like yourself had to come to Lincoln Prairie to see a bomb fac-tory."

She took a closer look at the contents of the cabinet. She might have thought some of the stuff was unusual, but she would not have associated it with building bombs. "Big bombs?" she asked. "Or just small ones like the two that went off here?"

"Small stuff," Tolley said. "He's got one of those text-books that were printed then banned in the sixties and sev-enties. Based on what we can see here and the two bombs that went off, he was still learning. Who knows what he might have done a few months or years from now. It's a good thing you two decided to come back here last night. The old lady was damned near dead, and God only knows where he was planning to hit next. Now if we could just find our arsonist."

Marti looked at the contents of the cabinet again. She shivered. Such an ordinary house until you came inside.

Fred Jhanke approached his house on foot. He had parked several blocks away and hadn't noticed any police cars as he walked. Instead of going to the front of the house, he

*turned on the street that ran behind it and took the shortcut
to the backyard. A police van was parked in the driveway.
They were inside his house! How dare they! Heart pounding,
he turned and hurried away.*

*He went to a cash station, withdrew the maximum, then
used a check-cashing card to get more money. He had to get
away for a few days, but where could he go? Not to Chicago.
That place was too dangerous. North, he could go north.
They didn't have a place there anymore, but he knew the Upper Peninsula well. There were a lot of summer places where
he could break in and stay. But . . . the thief. What about the
thief? He could not let him get away with taking that ring.
And if he left before he took care of him, he might not be able
to find him when he came back.*

*Fred decided to head north to an old camping ground
about fifteen miles northwest of Lincoln Prairie. The cabins
weren't winterized, and it would be deserted this time of
year. He stopped and bought food and blankets on the way.
Damn them! Damn them all! Invading his home, driving him
away. Who in the hell did they think they were? He should go
back and blow up their van. If it was still there tonight, after
he set fire to the thief's house, maybe he would. After all, it
wouldn't be the first cop car to go up in smoke today.*

Opal awakened to the sound of beeping. She was too tired to
open her eyes and see what was causing it. An alarm clock?
But where? And her arm, she couldn't move it at all. It
felt . . . something tight . . . bandages maybe. Where was
she? She could hear other sounds, people talking, something
like metal hitting against metal. She wasn't at home anymore. Someone had helped her. Where was she now?

"Opal? Are you waking up now, dear?"

A woman. She spoke with an accent.

"Do you know where you are, Opal?"

She tried to move her head from side to side.

"Opal, you're in the hospital. I'm Carmen, your nurse.
I'm going to take care of you."

The woman's voice was kind.

"I'm just going to check a few things here, dear. I won't hurt you. Everything is fine."

It was so good to hear someone speaking to her, even though she couldn't answer.

"Perhaps you'll have visitors later."

Fred. Where was Fred? Would he come to see her soon? Would he make her leave? She wanted to stay here. She wanted to stay. No visitors. How could she tell them? No visitors. Not Fred.

"I'll be back in just a little while to check on you again."

No. She didn't want her to leave. Please stay.

Opal listened to voices too far away for her to make out what they were saying. Voices. People. She wasn't alone. The woman must be nearby. She felt a sudden, crushing pain in her chest and the beeping got faster, much faster.

Marti made a detour to a florist that was open on Sunday and ordered a dozen roses for Momma to be delivered to the church for Momma's big day. She would get there on time, but just in case . . . She didn't get to the precinct until after eleven o'clock. Vik, Cowboy, and Slim were there when she came in. Cowboy tipped his five-gallon hat and said, "Good morning, Miz MacAlister-Walker."

She waited for some smart remark from Slim about the lateness of the hour, but Slim didn't say anything at all. And maybe it was her imagination, but the odor of Obsession for Men was not as overwhelming as it usually was. She helped herself to coffee and a doughnut. Thanks to a little extra shut-eye, she felt wide awake. She wasn't sure how long the feeling would last.

As soon as she sat down, Vik said, "Don't get too comfortable. We have a noon meeting with the lieutenant, and we've got to go down and take a look at the contents of Virginia's purse first."

"We don't have enough to hold Oona."

He tapped his pencil on a yellow legal pad. The top sheet was half filled with his squiggling handwriting. "Oh yes, we do. We've got a green sport utility vehicle with Wisconsin license plates registered to her nearest neighbor and a couple of witnesses who saw a similar vehicle at the forest preserve."

"Did the neighbor say they gave her the use of the car?"

"Yes, a week ago Thursday."

"Such a coincidence. Did she give us any trouble?"

"She came in squealing like a stuck pig. Her brother has called three times, but interestingly enough, he hasn't shown up. Their lawyer has called and insists on being present when we talk to her, which is fine with me. As I see it, that buys us a little time, if we need it. Whenever we do call him, he's not going to rush right down here. We can both play the cool-your-heels game."

With that taken care of, Marti turned her attention to the old woman. Poor old dear. Who knew how long she had lain there like that. It was a wonder she hadn't died. How could anyone treat his own mother like that? She knew it happened all the time, but whenever she had the misfortune to see it up close, look at frail and helpless old people who were neglected or abused, it still seemed incomprehensible. Helpless was the key factor, she had concluded, whether it was the very young or the very old. Those who felt the least powerful and most needed to control chose those who were weaker than they were to mistreat.

"Is there any word on Opal Jhanke, Vik?"

"The prognosis isn't good. She's in Intensive Care and in bad shape: dehydrated, dislocated shoulder, broken ribs."

"And her injuries were caused by her son."

"She's not responsive, so she can't tell us yet; but it fits. He builds bombs."

"And we haven't located him." That was a lot more important right now than whether or not they charged Oona Thornton Amstadt with Virginia's homicide. Oona wasn't likely to kill anyone else. Frederick Jhanke was.

Vik checked his watch. "We'd better get moving." He pushed his chair back. "Maybe we'll get lucky with Virginia's purse, and Tolley won't have any more surprises."

Marti gulped down the rest of her coffee, which was still hot but didn't burn her throat, and grabbed what was left of her doughnut. She took a closer look at Vik as they headed for the elevator. He had the usual dark circles under his eyes but no pouches. They had functioned long enough on sleep deprivation to make it a toss-up as to whether or not they could get by for a day or two on adrenaline, caffeine, and sugar.

"Did you go back to sleep after we talked this morning?"

"Until nine."

"Good." She had almost given up on getting enough sleep, but she felt like she had enough to get by, so Vik probably did too.

There was a small room where the evidence was kept where they could look at whatever they needed to without signing it out. Marti read through the list of the contents of Virginia's purse while Vik opened it. In addition to the usual—makeup, pen, checkbook—there were more papers inside.

"Too bad Jhanke and Virginia didn't know each other," Vik said. "If he had burned her place down, he would have saved us a lot of time."

Frederick Jhanke. Someone had to find him and soon. As far as they knew, he hadn't detonated any bombs in any crowded places, but who knew how long that would last. Opal Jhanke was real old. How old was her son?

"What do we know about Jhanke so far, Vik? How old is he? Did the two of you go to school about the the same time?"

Vik thought for a minute. "I'm not sure. I can't even place the name. We should get more information on him when we meet with Tolley and Lefty. It's their case too."

Vik took a thick stack of papers from Virginia's purse. They had been stapled together. From what Marti could see, most were typed, some were Xeroxed copies, and there were copies of newspaper clippings at the back. As Vik flipped through them, his expression went from boredom to interest;

and after a few minutes he was going back and forth from front to back and stopping to take notes. Eventually he said, "So that's it," and passed the papers to her.

"Don't make me read them, Vik. Just tell me."

"Land deals," he said. "Simple land deals. Nothing complicated, just inside information. Virginia's dad, the alderman, was telling his friend, the accountant, about potential land development months down the road. And, lo and behold, when the developers moved in and bought the property, guess who owned it?"

"Thornton," Marti said. "So why couldn't we see that?"

"Because it wasn't spelled out the way it is here. I don't know about the legality of any of it, and I don't know what can be done about it now, if anything, but that's not the point. The state's attorney's office can sort out all of that. Based on this, my guess is that Virginia didn't know a lot when she first suggested this pension. From the dates that these clippings were requested and documents were photocopied, it looks like she only realized what her father and Thornton had been involved in within the past year."

"And she didn't feel that her father had been adequately compensated, or that she was."

"That's my guess."

"So she put this together and went to see the daughter? Why not Thornton?"

"Maybe she saw him too, Marti. Maybe she showed this to all of them. Who knows. What we do know is that Oona saw Virginia a week ago last Thursday at the forest preserve, and that was the last day anyone saw Virginia alive."

Lefty and Tolley were already there when Marti and Vik went into the lieutenant's office. Marti was more than a little surprised to see fresh Danish and a basket with oranges, bananas, and apples. The lieutenant had outdone himself today. Someone had even slipped up and included sugar packets and little containers of cream for the coffee. Vik poured his own, added a reasonable amount of sugar, and filled a Styrofoam cup for Marti.

From where she was sitting, facing the window, she could see that the sun had finally come out. She hadn't paid much attention when she was driving in. She had been thinking of Theo. He'd come in and given her a hug and a kiss before he went to church. Mike had come in and hugged her too. Mike was such an affectionate child, but Theo, usually she had to hug him first.

The lieutenant was munching on an apple. "So you think the man who's setting off bombs might have set fire to a place in Pleasantdale. Why Pleasantdale? Does this mean he set the other fires too?"

Tolley peeled a banana. "I can't make any sense of it. I think he got angry for some reason, didn't have time to put a bomb together, or since we had the beat cops keeping an eye on the place, they scared him away. As for the fire, other than gasoline, which is a very commonly used accelerant, there is no similarity with ours. Our man has been building fires because he has to. This guy was angry. Those people were his target."

"So it's a case of whatever comes to hand?" the lieutenant asked.

"Probably. We don't know how he tracked these people down, how he knew they had been scammed by the same man as his mother, nothing."

"Why are you so certain that it's Jhanke?"

"Because they *are* certain," Tolley said. "And they saw him."

The lieutenant took another bite of his apple, chewed it, and said, "So what does that tell us? The MOs are different."

"What if he is the arsonist too?" Marti asked.

The lieutenant paused midbite and held the apple in the air. "Any reason why you think so?"

"Not really," Marti admitted. "Except that his car was seen near Eureka, and we had a fire there."

"Thin," the lieutenant said.

"I know," she agreed. "But what are the odds on having two lunatics go offtrack at the same time?"

"What would his motivation be?"

She thought about that. "The fire was set in anger. And the bomb . . . That guy who got killed went out on that motorcycle every night at ten or eleven o'clock. The bike was noisy. All the neighbors agreed on that and several seemed annoyed by it."

"And if you're already crazy enough to build a bomb," Vik said, "why not use one to get rid of a pest?"

"Someone who angered you," Marti said.

"That would also have to mean that he was angry about something related to those vacant houses," the lieutenant said.

"This is a nutcase," Vik said. "That's not too farfetched. Hell, the color of the house could have ticked him off, the fact that it was abandoned, an eyesore. You can't apply the usual kind of logic, sir. Everything this guy is doing is logical to him. His reasoning would probably seem silly as hell to us."

"If the arsonist and the bomber are one and the same," Tolley said, working it out, "he set off the bomb and set the last fire in anger. The other fires were set because that's how he gets off."

"And the mailbox bomb?" Vik asked.

"Practice."

The lieutenant looked at what was left of his apple and took another bite. "So what's he mad about?"

"Damned if I know."

"And if he stays mad?" Another bite and he was down to the core.

"I don't know that either."

The lieutenant tossed the apple core into a wastebasket and selected a navel orange. "Are we all in agreement that it is Frederick Jhanke?"

Tolley and Lefty weren't sure. Marti admitted that she wasn't either. Vik shrugged.

"Are we in agreement that we could have one perp and it could be Jhanke?"

They were.

"Why? What have we got?"

Tolley shrugged. "Marti's hunch."

Marti agreed that they needed something concrete to go on. "Were there any papers at the house? Any indication of next of kin? Anything?"

"We brought out a box of stuff. I don't think anyone has had time to go through it yet."

The lieutenant selected an orange. "Then maybe it's time we did."

Marti hesitated as she looked at the box filled with Jhanke's personal papers. She thought of his house, ordinary but isolated—creepy—then thought again of Pandora's box. After what they'd found in his house, what would they find in here?

"Why do people save so much stuff?" Vik complained.

"It's just one box, Vik."

"One damned box too many."

"Here." She took out a ledger and a couple of notebooks and tossed them on his desk. "You look at that; I'll go through these letters."

It took her about fifteen minutes to go through the correspondence. Some of the envelopes were yellow with age. The most recent were utility bills.

"What have you got?" Vik asked. There was a hint of smugness in his voice that made her think of a poker player with a royal flush. She went first anyway.

"Tax bills for some property in Wisconsin, the Upper Peninsula, or UP as people around here like to call it. There are, or were, a couple of cousins up there. The letters are dated thirty-five years ago and addressed to Frederick Senior. There's also a safety deposit box and several bank accounts. Mrs. Jhanke was receiving her husband's retirement pension as well as Social Security. I don't see anything to indicate that Frederick Junior was employed."

"Interesting," Vik said. "This one is a real killer."

Marti felt a little tingle of anticipation. "I'm right, aren't I? He's our arsonist too." She wasn't going to tell him that it wasn't a hunch; that there was just something illogical about having two crazies committing two different types of crimes within such close proximity, a copycat maybe, but not this. Then again, it was just as illogical that an arsonist would start making bombs. Maybe it was a hunch. She hoped that once she knew more about Jhanke, and knew for certain whether or not she was right, she could figure out why she was so certain that it was only him out there.

"Motive," she said. "Anger. What if the fires were displaced anger, and then something happened that made him direct his anger? Didn't Tolley or someone say something about a scam?"

"The pig people were scammed, but let me tell you about—"

"No. Wait. His mother. How old was the pig lady?"

"A hell of a lot younger than his mother. Mid-sixties rings a bell."

Marti thought of Momma. She was sixty-four. "No, that's not old," she agreed. "But if that woman was old enough to fall for that scam, Mrs. Jhanke certainly was."

Vik held up his hand. "Okay, okay. I give. You're right."

"How do you know?"

He tapped the books she had given him. "It's all right here. I think we'd better have another meeting with Tolley and Lefty and the lieutenant."

By the time they were ready to meet with Dirkowitz again, Vik had typed up a list of all of the fires that Jhanke had set, according to his journals and the newspaper clippings that were between the pages.

"Eleven people dead," Vik said, "including a cop. That couple with the pig got real lucky."

Marti read the article about Jhanke's grandparents again. "I wonder what they did to tick him off?"

"Maybe nothing," Vik said. "Maybe he was just perfecting his technique. Maybe he never thought about them at all."

Marti remembered something she had read once about polar bears. One of the reasons why they were so dangerous was because they never revealed anything with their eyes. There was no emotion, no feeling, nothing to warn someone that they were about to attack. She hadn't met Jhanke yet, but this was what he made her think of, a lethally dangerous polar bear who struck without reason, without warning, without remorse.

"So, where is he?" the lieutenant asked.

"We think Jhanke might have headed north," Vik said. "He spent summers in the Upper Peninsula until he burned down the cabin they owned there. It's a good place to run to ground. A lot of people have summer homes there, and they won't be opening them for a while. We've alerted the locals. We'll see."

"No chance he's still here?"

"That's always possible," Marti said, "but we don't think so. He's a loner. And it's not like he's worried about his mother. We've got an APB out on the car and Jhanke, based on the description that the people with the pig gave us. Our artist is working on a composite. We've got a man assigned to watch his house around the clock."

"What's this about his mother?" Dirkowitz asked.

Marti let Vik fill him in.

"Will she be all right?"

Vik shrugged, then shook his head. "It doesn't look good."

"Damned shame," the lieutenant said. "Lefty, how easy would it be for him to build another bomb without accessing the materials he has in the house?"

"It's possible," Lefty said, "but a hell of a lot easier to set a fire."

Marti glanced at Vik. He gave her a thumbs-up. She agreed. The odds were against Jhanke trying anything as complex as building a bomb. Not that that would make a difference to anyone trapped in one of his fires. She glanced at her watch. The Mother's Day program and church was at three and it was 2:35.

"This guy is a nutcase," Vik said. "You're telling me that

he's started three fires this week and detonated a couple of bombs. How likely is it that he can go into the woods for a while without doing what it takes for him to get off? It sounds to me like you're discounting the fact that the man's nuts."

Lefty rubbed at a stubble of beard with the index finger on his left hand, and Marti wondered if he had any feeling in his finger with part of it sliced off.

"We're doing everything we can," Lefty said.

Marti didn't disagree with that, but like Vik, she didn't think it was enough. "I think we need to go to the media with this one. If they put a pig on the ten o'clock news I'm sure they would be delighted to feature the man who burned down the pig's house."

"Two bad there weren't three little pigs," Vik said.

Marti kicked his ankle. "And the newspapers. Put a rush on the artist's drawing."

The lieutenant picked up the grenade. "MacAlister is right. Get on it. If we don't and something happens out there, our asses will really be in a sling." He pointed at Lefty then Tolley. "I don't want any more fires, and I don't want any more bombs. And I sure as hell don't want to up the body count. You see to it that that doesn't happen, and I don't care what it takes." He let the grenade fall to the desk.

Slim and Cowboy were still there when Marti went upstairs.

"What have y'all got this time?" Cowboy drawled. "You find that mad bomber yet?"

Vik launched into a description of Jhanke's "bomb factory," as the basement workroom was now being called.

"We think he might have struck not far from where your mother lives, Slim."

"My mother, Jessenovik? There haven't been any bombs over there."

"We think he does fires too."

"That fire Friday night? I keep telling her to sell that place and move into a condo, but she says it has too many memories."

"It's where you grew up," Vik said.

"No, it's not," Slim said. "I don't give a damn about the place at all. She bought it with her second husband, not my old man."

Marti realized how little she knew about Slim, how seldom he talked about himself or his family.

"Your dad was a preacher, wasn't he?" Vik asked.

"Right. Her second husband was too."

Marti noted that it was "second husband," not "my step-father."

Slim reached for his jacket. "Maybe now she'll start thinking about moving. That neighborhood is going to shit."

And on that note, Slim and Cowboy left.

Marti checked her watch again. The program at church had begun and she wasn't there, and there was no way that she would be. She pulled Virginia McCroft's file, flipped through the first few pages, and reached for the phone. There were only two cab companies in town, but even so, it took close to three-quarters of an hour to identify the one that sent a driver to pick up a woman at Thornton's place and drop her off at the forest preserve. Even then the person she spoke with had to call the driver to confirm that he was, in fact, the one who had actually picked up the fare because "sometimes someone else is closer." She wondered what kind of records they kept.

"The driver had to circle around because of the fire engines," she told Vik. "His description of the passenger fits Miss Oona."

Vik poured another cup of coffee, but he didn't lace it with extra instant or a lot of sugar. "Did the driver see her get into the sport utility vehicle?"

"Yes. It was dark when he dropped her off, so he waited until she was inside before pulling off. It was also the only vehicle in the parking lot."

Vik came close to smiling. "We've got a lot to talk about when we get around to questioning her."

Marti checked her watch again and wondered what she

was missing, besides the expression on Momma's face. Had they given her the roses yet? "Damn."

"What?" Vik asked.

"It's Mother's Day and I was supposed to be at church at three."

"MacAlister, Mother's Day is next Sunday."

"It is? Vik, if you weren't married I'd hug you."

Vik almost broke into a smile.

Fred sat on the floor in a corner of the small cabin. The place was empty but there was a fireplace, not that he could build a fire and let them know someone was in here. He wrapped up in the blankets and poured hot coffee from a thermos. They were at his house. They must have found Mother. Was she still alive? She should have died in her bed, like Father, with a plastic bag over his head. As sick as he was, how frightened he had been. Mother was always frightened. Still . . . no matter. He didn't have to worry about her anymore. He didn't have to worry about either of his parents ever again. He looked about the room. Cobwebs, dust. How could anyone live like this? He put the coffee down and began scratching his arms. One day. He could do this for one day. He would have to. Tonight he would set his last fire in Lincoln Prairie. First thing tomorrow morning he would draw everything out of the bank and get what was in the safety deposit box, then he would head for California.

Marti and Vik met with Oona and her attorney in a small room with pink walls and glass windows, where they could not be heard but they could be seen. Oona's eyes were red and swollen. Her hair hung in brown disarray.

"How could you do this to me? My father is dead. How could you do this to me now?"

Marti said nothing. This was a different Oona, emotional but not defiant. Maybe they could deal with this Oona, get to the truth.

"I have babies at home," she said. "I've got a funeral . . ." She began to cry.

Marti spoke to her attorney. Maybe they could resolve

this without too much hassle. "We have sufficient evidence to place Mrs. Amstadt at the scene of a homicide with the victim, Virginia McCroft. We have sufficient evidence to prove motive."

"Could you be more specific?"

Marti didn't recognize the attorney. He was a young man, with light brown hair that fell across his forehead. He had large hands and wore a wedding band.

"Mrs. Amstadt's father was paying Miss McCroft for keeping certain family secrets. Miss McCroft was in need of additional funds and was asking for more."

"And not getting one more cent," Oona said. "My father is dead because of her."

Marti didn't bother to remind Oona that Virginia had died first, and from the looks of it, she had killed her. She checked her watch. Three-thirty.

The lawyer reached out and patted Oona's hand. "Just stay calm."

He turned to Marti. "Could you be a little more specific as to how you have determined that my client was with the victim?"

"She was seen by three witnesses. We have identified her and the vehicle she was driving."

Oona sobbed loudly. This was very different from what Marti had expected. "My father," she said. "My father. I want my husband. I want to see my babies. Andy needs me." She looked at Marti. "You sonsabitches, my father is dead! He's dead! My father!" That was more like it. She began sobbing again.

"Can I have a little time with my client?" the lawyer said. He spoke quietly and seemed totally unperturbed. Maybe he would have a calming effect on Oona.

While they waited, Vik said, "Let's hope he talks her into cooperating. Even if we find out that she was carrying a gun when she went to see Virginia, a lot of farm people keep guns to get rid of pests. That doesn't necessarily make it premeditated."

Marti couldn't believe Vik was saying this. Oona wasn't

the type to gain his sympathy. She thought of the child's table in the great room and the basket with coloring books and crayons. That was it, she decided. She wondered why Oona had waited so long to have children.

Mildred Jessenovik was there when they reached their office. She was leaning on a walker and another woman was with her. It was the first time Mildred had come to the precinct since Marti had worked here.

"Is everything okay?" Vik asked.

Mildred nodded. She was a petite woman with short, blonde hair becoming white and a face almost untouched by wrinkles. She wore a touch of lipstick but no other makeup as far as Marti could tell. When Mildred and Vik looked at each other, it was as if a pleasant secret passed between them. They both smiled. It was an intimate smile, like a kiss.

"What brings you two here?" Vik asked.

"We're going to go out for coffee," Mildred said, "while Essie has a little talk with Marti."

Essie. Virginia's friend.

Vik gave Marti a look filled with questions. She made a motion with her thumb that said get out of here. He grabbed his trench coat. "Did you say coffee? Let's go."

Mildred came over and gave her a hug. "I can't believe how well he behaves for you," she whispered. She and Marti laughed.

Essie Wojtowicz was slender to the point of being skinny. She was a nervous woman who fidgeted with her hands as if she were looking for a cigarette. Up close, Marti could see the gray that streaked her blonde hair. There were lines at the corners of her mouth, as if she frowned or laughed a lot.

"How can I help you?" Marti asked.

Essie sat with her head down, twisting her hands. She took a deep breath. "It's about Virginia."

"Can I get you some coffee?" Marti asked. She had all day to talk about Virginia.

Essie shook her head.

"You were friends," Marti said.

Her chin trembled as she nodded.

"It's all right, Essie. We're alone. No one can hear you."

"It's . . . it's about him."

Marti waited. Essie plucked at her sweater even though there were no fuzz balls. It was a lovely turquoise sweater that brought out the blonde highlights in her hair.

"He . . . we . . . he was so mysterious . . . different. He wasn't like the other boys. It was as if he was . . . dangerous . . . but of course we knew he wasn't . . . but thinking so was a delicious kind of fun."

Marti wondered who *he* was, but didn't ask.

"One day I met him . . . Lynn had—she was Virginia's friend—Lynn had met him a couple of times, said he wasn't her type . . . but he was . . . he was . . . nobody else in school was like him . . . they were boys . . . but he . . . he was a real man."

She was pulling at the sweater now, tugging hard enough to tear it.

"It was so scary . . . so daring . . . to meet him. I wasn't afraid, not of him. . . . Lynn had met him . . . said it was fun. But my parents . . . they would have killed me if they'd found out . . . and my friends . . . I wasn't like Lynn. I was always . . . just me . . . not the life of anything . . . and Virginia . . . Well, he hadn't asked her . . . At least not yet."

She stopped talking, stopped plucking at the sweater for a moment. "It was the only time in my life that I'd ever got asked to do something special that Virginia hadn't already done." She sounded sad. "It was the only time a special boy ever asked me out at all. And this one, Virginia liked him. She liked him a lot."

She sat very still, then squeezed her eyes shut. She took several deep breaths and opened her mouth, but nothing came out.

"It . . . he . . ." She gulped in a deep breath of air. "Rape . . . but he . . . he . . . couldn't . . . so he tried—"

She clutched the sweater so tightly that her fingers were white. "He couldn't." She began shaking, first her shoulders, then the entire upper half of her body. Marti wanted to hold her, but she did not want her to stop talking.

"He tried ... he tried to use ... something else. ... I screamed ... he covered my mouth ... thought he was going to kill me ... I bit his hand ... and ran."

Essie wrapped her arms around herself and sat there, shaking.

"It's all right," Marti said. "He can't hurt you now." Who was "he"?

"It was Jimmy," she said.

Jimmy? Where had she heard that name? She couldn't place it, but she had heard that name in the past few days. She had heard someone mention that name.

Marti pressed Kleenex into Essie's hands. "Jimmy who?"

"Horace Warren. Nobody called him that though. He'd fight anyone who did. Jimmy, we called him Jimmy."

Jimmy. Why couldn't she remember? Maybe it was in her notes.

Essie wept silent tears that streamed down her face until the sound of her noiseless crying seemed to fill the whole room. Marti pulled a chair up and held her until she calmed down.

"Did you tell anyone?"

"It was ... rape ... almost. Good girls didn't get raped."

Marti understood that. In those days, it would have been considered Essie's fault.

"I should have told Virginia though." She trembled again. "Poor Virginia."

"Did he do the same thing to her?"

"Yes, but I think ... I think he succeeded, but with ... with the thing."

"What thing?"

"I don't ... I ... It looked like it was supposed to ... but it was made out of wood ... and big, way too big."

"Wouldn't Virginia have screamed too?"

"Yes, but no one would have heard her."

"Why not?"

"We were at his house. In the basement. Nobody else was there."

"Essie, during this time, did you know anyone named Frederick Jhanke?"

"Jhanke?" She seemed puzzled. "I can't remember anyone by that name. Of course we all kept to our own little groups. Should I know him?"

"Perhaps not."

By the time Mildred and Vik returned, Essie was sipping hot chocolate. Marti had found a couple of packets in Traffic's office while she was looking for tea bags. Essie didn't drink coffee.

Essie hadn't married either. She lived alone in a small apartment. She still seemed so upset that Marti was concerned about her being alone.

Mildred took one hand off her walker and patted Essie's shoulder. "Essie's going to stay with us for a few days, Matthew."

Vik looked from one of them to the other, but he didn't ask why until Mildred and Essie were gone.

"Mother of God," he said. "Holy Mother of God. I always thought she was a pain in the ass, the way she was always so overprotective of everyone's kids. And afraid, afraid of her own shadow. You should see where she lives. Fourth floor, door has more locks than a fortress. You have to get buzzed into three doors before you can enter the building."

"Do you think it has anything to do with Jhanke setting the fire there?"

"I don't know. What did Essie say? Did you ask her?"

"His name didn't mean anything."

"I never hung out with the Warren kids. They weren't into sports and their old man was a drunk. Never caused any trouble, but a drunk." Horace too. He thought for a few minutes. "Damn. We've got Virginia's body in the basement of the house where she was raped years ago by a man long dead. And we've got Jhanke setting fire to the place four days after she died. Maybe there's no connection. Who knows. There's nothing about Essie or Virginia in his journals." Vik put his chin in his hands and looked down at his desk. "Essie. My God, why didn't she tell anyone?"

"Good girls don't get raped, Vik," Marti reminded him.

"But they do," he said. "We know they do. Hell, if it was about sex appeal, he would have left Essie alone."

"It's about power, Vik, and if Essie was as timid then as she is now, this guy would have found her irresistible."

"Then why Virginia? She wasn't like Essie at all."

But she must have been, somewhere inside. Had their rapist seen that vulnerability? Maybe he was just figuring out how to entice girls to go with him when he got Essie to go to the Warren place. Maybe the rapes began with Virginia.

"Do you remember someone named Lynn who might have been good friends with Virginia?"

"Lynn. It must have been Lynn Wiley. She died a few years ago, cancer." He thought about that for a minute. "He didn't rape her too?"

"It doesn't sound that way." But there had been enough spoken, enough remembered. *More than enough,* Marti thought.

Oona's lawyer sent for them a short time later and asked to have someone there to record a statement. Oona had quieted down. She looked exhausted. For the first time, Marti felt a twinge of sympathy.

"Oona," the lawyer said. "Why don't you tell them."

"She wanted more money," Oona said, almost without emotion. "Poppa wanted to give it to her. He said she had it coming and now that she had found out about all the land deals with her father, we should give it to her. He said that even though her father died before a lot of the land was sold, he had cheated him by cheating her."

Marti had never seen her this calm, but she knew it was most likely delayed shock because of her father's death and being incarcerated so soon afterward.

"He was right. Andy was right. He thought we should pay her off too. I don't know why I was so stubborn about it.

Lord knows we don't need the money. She wasn't asking for that much, just a thousand a month instead of five hundred. We could have done that easily enough. I don't know why I wouldn't. She was just so demanding. It rubbed me the wrong way and I refused. Maybe if I hadn't, neither she nor my father would be dead." She sat very still and looked down at her hands.

"Tell me about that Thursday night," Marti said.

"We had talked on the phone. She talked. I yelled. She said she would go to the police. I told her she couldn't, that she didn't have proof, and she said oh yes she did. So we agreed to meet at the forest preserve."

"Why there?"

"She said she had to meet someone else there."

Jhanke? "Did she say who?"

"No, but I was a few minutes late and she was damned mad and in a hurry. She kept walking toward one of the paths and looking somewhere and coming back. She said he was late."

"He?"

"Yes." Oona looked at her lawyer. He nodded.

"This sounds so childish," she said. "At first we sat in my chair—my friend's car, mine was in for a tune-up. Then she looked at her watch, got out, went over to check whatever she was checking. I got out too. We were parked side by side, and she left her purse and her keys in her car. She gave me this Xeroxed set of papers that she said was proof. I didn't know what it was, what I was reading. I got mad, real mad, called her a few names, called her a bitch, then a whore. Something about whore set her off. She hit me. I hit her back, hard across the face. She ran toward the trail. I locked my car, got in her car, and took off. I left her stranded there." Her voice broke. "It was getting dark. She was a woman. Alone. I took her car and left her there. And then she was dead. My fault," she said. "All of it. My fault. When Poppa found out she was dead and I had driven her car home, he made me tell him." She wiped at her eyes. "He didn't get angry, he just gave me that sad look of his and said, 'Oona, why can't you ever just use your head? Why don't you think first, just once in a while? Why couldn't you just give her the money, Oona? She was just trying to take care of her mother.' "

She dabbed at her tears and sniffled. "And now he's dead. They're both dead."

Marti almost pointed out that Thornton did smoke and did have emphysema and was as responsible for his death as anyone else, but then again, guilt seemed to become Oona. She wore it well. Too bad they couldn't hold her for a few more hours. Then she thought of Oona's kids and was glad she could go home. Still, a few more hours . . . she was beginning to think like Vik.

Fred couldn't stand being in the cabin. It was cold. Dirty. He had no way to prepare food. He was hungry. He had to use the outhouse and it smelled. Damn. There was no way he could go back. But he had to. They had taken over his house, and if they knew where he lived, they must know what kind of a car he drove too. What if he was in a different car? Maybe that would work. He would have to risk leaving here.

An hour later he was in Kenosha. He had stopped at an ATM again and cashed two more checks for cash. He had fifteen hundred dollars, enough to buy some kind of car, but if he did, he would be remembered. He drove around the most impoverished neighborhood he could find until he saw a car with a FOR SALE sign. The car was a small Honda, yellow and rusty and old. He hoped it would start and run long enough to get him back to Lincoln Prairie and then out of town, Chicago maybe. He could buy another car there and drive to California.

The car was parked in front of a house with peeling paint and sagging steps. Even though it was getting dark, three dogs and five children were playing in a yard that was more dirt than grass. He didn't want to go inside. He called to one of the children and asked to speak to the car owner. The child ran inside and a few minutes later a middle-aged man with a drooping moustache came out. He was wearing a T-

shirt with the sleeves torn out and jeans with holes at the knees.

"I'll give you this car and two hundred dollars for that car."

"This car?" the man asked.

Fred was hoping for someone who wasn't too smart, but knowledge filled the man's eyes. He was smart enough to know that a deal this good could only mean one of two things—just trouble or trouble and the cops.

"I've got the title," Fred said. "I'll sign it over to you and give you the two hundred. Have you got the title for that?"

"Sure," the man said, "but it will cost you the car and four hundred dollars."

Fred thought about coming back and burning the man's house down with the dogs and the children inside. Too bad he wouldn't have time.

"Three hundred," he said, then added, "there's another car a couple of blocks from here," hoping the man would think about being too greedy and ending up with nothing at all.

"I'll be right back with my title," the man said. "You just wait right here."

Fred drove off without it.

Vik paced the distance from the coffeemaker to his desk twice.

"Sit," Marti ordered. She couldn't stand any pacing today.

"Damn!" Vik said. He sat on the edge of his desk. "Leave it to Virginia. We no sooner clear one suspect and come up with another than we get someone else out of the blue. Who in the hell was she going to meet at the forest preserve? What he? Jhanke? Why Jhanke? If not Jhanke, then who?"

He got up, stretched, and walked over to the spider plant to give it the dregs from his coffee. He snapped off a couple of plant babies that were dangling from the mother plant and crushed them. "Damn!" he said again.

Jimmy. The name came back to her again. Marti could not think of where she had heard that name and she didn't have anything on it in her notes. She mentioned it to Vik.

"Virginia's mother," he said.

Marti remembered as soon as he said it. She hated loose ends.

Geoffrey stayed in bed until Sister Hawkins got home from church about five and began playing gospel music—loud. How he hated it here. He was going to go home. To hell with the cat, to hell with the birds, to hell with Aunt Precious. There was room enough in Mama's house for them all. He had his suitcase out of the closet before he remembered that he had to see Deacon Evans today. He didn't know why the old man thought his work week included Saturdays and Sundays, but they would get that straightened out today. He had had enough. He was going to quit. He was going to quit and go home.

The deacon was in his office reading the Sunday paper when Geoffrey walked in. There were several Chinese food containers on the old man's desk, reminding Geoffrey that he hadn't eaten since breakfast.

"Mind?" he said.

"Help yourself."

While he ate, the old man pulled a folder out of a drawer. "There's been something I've been meaning to talk to you about." He flipped open the folder.

Geoffrey recognized his spreadsheet. He didn't care if the old man had caught the math calculation. As soon as Evans said something, he was going to tell him just what he could do with this job.

"I saw your mother at church today," Deacon Evans said, "her and Precious."

Not that again. Evans didn't have to live with either of them. What did he know?

"Neither of them's had much bragging rights, but they are good, decent women. They loved their husbands, and they both raised you children, and they are deserving of more than they got."

Evans put the spreadsheet to one side. There was a copy of a deposit slip beneath it. "Now I know it's hard sometimes for a man raised mostly by his mother. But a man has to stop being a boy one day and start doing his mama proud. And it's time you did that, son. It's time you did that."

Just who in the hell did he think he was? He wasn't nobody's daddy. Never had been. Geoffrey started to say something, but before he could, Deacon Evans raised his hand to silence him.

"Now, I do need some honest help around here, and I think with a little effort you can become that. Your daddy was an honest man. Kept his rental units clean and roach-and rat-free and in good repair, never charged enough rent, let alone too much. A good, God-fearing man, Henderson was. Raised his sons to be honest men, and he would be dishonored and ashamed if his sons turned out any different."

He closed the folder. "Now, what I think has to happen here is that you need to go spend the day with your mama and your auntie. Tomorrow, you get back to work. You might not know nothing about computers yet, but you're smart, too smart maybe, and you'll learn. As for this," he tapped the folder with a thick, blunt, yellowing fingernail. "We'll forget about this. For now." He slid the folder into the drawer. "You go on home now and be a good son to your mother."

Geoffrey left quietly. He didn't want Mama to know what was in that file. He got into the car and just sat there. What had he gotten himself into? He had no scam, no home, no nothing, just some church sister who woke him up at an ungodly hour, an old man who expected him to do real work, and Mama, and Aunt Precious too. He started the car. Maybe this was his lucky day after all and when he got to Mama's, not only would he have collard greens and dressing and ham, but Calvin would be there to find fault and Miles Davis would pee on his shoe.

* * *

A doctor was with Opal Jhanke when Marti and Vik walked into her hospital room. He looked at them and shrugged. Opal was breathing on her own. Her eyes were closed and she appeared to be sleeping, but Marti couldn't tell the difference between sleep and a coma. The doctor checked the machines that beeped and hummed. When he was finished with his brief examination, they followed him to the desk and waited while he made a few notes on a chart.

"She's not doing well," he explained, when they identified themselves. "There was no order not to resuscitate, and so we did. She does not require assistance to breathe although we are giving her oxygen. There is brain activity. All of her organs are functioning. She is stable. We shall see."

"How long will she be like this?"

"She has experienced a great deal of trauma. If she can hold on for a few days, and rest, perhaps she will recover. Who can say?"

Marti got into Vik's car on the passenger side. For one of the few times since they had been working together, she wasn't the duty driver.

"Roll down your window and listen," he said, as he turned the key in the ignition. "I think something's wrong with the transmission."

Marti listened. The engine seemed to hesitate when he pressed on the accelerator and there was a rattling noise, but she didn't know what that might mean.

"It sounds like you should take it to the shop and find out what's wrong."

Marti didn't say anything about Vik's driving until after he'd made three lane changes without signaling and come to a rolling stop at a stop sign.

"When we get back to the precinct we'll take the un-marked vehicle and you can drive, MacAlister. Right now I'm trying to figure out what's wrong with my car."

"And how does going through stop signs, exceeding the speed limit, and making illegal turns help you do that?"

"I need to see how the car responds under adverse driving conditions."

"The only adverse driving condition I can identify is the driver. Next you'll be driving the wrong way on one-way streets."

"That's not a bad idea."

They drove the rest of the way in silence. Their first stop was the nursing home.

"We'll probably get as much out of these two birds as we did with Mrs. Jhanke," Vik complained. "We've already seen enough of them to know what the odds are that they'll say anything intelligent. I can't come up with any connection between Jhanke and Virginia. I don't think there is one. And guess what: I think the odds are almost nonexistent for finding out who offed her and why. Know how I feel about that?"

"Yes," she said. "Like I would if someone I went to school with died and I couldn't get to the bottom of it."

An older man was sitting with Mrs. McCroft, who was lying back on her pillows. She smiled and fussed with a pink, ruffled bed jacket when she saw them. The man introduced himself as her nephew from Minnesota. "I've come to take Libby home and make arrangements for Virginia to be up north with the rest of the family," he said.

"We're moving," Mrs. McCroft said. She sounded excited. "Don't forget to get Virginia's school records."

"Her high school records?" Marti asked.

Mrs. McCroft seemed puzzled, then she brightened and said, "Oh yes, that's right, Virginia is in high school now."

"I think she's with Essie," Marti said.

"Oh, that's good. Essie is such a sweet, obedient child, not headstrong like Virginia."

Vik gave her a look that suggested that this was all a waste of time. Marti ignored it.

"Yes, we all like Essie," Marti agreed. "She's not like Lynn at all, is she."

"Virginia's not with Lynn, is she?"

"I'm not sure," Marti said. "She did say something about going with Lynn to see Jimmy."

"No," Mrs. McCroft whispered, "not him. He's not a very nice boy."

"Have you met him?"

"No, but the girls whisper when they talk about him so I can't hear what they say." She turned to her cousin. "How is Flossy going to travel? She's never even been outside without a leash."

Her nephew patted her hand. "She'll do just fine," he said.

Marti checked her watch. It was getting late. If she was going to see Mrs. Rosenblum before bedtime, she would have to see her now. The same nurse was there when she went to her room. Mrs. Rosenblum remembered them. Marti wished Mrs. McCroft's mind was as good.

"It's so nice to see both of you again. Stanley was here yesterday and I told him I had seen you. He wasn't the least bit interested, but you know Stanley. Always preoccupied. I thought he might come today, but he usually spends Sundays chatting with friends. At least that's what he says. 'I was chatting with my friends, Mother.' As if he has so many that it would take him all day. If you see him before I do, would you please tell him that I need more of the lavender bath salts. They're so hard to find. I'm not sure where he gets them now, but I'm almost out."

"Perhaps you could call him," Marti suggested.

"Oh, no, dear, the line is tied up."

Marti wished she had a specific question to ask. When Mrs. Rosenblum began talking about her late husband, Marti made an excuse and they left. Vik gave her a look that said, *Waste of time,* but he didn't say it out loud.

"So," Vik said, as they headed back to the precinct. "What do you know now that you didn't know before we came here?"

"That Rosenblum likes to talk on the phone."

And more: She knew that neither Virginia nor Essie had gotten over their experiences with Warren. She knew that Virginia would have had a strong and negative reaction to seeing what was on that diskette. What she didn't know was if, or how, or why that was important.

CHAPTER 38

Fred waited until it was dark before returning to Lincoln Prairie. The car didn't make any noise. Its engine was in better condition than he expected, but he thought by the smell that something was wrong with the electrical wiring. No matter. He only needed it until tomorrow. Even if it was something major, nothing would happen unless there was a spark and some fuel.

The police van was no longer parked in his driveway, but he drove past anyway. They were trying to trick him. He knew that someone was waiting inside. When he drove by the house where the thief lived, the tan car was not parked outside. He turned the corner a few times. When he passed the house he had burned down, he slowed to see the damage. The place had been gutted. Too bad he hadn't been able to stick around. He watched for police cars, but there were none. When he finally did spot one, he pulled in front of it. Nothing. They were watching for the car, not him.

He drove past the thief's house one last time, still no car. He was leaving tomorrow. If he had to burn the place down without the thief inside, so be it. He thought of the block-long building where he had seen the man park and drove past that place too—no car. This would be an easier place to set a fire. And bigger—an entire block in flames. If he succeeded, it would be the most beautiful, most spectacular fire—better than the fire at the Warren place, bigger and better than any fire he had ever set in his life. A fire that nobody in Lincoln Prairie would ever forget.

* * *

Marti returned to the precinct and went through her notes. There had to be something she was missing. She felt as if she had overlooked something somehow, but she couldn't figure out what it was.

"We've covered everything, MacAlister. I'm sure of it."

It didn't seem possible with all they did know that she couldn't find a motive or identify a suspect in Virginia's death or determine if the diskette was important.

"Jhanke couldn't have killed her," she said. "Nothing connects them but the fire, and she was long dead by then. Rosenblum doesn't have a motive."

Vik threw up his hands. "Marti, the mayor had it right. Virginia was a public nuisance. What can I say? She still is. And I'm starving. I'm ordering in. What do you want?"

"Burgers," she said. "And lots of fries. And order a salad, so I can tell that to Joanna if she asks, then cancel it." Joanna could always tell when she lied.

Her neck ached. She did some stretching exercises that didn't help and wished Ben were here to massage it. "So Virginia finds this diskette somehow. It sets her off, gets her to remembering what happened between her and Warren, whatever. For some reason she decides to go to the Warren house." That did make some sense. "She needed closure. She was in a relationship with Rosenblum and somehow came in possession of this diskette. You know, Vik, I thought that idea of yours, about kids putting it in her mailbox as a joke, sounded unlikely. But the more I find out about Virginia, the more possible it becomes, if only because of the odds of her stumbling over it any other way. So maybe the diskette sets her off; she realizes she needs to get over it, get on with her life, thinks that confronting what happened at the Warren place will help. She arranges to meet Oona first because she also has to get her finances in order. Oona upsets her; she has to get away from her. Mean little Oona takes the car."

"That sounds plausible, MacAlister. It sounds good. I know it's not quite as tight as you like it, but we're not dealing with two competent minds here. That brings us to the gun. Why did Virginia take a gun with her?"

The gun was part of what was wrong. "Maybe she brought the gun for protection."

"I can buy that. But from what? Did she think Oona was a threat? Or did she plan to meet someone in that house? And if so, who? It couldn't have been Warren."

"Vik, shut up. We're getting nowhere. Let's focus on Jhanke for a while." She filled her coffee cup again and wondered how many cups she had had today. She was beginning to feel wired.

She put in a call to the locals in Pleasantdale.

"Now what?" Vik asked, when she hung up.

She dialed again. "I'm going to talk with the people who own the pig."

When Mrs. Nordstrom came to the phone, Marti asked about Fred.

"He wanted to know who took the candleholders," the woman said. "Babette and I were on the ten o'clock news and in all the newspapers and he saw us. Oh, and watch the news tonight too. We're on again. Babette saved our lives, you know. She smelled the smoke and woke us up just in time."

"What did you tell this man about the candleholders?"

"He wanted me to describe the man who installed the alarm. He said the same man had taken advantage of his mother and had her watch. He wanted to know what the man looked like, so I told him as best I could remember."

"What did you tell him?"

"That the man was nice-looking and smooth-talking and colored."

"Colored?" Marti asked.

"Yes, he had real light skin and nice hair, like mine, but I'm sure that even so he was colored."

That was it! That was why he'd set the fire on the South Side. But—wait a minute—Jhanke's house—his kitchen—

hadn't she—yes—she was certain she had seen a pair of candleholders on Jhanke's kitchen table.

"Were the candleholders ever returned?"

"No. To tell you the truth, I thought they were ugly; but my husband, well, they had belonged to his great-grandmother."

Marti asked the woman to describe them, and as soon as she hung up she sent a uniform over and had them brought in.

"How else could Jhanke get the candleholders, Vik? He must have met up with whoever took them. And whoever took them was black. That's why he was in that neighborhood on the South Side. That's why he set the fire."

"But nobody was in the house, MacAlister. Why set fire to an empty house when you've got a target? We know he's killed people before. In a couple of cases we can even figure out why. This was a vacant house, MacAlister. No victim. No target. Not his MO."

She didn't know the answer, but she was damned eager to talk with Jhanke. Too bad his mother couldn't talk to them. She called the hospital again. No change. Marti picked up one of the candleholders. It made her think of an illustration in one of the books she used to read to the kids. Someone jumping over a candlestick. In the book it was just like this one, saucer-shaped, with the candleholder in the middle and a curved handle her fingers could hook around. Jack-Be-Nimble—that was it. This Frederick Jhanke was nimble too—so far.

When Fred drove by the house at quarter past nine, the tan car was there. He didn't want to set the fire this early because he didn't want anyone to notice it before it had had a chance to burn. He hadn't been able to check out this house either. He would be working blind. No matter. It was too late for any of that. This was something he had to do, and he was going to do it now. He drove around the block again. The street was quiet, but there were still a lot of houses with lights on. Too many. He might have to settle for setting this

*one, knowing it might be controlled before it could consume
the entire building, and then setting another fire at the
building with the apartments and storefronts. The more he
thought about it, the more he liked that idea. Everyone
would be at this fire. Nobody knew he had any interest in the
other place.*

*He drove over to the block on Sherman where the thief
had parked his car. A quick drive around the block and he
could see that he would have no problem at all. What if he
started this fire first? It would pull the fire equipment here
and be much too big to put out. Then there would be a better
chance for the other fire to get a good start. Maybe more
than one house would catch fire there, with everyone busy
here. He pulled into the alley, got out the sack with the gasoline can inside, chose what he wanted to use with it, and decided to start the fire in the rear of an empty storefront right
in the middle of the block.*

It was a little before ten when Slim and Cowboy came in.
Slim still didn't have anything to say to Marti, but Cowboy
tipped his hat and grinned before making another pot of
coffee.

"What brings you two in?" Vik asked.

"The nighttime is the right time," Slim said, "to be without the one you love and with a hooker or two." He did a little dance step, but didn't even glance in Marti's direction.
She had expected a little hostility, but this was excessive.

"Or three hookers," Cowboy said.

"No." Slim disagreed. "Three's a crowd."

To Marti's surprise, Slim and Cowboy actually sat down
and discussed a strategy for the night's work. They were still
certain there were at least a couple of underage ladies of the
night out there, and they were devising an action plan of
sorts.

On their way out, Slim said, "Boy, those things are pop-
ping up all over the place."

"What things?" Vik asked.

"Those candleholders, the ones on Ms. MacAlister-

Walker's desk. My mother's new tenant had some that were something like that when I was there the other day."

"What day?" Marti asked.

"Hell, I don't know. She had the downstairs converted into two apartments, and I went over and did the blue shirt routine with the new tenants."

"And one had candleholders that looked like these?"

"Yes, Officer MacAlister. Occasionally I do employ my powers of observation and do, in fact, remember what I see. Why?"

"Because if you're right I think your mother's house might be the arsonist's target."

Fred returned to Eureka, turned down an alley, parked in the driveway of an unlit house. It was a little after ten. He hadn't stayed to watch the first fire and it was the biggest place he had burned yet. He couldn't hear the fire engines yet, which meant he was getting a good start. After he finished here, he would find a place there where he could watch. Both fires were sure to be in the morning newspaper.

He took the plastic bag with the refilled gasoline container out of the trunk and slung it over his shoulder. This one wasn't going to be as easy. The house was well taken care of, and he didn't think he would find an unlocked door. There were sensor lights outside. Fred stood on the side of the garage that belonged to the house that faced the next street while he tried to figure out what to do. This wasn't like any house he had lit up before. This wasn't a house he would choose. It had been chosen for him, and there had to be a way to get it to burn.

Geoffrey was watching the ten o'clock news. He didn't usually, but he had left the remote on the coffee table and didn't feel like getting up. When he saw the pig again, and then the house burning, he sat bolt upright. Their house was torched last night; the house just around the corner was torched the night before. That fool saw him leaving here and wanted a watch. But he gave him the ring. No, no. None of this made any sense. He was just tired, And depressed. Mama thought he should give this a try for a little longer before moving back home.

No, that man wasn't about nothing. He'd given the man his ring back; the fool was just confused about it being a watch. No, it wasn't about the ring. What was it the man had said? He couldn't remember exactly, but he could remember how he had said it; and now that he thought about it, it had sounded like a threat. It was a threat. No. No. He was just jumpy tonight. Jumpy because an eighty-year-old man had caught him out. Jumpy because he was stupid, not because he had any reason to be.

He jumped at a knock on the door.

"Mr. Bailey?"

It was Sister Hawkins, but she was whispering.

He opened the door. "Yes, ma'am?" He whispered too.

She was wearing dark slacks and a sweater. It was the first time he had seen her wearing anything other than a skirt and blouse or a dress.

"Mr. Bailey, there is a man acting suspiciously near my property. I just put a call in to my son. Would you please come with me? We did just have a fire in the neighborhood."

Geoffrey grabbed his jacket, put it on over his pajamas, and stepped into the hall. Sister Hawkins had a gun. A big gun.

"Ma'am, I don't think you want to walk around outside carrying that." And he sure as hell didn't want to walk out there with her. "There are too many folks out there with guns now. One of them might think . . ."

"Mr. Bailey, come along. I am going to protect my property."

"Yes, ma'am." Bossy old biddy. How had she managed to snag two husbands?

"I'm going to cut these lights off. Don't make any noise."

Geoffrey stayed well behind her as she made her way along the hall that separated his apartment from his neighbor's and to the back of the house. When she unlocked the door, he said, "Are you sure you want to do this if someone is out there?"

"God save me from fools," was all that she said.

She peered out, then came back in, and locked the door again.

"See, what did I . . . ?"

"Shut up, Mr. Bailey."

"Yes, ma'am."

"Where is that son of mine? We are going to the front of the house and then outside and around to the back."

"But I . . ."

"Come along, Mr. Bailey, and don't 'ma'am' me anymore; just shut up and do as I say."

It was cold outside, too cold for the light jacket Geoffrey had grabbed, and his pajamas were silk. He shivered as he kept to the side of the house and well behind Sister Hawkins. When she said, "Don't move and put your hands up," Geoffrey did; then he saw there was someone standing in front of her.

Fred was so intent on pouring the gasoline that he didn't hear anyone come up behind him. When a woman's voice said, "Put your hands up," he wanted to laugh. Maybe he should just turn around real quick, throw some of the gasoline on her, and toss a lit match.

"I have a gun," the woman said. "And I know how to use it. I've used it before, and I'll use it again. Now, put down the gasoline can."

Fred did. Now what? Would she shoot? No, she was a woman. She was bluffing. She had a toy gun, and she was bluffing. That wasn't what mattered anyway. She had caught him and he didn't want to get caught, not now. Better to just get away.

He took a step forward, tripped over the gasoline can, and went sprawling. He picked himself up and ran. There was a loud bang and a sharp pain in his arm that seemed to happen all at once. She had shot him. He kept running.

When he reached the driveway where he had parked the car, he jumped inside, turned the key waiting in the ignition, and backed out. The pain in his arm as he turned the wheel was so bad he almost screamed. The smell of gasoline was so strong he wanted to puke. The explosion came all at once.

"Matthew Jessenovik, I am not going to get into that car with you again! You drive like a maniac. We are going to take the unmarked car. I'll drive."

"Damn it, MacAlister, I still haven't figured out what's wrong. If you don't want to ride with me, fine, go by yourself. I'm taking my own car."

"Damn." She relented. "Damn, damn, damn. If we have an accident . . ."

"I haven't even gotten a ticket in the last twenty-five years."

"Of course you haven't, you're a cop."

By the time they pulled up behind Slim and Cowboy, Marti could see the smoke and the glow from the fire. Slim jumped out of the car before it came to a complete stop and ran to the house, calling for his mother. A woman came from the side of the house, and he grabbed her in a tight hug. Then he stood away from her and they talked. The woman was holding a gun.

Marti rolled the window down. "Gun!" she yelled. "Gun! Get her weapon, Slim! Get her weapon!"

"It's okay," Slim called back, "it's my mother. She's licensed."

The woman put the gun in her pocket.

The fire was extinguished quickly. Tolley pulled up while the firefighters were working and consulted with the lieutenant in charge.

"Looks like we got a crispy critter this time," he said, when he walked over. "Second fire of the evening. Had another one over on Sherman."

"Anyone hurt?" Marti asked.

"No. That one hardly got started. A tenant spotted it when he was taking out the garbage. Besides, the whole place was built with fire walls."

"Think we got lucky this time?" Vik asked.

"What do you mean?"

"Could the crispy critter be our arsonist?"

"No way to tell, except maybe by the dental work eventually. If it is him, he's not driving the same car. We do have quite a gasoline spill behind this house to neutralize though. That's what Jhanke used the last time."

Geoffrey looked at the car in the alley. It was engulfed in flames. God help the man who was inside. Everything seemed to happen at once. Smoke, fire, sirens, voices, people shouting.

"Not another fire," someone said. "There's a fire over on Sherman too."

"Another fire here and one over there too? You think this is a riot?"

"No, fool. There ain't no stores around here to loot."

Geoffrey turned and walked back to the house. Even though he hadn't gotten a good look at the man with the gasoline can, he had recognized his voice. He knew what the man was trying to do: get even. He knew that the fire on Sherman was at Deacon Evans's place. The man had followed him there. All this because of a fake security alarm. All because of him. All because of his game. That's all it was, a game. He didn't need the money. He just had to out-hustle his old man.

There was a knock on the door. Not again.

This time it was Sister Hawkins's son. Geoffrey let him in. His ass was going to jail now, no doubt about it.

Officer Ross walked about the small apartment, looked in his drawers, his closet, said nothing. Geoffrey sat on the couch, waiting to be arrested.

"So," the cop said, "who was your friend? Why was he going to burn my mother's house down?"

"I don't . . ."

The cop was beside him in two steps.

"I think we'd better reach an understanding, Mr. Bailey. Number one, I don't tolerate any lies. Number two, we're talking about my mother."

"Yes, sir."

"Now, let me ask you that question again, and this time, don't begin your answer with anything negative. And while you're at it, explain about those candleholders that aren't here anymore."

He knew. Bailey told the cop the whole story.

"If Jhanke was in that car, Vik, we'll never know what really happened," Marti said, as she sat at her desk. She took out her notebook and got a legal pad out of the drawer.

"If that was Jhanke, MacAlister, we probably don't want to know what really happened."

"Speak for yourself."

Marti liked working at night. The precinct was quiet. The phones were still. There were no distractions. Her annoying and insulting office partner, Slim, was downstairs with his mother while she made a statement. No Obsession for Men, so her sinuses were clear. And, thanks to action and adrenaline she was wide awake. It didn't get much better, at least not at work.

"Too bad about Opal Jhanke," Marti said. "On the one hand, you want her to make it; on the other, what happens to her if she does? Dead or alive, her son won't be around."

"MacAlister, he wasn't exactly a good boy. Not having him around shouldn't be too much of a hardship."

"You're right. It's just hard to think of growing old and being alone."

"You're getting morbid. We've been dealing with too many old people."

"That Mrs. Rosenblum is a quaint old bird, isn't she?"

Vik grunted. He didn't like too much small talk when he was writing reports and she'd pushed it.

"Stanley is chatting," Marti mimicked. She put that in her

notes, then thought, *Chatting, chat room.* "What's a 'chat room,' Jessenovik?"

"I don't know."

"In a chat room," "going to a chat room." She had heard those expressions before. She kept writing, but it nagged at her because she didn't know what they meant. It was three in the morning. There wasn't anyone at this hour she could ask.

"Computers," Vik said.

"What about them? We don't have one. Try elderly electric typewriter."

"Computers as in chat room."

Marti spelled *incendiary* wrong. She crossed it out and tried again. "How do you spell . . ."

"Rosenblum," Vik said.

"Mrs. or Stanley? In . . . what—?"

"MacAlister, pay attention!"

"Can't. It's past midnight, way past midnight."

"You're not authorized to turn into a pumpkin." He stood in front of her desk, diskette in hand.

"Not that again, Vik. Help me spell incen—"

"MacAlister, pay attention. I don't know what Mrs. Rosenblum meant by chatting, but 'a chat room' has something to do with a computer. I'm not sure what, but for some reason I'm making a connection—"

"You just want that damned diskette to be important!"

"No. That's not it, And remember, she said something about the phone line being tied up."

"Because they only have one line."

"Maybe," Vik agreed. "Let's have a talk with him anyway." He rubbed his hands together.

"Anticipating the joy of waking someone else up at this hour of the morning, Jessenovik?"

"It's more like misery loves company, but let's go."

"Okay, but you're not driving. You deliberately went through that red light."

"What red light?"

* * *

Rosenblum was a sound sleeper. It took at least five minutes of steadily applying the finger to the doorbell to awaken him. When he did peer at them from the other side of a security chain, his eyes were only half open.

"In the basement," he said, as he let them in.

"Computer?" Vik asked.

"Umm. Dozed off in the recliner right in the middle of a chat."

"A chat?" Vik said.

"Ummm."

It was time to advise Mr. Rosenblum of his rights. Rosenblum led the way into the living room and turned on a lamp. The fringed shade was old and yellowing, the bulb dim. It made Marti think of gaslights, and the room seem even more Victorian. Vik recited Miranda.

"You understand these rights as I've read them to you?"

Rosenblum nodded.

"You don't have to say anything else without an attorney present, sir. We are going to ask you to come in for questioning now."

The harsh overhead light in the interrogation room exaggerated the thin planes of Rosenblum's face, elongating his chin and his nose. He was not an attractive man and became less so without the Victorian quaintness of his home.

"So," Vik said, "from what your mother told us, you spend the whole day Sunday on the computer, in this chat room."

"There are so many chat rooms to visit."

"Do they have one on pornography?"

"They have sites . . ." He stopped. His eyes narrowed as he looked at Vik. He didn't say anything else.

"Those . . ." Vik groped for the right words. Marti couldn't help him. She didn't know any computer terminology either.

Vik took the diskette out of his pocket. "Why don't you just tell us about this?" he suggested.

Marti thought all diskettes looked alike, but she could see

from Rosenblum's expression that this one did mean something.

"What exactly was your relationship with Virginia McCroft?" she asked.

"That's personal."

"Well, she's dead now and I know quite a bit about her that's personal. So tell me about this."

"We weren't . . . intimate," he said. "Not like that."

"Then what were you?" Marti couldn't see any reason to be delicate about it. She could tell by the way he kept looking at the diskette that he knew what was on it.

"Affection," he said. "Virginia wanted affection."

Marti took the diskette from Vik and held it up. "And when she saw this?"

"It was . . . She was . . . We spent a week trying to work through it."

"How?"

"We talked . . . she cried . . . She seemed to understand that I do have needs, needs that she couldn't meet. It was the diskette itself that troubled her. She kept saying it was rape. I told her it wasn't, but to her it was. I really didn't want to break up with her . . ."

Marti wanted to say of course not, not with the cash she was bringing in.

"I suggested a therapist. I mean, most women her age have some interest in more than just . . . what we were doing. She said that she couldn't tell anyone."

"Tell them what?"

"I didn't know. She said she had to go back to that house. That she would be okay if she could just go back. She said that I had to go with her, that she could not go there alone."

"What house?"

"That house."

"What house?"

"The house where she died."

"That's why you went there?"

"I agreed to meet her there. I was running late and when I did get there, she was hysterical. I'm still not sure what happened, what she was talking about. She kept saying, 'He'll hurt me again. He'll hurt me.' She was crying and I took her by the shoulders and tried to get her to tell me what was wrong, but she was crying and shaking. I had never seen her like that. She kept saying he was going to hurt her again. Then there was a noise, a rat maybe, and she pulled out a gun. Virginia! She was waving a gun around. It scared the hell out of me. I had never seen a real gun before. I told her I was getting the hell out of there. *She had a gun!*"

Rosenblum stopped talking and squeezed his eyes shut. His hands were clasped on the table. When he sucked in his breath, it was almost a sob.

"She told me I couldn't leave her. That I was the only man who had ever . . . we didn't do anything, we really didn't, but she said I was the only man . . . could . . . had ever . . . but she had the gun. I tried to leave. She said she would kill herself if I did. She was so upset, crying, shouting at me. She put the gun to her head. She said she would shoot. I tried to get her to calm down. I told her that I would protect her from this man, that I would do whatever she wanted me to, anything. I begged her to put down the gun. I was scared. God, I was so scared."

He ran his fingers through thinning hair, then focused on a place on the pink wall, blinking rapidly. "She did hold the gun down. And I don't know what made me do it, but I thought if I could just get it away from her, just get close enough to hold her the way she liked to be held . . . but somehow . . . I don't know. She didn't let go of it. And she was trying to pull it away from me and the gun . . . it went off."

He wiped at his eyes. "I don't understand why all of this happened, not over that." He held out his hand as if he was reaching for the diskette. "All because of that. I don't understand. Why did she have to go there? Who was she talking about? And that gun. I didn't even know she owned one. I had never even seen a gun before. I didn't know what was happening to her, what was wrong. I should have got there on time. Being in that basement alone made her crazy. Virginia was always so calm, so controlled. What could he have done to her, whoever he was? What could have happened to make her like she was that day?"

Now he was crying. Marti gave him some Kleenex.

"It's my fault. If only I had gotten there on time, she wouldn't have gotten so upset. Who is he?" Rosenblum asked. "How did he hurt her? Why was she so afraid?"

Marti didn't say anything, even though she knew most of the answers.

"Why didn't you tell anyone she was there?" Vik asked. His voice shook. He was angry. "You could have called anonymously. You didn't have to tell us who you were. Why did you just leave her there like that?'

Rosenblum put his hands on the table, fingers splayed. They were large hands, with hairy knuckles, that went along with the hair that curled below the cuff of his shirt and the hair in his nose and his ears. "I didn't want my mother to know. She always manages to find out everything. Even in that nursing home, she knows."

Why him? Marti wondered. If Virginia went to the prom with the captain of the football team she had to have something going for her, even if it was just looks. How could she have ended up with such an unattractive, unappealing, totally selfish man?

When they got back to the office, Vik sort of slumped in his chair. He looked pale and sweat was beading on his forehead.

"Are you okay?"

He shook his head. "No, I'm not okay. How can anyone listen to all of this, find out all of this, about Essie, about Virginia . . . and be okay? Horace Warren, that *dupajas skurvie sen,*" he said, cussing in Polish. "All of this seems so crazy, so damned insane. What if there had been a rape hot line then, someone they could talk to, someplace they could go? Virginia was a tease, a flirt, you name it, but a lot of girls were. Nobody ever said she put out. Maybe what she did do wasn't nice, but most of it was in fun and most of us took it that way. She should have had someplace to go. And Essie, she never even told Mildred until this weekend. She's not a bad person. Would have made a good mother. What a waste."

They sat in silence until Slim and Cowboy came in.

"We nailed them," Cowboy said. "We got those little girls, and we nailed those bastards good."

For the second time in one day, Vik came close to smiling. "I owe you two a drink," he said. "I owe both of you a drink."

After Slim and Cowboy left, Marti thought about going home. There were only a few loose ends. She could take care of them in the morning. Instead, she went through her in basket. The first reports on the motorcycle bombing were in. She'd almost forgotten about that. She glanced through them.

"Check your in basket, Vik. They found enough of Malcolm Fletcher's jaw to make a positive ID."

Vik scanned his copies of the reports. "If we could just pin a motive on Jhanke, we'd have this one wrapped up too. Why would he risk calling attention to himself by blowing someone up so close to home?"

Marti thought back to her conversation with Ben while they were having lunch at the Barrister. "Because he was threatened," she said. "Or angry, or afraid."

"But why?"

She flipped through the reports until she came to the profile on Fletcher.

"They were close to the same age. Fletcher was a widower. His parents owned his house and had left it to him, same as Jhanke. I'd guess Fletcher and the Jhankes were the only ones on the block who had lived there for any length of time."

"Maybe he knew something. But what?"

Marti thought for a moment. "The first time we went to Jhanke's place, he said he lived there alone, but he didn't. Maybe Fletcher knew that. Maybe he knew Opal was there. The way he was treating his mother, that could have been enough, then again, he could have just got fed up with the noise." She put the reports into a manila folder. "I don't know about you, but I'm ready to pack it in. We can work on this one in the morning."

Opal Jhanke heard a sound like the pages of a book rushing in the wind. She felt as if she was being pushed through a tunnel. Then the noise subsided and there was a light, dim at first, then brighter. As she moved toward the light, she heard her mother singing. Mother's voice was so clear and sweet, just as she remembered, and the light so bright and warm. Opal smiled. Here I come, Mother. I'm coming.

As she drove home, Marti thought about Fred Jhanke. For someone she had never met, she had a very clear impression of a man with eyes like a polar bear, eyes that never showed any emotion, a person with feelings that never extended beyond himself, a man who was the center of his own universe and was all that mattered within it. Was fear, or anger, or resentment all it took to set him off? Could some slight, some minor insult or misunderstanding, result in a fire, a death? With the exception of the people who owned the pig, not once in this investigation had she come across one person who had had any recent contact with Jhanke. Despite his isolation, he had set fires, detonated bombs, and killed. What had gone on inside his head that had made him do this?

She had gone to his house, entered his "factory," gone through his belongings, even tried to offer some small comfort to his mother. Did he know any of this? How would he have reacted if he had? Would he have tried to set fire to her house, blow up her car . . . Marti stopped in the middle of the street. Behind her, brakes squealed.

Jhanke couldn't have gotten anywhere near her house, not with Trouble patrolling the premises and the alarm system. Her car hadn't been tampered with either. But what if. No. If she called this one in, they would think she was crazy. She would be the butt of every joke at the precinct. But if she didn't, and she was right, she would be dead.

* * *

Vik stood beside her, shaking his head. "I don't believe this," he said. "I just don't believe this."

The bomb that had been found attached to the rear wheel of their unmarked car was small and deadly. Tolley had not laughed when she called him. Nobody at the precinct would be laughing at her tomorrow. Tonight she was going home, to safety, to love, to her children, to her mother, to Ben.

MONDAY, MAY 3

Marti felt exhausted when she came into work in the morning. Vik looked worse than she felt. Slim and Cowboy had come and gone, and the precinct was so quiet it sounded more like the middle of a night than the beginning of a day. An occasional voice, the elevator door, footsteps in the hall that were hushed by the carpet. She inhaled the aroma of Cowboy's strong-brewed coffee because it was too hot to drink and sat back and let the cup warm her hands. The sun was out. No overcast skies today. Just reports. She didn't feel the usual euphoria that came when a case was closed. Fred had been identified through dental records. At least they wouldn't have to go through a trial. It was all over but the reports.

She had been wrong about yesterday. It wasn't Mother's Day and she was glad of that. There were too many mothers involved in this case. At least Opal Jhanke was at peace now. She didn't want to know what kind of hell Fred Jhanke had put his mother through. Mrs. McCroft would be going home to Minnesota, and within the confines of her dementia Virginia might never die. Mrs. Rosenblum still had her son, and all of her illusions about him were intact. As for her mother, she hadn't missed Momma's big day at church.

"Why did Virginia go back to that house?" Vik asked. It was the first time he had spoken of it today.

"I don't know." She didn't understand all of this. She had never been raped. She thought that somehow Virginia was trying to bring some kind of closure to what had happened to her years ago; that perhaps, once she went into the house and was alone, it had overwhelmed her again. Somehow, that made sense. Just as the orderly clutter in that house did now, with every space filled; the planner with every detail of her life organized and in order; Virginia's life, filled with things to do, places to go, people to see, but no friends. Everything about Virginia made sense somehow; but the more she thought about it, the less she understood why.

"Poor Essie," Vik said. "She drove Mildred and damned near everyone else crazy the way she worried about their kids, especially the girls. Mildred said more than once that there had to be a reason for it. Everyone thought it was because she didn't have any kids of her own." He shook his head. "Good person, Essie—fussy, real mousy, and a worrier, but good people." He picked up an empty Mello Yello can and crushed it. "If I had known when it happened, what he did to her, I would have beat the shit out of him."

Marti worked on her reports until Slim came in and the scent of Obsession for Men cologne began clogging her sinuses. She didn't look up.

"I need to talk to you two," he said.

Cowboy wasn't with him. It seemed odd, seeing one of them without the other. Marti wondered if they hung out together when they were off duty, not that she would ever ask.

Slim sat on the edge of Vik's desk. He didn't flash the dimpled smile. "Got a problem," he said.

"What's that?" Vik asked.

"This guy is staying at my mother's house. He's renting one of her efficiency apartments. He's the son of her church sisters. They go back years and years. Nice enough guy, but stupid. Real stupid."

"How stupid?" Vik asked.

"His family is loaded, really loaded, but this fool has to trick little old ladies out of their money."

"Sounds like a mean bastard to me," Vik said. Slim's timing was off if he was expecting any sympathy for a street hustler.

"No, man, he's just a con artist," Slim said. "It's just a game with him. He doesn't want their life savings. He just wants the thrill of victory, a little cash, maybe a piece of jewelry . . ."

"Or a set of candleholders?" Vik said.

"Something like that."

"So what do you want from us?"

"He's somewhat involved in your case. At least he might have some information. I don't know if it will be useful or not, but you should talk to him."

"And?"

"I'd appreciate it if you would kind of keep the whole thing under wraps."

"Why? So he can take advantage of somebody else?"

"No, man, I've got him in check. He won't be doing anything with little old ladies but helping them cross the street. Come on, Jessenovik. I could really be in big trouble with my mother."

A smile played about the corners of Vik's mouth. "And why is that?"

"She introduced me to him a couple of days ago. You know, the blue shirt routine," Slim said. "She would really be upset if she finds out I didn't check this guy out."

Marti burst out laughing. "Am I hearing this right?" she asked, when she caught her breath. "You want *me* to help *you?*"

He nodded.

"Well, Amos Dent Ross," she said, "I'll have to think about that."

She could see that he was stunned that she knew his full name. She had been saving that since winter. He'd been Slim or A. D. Ross ever since he came on the force.

"Oh, that's right, it's Slim. Sorry." She sniffed and wrinkled her nose as if she smelled something bad. "You're getting kind of heavy-handed with the cologne," she said. "What's the matter, too busy to bathe?"

Slim took a couple of steps back and just looked at her.

She hoped he was realizing that she wanted a lot more respect than she had been getting and a lot less of his Obsession for Men.

"Yes, ma'am," he said, and gave her a small salute.

"Why don't you give us this guy's name."

"Oh, he's right outside. He really wants to talk to you."

"Give me a few minutes," she said. "I've got to think about this."

Vik gave her a thumbs-up. She winked at him and smiled.

Marti waited until Vik left the office to give Geoffrey Bailey her full attention. He was tall, slender, and light enough to pass for white if he wanted to. He had dressed for the occasion, pin-striped suit, light blue shirt, navy blue tie with tiny red triangles. He even smiled. Momma would have called him a dandy. Marti leaned back in her chair.

"So, Mr. Bailey, Officer Ross says you have some information that I might find useful."

His smile broadened. "I think we can reach an accommodation, Officer."

"Mr. Bailey, let's understand each other. You're going to tell me everything illegal that you have done to defraud the elderly or anyone else in the last five years. Every scam, got that?"

She waited until he nodded. "When you've done that, we will discuss the scam that specifically involved the late Mrs. Opal Jhanke and the deceased Fred Jhanke."

The smile was gone.

"At that point I will take you downstairs to be booked, printed, and photographed. Then, if you are very well behaved and I do not feel that you have withheld any information, you will be released on your own recognizance."

"But—" His eyes widened.

"If, within the length of time it takes for your case to be processed, I am satisfied that you are indeed repentant and not likely to resume your . . . career, I *may* suggest to the state's attorney's office that the charges against you be dropped. However, please remember that any time any scam is perpetrated that remotely fits your profile, your photograph will be on file, and I will be right here, waiting."

It was a little after six when Marti got home. Momma was in the kitchen with Lisa. Joanna was setting the dining room table for dinner. Marti stood in the hallway. Momma was showing Lisa how she wanted the tomatoes sliced. Lisa was like Sharon in many ways—neither of them liked to cook. As she watched, Marti thought back to the bright yellow kitchen she had shared with Sharon until the intruder came. Instead of Boston ferns, Joanna's sun catchers hung at the windows. Wallpaper reminded her of Momma's kitchen when she was growing up. The house had become home the first time she came into this room.

Momma inspected the tomato wedges. "There. That's fine. Now let me show you what I want you to do with the lettuce. I really need someone in the kitchen to help with the salad. The boys are getting good at helping with dessert, and Joanna is going to make sure there are plenty of fresh vegetables."

Momma and Lisa moved to the sink without noticing that she was there. Above the sound of running water, Momma said, "How did you do on that math test today?"

"So-so."

"Well, that might get better now that you're doing your homework. If not, we can get you some tutoring."

"I'm going out Friday night."

"Good. It's time we began meeting your friends."

"Oh, well, I was going to meet him there."

Momma wiped her hands on her apron. "No, child, you are bringing him home. He can pick you up right here."

"But Sharon—"

"This is not your momma's house. That is not how we do things here."

Lisa washed the lettuce, put it in a bowl, and added the tomatoes.

"You all right, girl?" Momma asked.

"You're too strict here."

Marti almost held her breath as she waited for Lisa to announce that she was going back to Sharon. She saw the way Lisa's shoulders went rigid and remembered Sharon doing the same thing. What would happen to her if she left here? As concerned as she was about Lisa's influence on Joanna, she did not want this child to go.

Momma reached for the cucumbers.

"I don't think I've got a date. No way he'll pick me up at home. Especially not with Ben here and maybe Marti."

"That might be a good thing," Momma said. "He might not be someone you really need to be going out with. Slice these real thin. Then I'll show you how to make my special dressing."

After a few minutes, Lisa said, "Maybe I'll just go to Joanna's game Friday night. I think they're all going someplace afterward."

Marti was not surprised by her sense of relief.

Marti could hear the ring announcer before she reached the den. Momma was watching a wrestling match. She took the box from her pocket and sat beside Momma on the sofa. "Why don't you put your feet up?"

"Lord, child, if I did that I'd be sound asleep in no time."

"That doesn't sound like such a bad idea."

"I know, child, but I sure don't want to miss the matchup between the Marvelous Monster and Deadly Dan Danger."

Marti laughed and gave her a hug. "I thought yesterday was Mother's Day. I wanted to give you this, and there was no way I could get home. The Job, Momma, the Job. It keeps me from doing a lot of things."

"Child, I want you doing that job, getting those fools off the street. What would it be like, Marti, not just here but anywhere, if your job didn't get done? I can tell you one thing: Sister Shirley is sure glad you were on the case."

Marti laughed. "Momma, Sister Shirley did not need me. She knew just what to do with that Smith & Wesson. Slim's mother is something else. Just like you." She gave her the box.

Momma held up the necklace, with the little gold charms and birthstones. "This is you, and your brother, Nathaniel. Here's Theo and Joanna; Ben and Mike . . ." She looked up.

"Sharon and Lisa," Marti said.

Momma's eyes filled with tears. "Thank you, child, for knowing how much I love both of them too."

The boys were upstairs. Marti could hear Ben's deep, rumbling laugh and Theo's and Mike's higher-pitched giggles. Again she stood in the doorway and watched, feeling a sense of peace and contentment that she hadn't known in a long time. The three of them were sprawled on the carpet. Newspaper had been spread and each boy was working on a model airplane. After four years, Theo was finally completing the Cub Scout project that he and his father had been working on when Johnny died. She didn't understand any of it, why the airplane had sat on the bureau for so long and then been packed and left in the box. Johnny would be pleased, knowing it was finally complete, and he would be proud of this self-sufficient little boy who carried his father's likeness in the planes and angles of his face, maintained his father's silence, and kept his father's memory in his heart.

CHAPTER
41

It was almost ten o'clock when Vik and Mildred got home. They had attended evening mass together. Then he'd driven to a Polish restaurant in the city. It had been a long drive, but Mildred had enjoyed being out and the food was good. Tomorrow was Mother's Day. They would go to mass again with the children and grandchildren, and there would be a big dinner with the in-laws. Tonight was their time, his time to be with her without sharing her with anyone.

The walker thumped as she went ahead of him and into the bedroom.

"Oh, Matthew!" she exclaimed.

He had taken one of their wedding photos to a florist and asked her to make an arrangement that was like Mildred's bouquet. There was a bottle of champagne cooling in an ice bucket. The bed was turned back, and the white negligee she had worn on their wedding night was folded on the pillow.

"Moja serce," he said, taking her in his arms. *"Moja serce."*

MOTHER'S DAY, MAY 9

The house was quiet. Momma was dozing in her new recliner. Marti had her feet up on her new hassock, and Ben's
tongue was teasing her ear. It had been such a good day with
all of the church members welcoming Momma. Slim had
even come to services with his mother, although they attended a different church, as did the infamous Geoffrey Bailey, who was there with his mother and aunt. Just about
everyone she knew had come to welcome Momma. Everyone except Sharon. And although Momma hadn't said anything yet, Marti knew she had been waiting for Sharon to
come and had been more than just disappointed when she
did not.

Ben was working his way under her blouse when they
heard the children coming downstairs. He grinned as he removed his hand and mouthed the word, "Later."

Theo came in first, carrying flowers. He gave Marti a
pink rose, then woke up Momma.

"Well, if you children aren't sweet," Momma said, rubbing her eyes.

Mike gave them each a box of chocolates. Joanna gave
her a bottle of perfume, Elige by Mary Kay, something she
hadn't tried before, probably to distract her from vanilla.
Then Joanna and Lisa brought in all the fixings for ice cream
sundaes.

"We all wanted to talk with you about something,"
Joanna said. "Theo is first."

Theo looked down and scuffed his shoe on the carpet.
Mike grinned and poked him in the ribs. Theo licked his lips

a few times, then pressed them together. Finally he said, "We, umm, well, Mike and Patrick and Peter . . . well . . ."

Marti wondered what the boys next door had to do with this.

"Well, they all call their father Dad, and Peter and Patrick call their mother Mom. And I, well, I called my father Daddy because I was little, and Mike called his mother Mommy because he was little . . ." His voice trailed off and he shifted from one foot to the other. He didn't look at her or at Ben. "Anyway, instead of Ma and Dad and Ben and Marti, we thought we should all call you the same thing—Ma and Dad. Lisa, too. Is that okay?"

Ben all but leaped from the couch and lifted Theo high in the air. "Is that all right?" he said. "Is that all right? You bet."

Marti wiped tears from her eyes and she gave Mike a big hug. How dear he had become to her. She looked up at Lisa. How amazing, all the different ways that one became a mother and a house became a home filled with love.

The girls dished up the ice cream.

"Ma, do you want chocolate, vanilla, or strawberry?" Joanna asked.

Marti looked at Ben. He broke into a wide grin. "Vanilla," she said. "And I think we'll take ours upstairs."

Don't miss these spellbinding Inspector
John Rebus novels from acclaimed,
award-winning author

IAN RANKIN

"This is crime fiction at its best."
—*Washington Post Book World*

"A brilliant series....The work of a master."
—*San Francisco Chronicle*

KNOTS AND CROSSES
Rebus's city is being terrorized by a baffling series of murders, and
he isn't just a cop trying to catch a killer—he's the man who holds
all the pieces of the puzzle...

TOOTH AND NAIL
Sent to London to help catch a vicious serial killer, Rebus must piece
together a portrait of a depraved psychopath bent on painting the
town red—with blood...

MORTAL CAUSES
A young man's tortured body is found in a medieval cellar far
beneath the Edinburgh streets, and to find a killer, Rebus must travel from the city's most violent neighborhood to Belfast, Northern
Ireland—and make it back alive...

HIDE AND SEEK
In an Edinburgh housing development, a junkie lies dead of an over-
dose, his body surrounded by signs of Satanic worship. Rebus knows
it was no accident. Now, to prove it, he's got to scour the city and
find the perfect hiding place of a killer...

**AVAILABLE WHEREVER BOOKS ARE SOLD
FROM ST. MARTIN'S PAPERBACKS**

From the acclaimed author of *Flat Lake in Winter*
comes a gripping legal drama that's
"just like Grisham."*

FELONY MURDER

Joseph T. Klempner

A small-time lawyer in private practice, Dean Abernathy has a
big case on his hands. His homeless client has confessed to
killing the police commissioner, claiming it was an accident.
But Dean thinks there's more to this case than anyone's admit-
ting. And with the help of a gutsy single mom, he's about to dis-
cover that behind the notorious blue wall of police silence
stands a conspiracy so menacing, that the deeper he gets into
it, the more he realizes he'll be lucky to get out alive...

"A book you can't put down...A winner."
—Edwin Torres, State Supreme Court Justice and author of
Carlito's Way

"[A] tautly woven legal drama."
—*Booklist*

Kirkus Reviews

FM 2/00

Winner of the Edgar Award for Best First Novel, author Eliot Pattison masterfully scales the heights of the genre with this gripping thriller that follows the tradition of *Gorky Park* and *Smilla's Sense of Snow*.

THE SKULL MANTRA

Edgar Award Winner

ELIOT PATTISON

When the grisly remains of a corpse are discovered, the case is handed to veteran police inspector Shan Tao Yun, a prisoner deported to Tibet for offending Beijing. Granted a temporary release, Shan is soon pulled into the Tibetan people's desperate fight for its sacred mountains and the Chinese regime's blood-soaked policies when a Buddhist priest, whom Shan knows is innocent, is arrested. Now, the time is running out for Shan to find the real killer... An astonishing, emotionally charged story that will change the way you think about Tibet—and freedom—forever.

"Superb...breathlessly suspenseful." —*Kirkus Reviews* (starred review)

"A top-notch thriller!" —*Publishers Weekly* (starred review)

"Pattison provides truly remarkable transport...a riveting story."
—*Booklist* (starred review)

"A stark and compelling saga...As in Tony Hillerman's Navajo mysteries, Pattison's characters venerate traditional beliefs, and mystical insight as a tool for finding murderers." —*Library Journal*

"A thriller of laudable aspirations and achievements." —*Chicago Tribune*

"One of the hottest debut novels of the season." —*Minneapolis Star-Tribune*

AVAILABLE WHEREVER BOOKS ARE SOLD
FROM ST. MARTIN'S PAPERBACKS

SM 10/00

A COLD DAY IN PARADISE

Steve Hamilton

Other than the bullet lodged less than a centimeter from his heart, former Detroit police officer Alex McKnight thought he had put the nightmare of his partner's death and his own near-fatal injury behind him. After all, Maximilian Rose, convicted of the crimes, has been locked in the state pen for years. But in the small town of Paradise, Michigan, where McKnight has traded his badge for a cozy cabin in the woods, a murderer with Rose's unmistakable trademarks appears to be back to his killing ways. And it seems as if it will be a frozen day in hell before McKnight can unravel the cold truth from a deadly deception in a town that's anything but Paradise.